The Ripple Affair

The Ripple Affair

Book 1 of The Ripple Affair Series

Erin Cruey

Acknowledgements

To God, my inspiration and greatest love. There are no words that can adequately describe how good You are to me. I am so grateful for all that You've done (and are still doing) in my life.

To Mom, my best friend who has patiently endured ten years of listening to me ramble on about story ideas. Your patience knows no bounds and if there was ever a person I wanted to make proud and be like, it's you. I love you, Mommy!

To my family and friends, thank you for your support and encouragement.

To my readers, both past and present, thank you for giving me the opportunity to write. I hope you enjoy reading this story and all the stories that follow.

A Cast of Main Characters

From the Kingdom of Audlin...

Arden Engel VI, the King:
Tough, strong, and loyal to his people, Arden is the current ruler of Audlin. Longing to see his kingdom prosper after his departure, he works tirelessly to train his youngest son, Edward, for the throne. His hard work is only a cover for his frustration, however, and he begins to doubt Edward will ever be ready to ascend.

Maria Engel, the Queen:
Maria is a typical queen-gracious, diligent, and kind-but beneath the proper exterior is a woman who is clever and loyal to her family. Unlike Arden, she believes Edward has the capacity for greatness, though that never stops her from worrying about him.

Stephen Engel, the Brother:
The firstborn of Arden and Maria, Stephen had a penchant for books and learning. Often seen as the favored son of Arden, Stephen was destined for the throne of Audlin until an unfortunate accident cut his life short.

Edward Engel, the Prince:
The youngest of Arden and Maria, Edward was once seen as bound for a life as a knight. Strong, brash, and at times arrogant, Edward's destiny seemed simple until his brother's untimely death. Now the next heir to the throne, Edward finds himself at odds with his own future-as a prince who acts without wisdom and as a future king nobody believes in. His only comfort is his fiancée, Antoinette, but even she is unaware of the past that plagues him and the future he fears.

Marcus Peterson, the Knight:
An archer and swordsman from the port city of Circh, Marcus is the youngest member of the royal guard in charge of protecting the royal family. Loyal, honorable, and faithful, Sir Peterson is the purest example of what it means to be a knight.

From the Kingdom of Edeland...

Susanna van Echt, the Mother:
The queen of Edeland, wife to King John and mother to Antoinette, Caspar, Bernette, and Robert. She is meticulous and proper to the point of being a bane to her daughters and insists that everything be perfect lest her wrath fall upon them all.

Antoinette van Echt, the Betrothed:
The fiancée of Edward Engel and eldest daughter of King John and Queen Susanna, Antoinette is charming, beautiful, and kind. She is one of the few who support Edward in who he is and not who he should become. She has the ultimate faith in her husband-to-be and longs for the day she can be with him and spend the rest of her days by his side.

Bernette van Echt, the Sister:
Called Bernie by most, she is the youngest daughter of King John and Queen Susanna and sister to Antoinette. Smart and witty, Bernie immerses herself in books, desperate to hide a growing insecurity about her appearance.

From the Kingdom of Hugellia...

Erick van Ketten, the Ruler:
The king of Hugellia and father to Maria, Ulrich, and Ambrose, and stepfather to Aldaric, Erick has been king for a long time and sees himself as one of the wisest in history. Hugellia has never been so prosperous, and he is certain it will stay that way.

Aldaric van Ketten, the Ambassador:
The stepson and biological nephew of King Erick, Aldaric works as an ambassador for Hugellia in hopes of building alliances for trade and the country's defense. Wise and discerning, Aldaric works hard for the benefit of his people, though his family sees it as nothing but a quest for a lost throne.

Emmerich van Ketten, the Cousin:
The only child of Aldaric and Anna van Ketten, Emmerich is often mocked for his lack of a royal title and is seen by many as a bore due to his love for learning. A passionate man with a heart for justice, he dreads the upcoming wedding between his cousin, Edward, and Antoinette, the woman he has loved since childhood.

From the Kingdom of Verloris...

Malina Serus, the Mistress:
A daughter of King Calimus, Malina is a princess of Verloris who meets Edward during a storm. Though she is not guaranteed a throne in her own country, she hopes to find a throne in Audlin. Charming, confident, and deviously deceptive, Malina will stop at nothing to get what she wants.

Vacius, the Shadow:
A member of the Velori, a mysterious organization that little is known about, Vacius is a warrior bred since childhood for battle, and Malina takes full advantage of his skills.

Chapter Index

Book One: The Ripple Affair

"In love, there is patience."

Chapter 1: The Prince and the Princess

She's beautiful.

The young man leaned against a marbled pillar, watching the woman from a distance. She stood there, talking, her emerald dress matching the summer trees that swayed in the gardens outside. Her long, dark tresses flowed to the middle of her back, a simple, shimmering headdress adorning the top of her head that matched her light eyes. Her skin looked as soft as milk, and the man yearned for his senses to be immersed in her flowery scent.

I can't believe she's mine.

Her voice echoed in the hall where they stood, like a simple melody that was barely above a whisper. The man sighed and closed his eyes, listening. He imagined himself there with her, talking, holding her in his arms and caressing her face. He was enjoying the fantasy, so close to the reality he shared with her for years, until he heard the voice stop and call his name.

"I know you're there, Edward."

It was followed by a playful laugh. He opened his eyes, a guilty expression coming across his face as he strode to her, hugging her from behind. She looked up, smiling, as she leaned back and kissed his cheek. The old woman beside them bowed her head, clutching the cream linen she held in her arms to her chest.

"Your Majesty," the woman whispered.

Edward turned to her in greeting. "My apologies, fine seamstress. I see my musings have interrupted your conversation with my fiancée."

"Of course not, Your Majesty." The peasant lifted her head. "His Highness is always welcome to come and go as he pleases."

The young woman touched Edward's chin with her fingertips, gazing at his strong features. His eyes were as blue as the sky, his face matching those of the ancients. "We were discussing table cloths for the reception," the lady answered. "Does the linen suit you?"

Edward barely glanced at it, his eyes wanting to remain on his future bride. "If that is what you wish, then take it."

"It will do then," the lady replied to the older woman. "Thank you, Margaretha."

"Of course, Miss Antoinette." The lady curtseyed.

Edward's eyes turned to the old woman, glowering. "Excuse me?"

Margaretha lifted her brow, confused. "Your Majesty?"

"Your mistress is a princess of our fine neighbors in Edeland," Edward replied, his voice stern, "and your future queen here in Audlin. You will address her as such."

Antoinette looked to Edward and frowned, her hand returning to her side.

The old woman's lip quivered, but she nodded and bowed again. "Of course. Forgive me, Your Majesties." She lifted her head and drew the linens close. "I will prepare the order right away. Good day."

She hurried off, leaving Antoinette and Edward alone.

The prince relished the moment. "Finally!" he whispered as he bent down to kiss the woman in his arms. "I thought she'd never leave."

Antoinette put her hand up, blocking his kiss. She looked at him, her face full of disappointment, and sighed. "You're too hard on them."

"Them?" Edward asked, perturbed. "The servants?"

"Not all of them," Antoinette cleared, "but with that one, you were."

Edward's brow rose in defense. "What did I do?"

"You know."

Edward shook his head, rubbing the bridge of his nose. He loved Antoinette, surely, but sometimes she forgot her place. She was royalty, not a commoner. "You do a disservice by letting them call you by first name. You will be the most powerful woman in this kingdom. You should act as such."

Antoinette crossed her arms in a huff. "I should act arrogant?"

"No, I didn't say that." Edward softened his face as he looked at her pouting lips, lips he longed to taste instead of argue with. "I only meant you are a woman of privilege. Don't be ashamed of it."

"I'm not ashamed," Antoinette replied, putting her hand in his and holding it. "They work hard, Edward, even more so than us, and are we really so different from them? They are peasants, we are nobles, but we're both human beings-the same wants, needs, joys, and hurts. The only thing that separates us is the card life has dealt."

She wrapped her hands around his waist, drawing him in, gazing into his eyes and smiling. He held her back, relishing the warmth of her touch. "All it takes is a simple change to put us where they are. We are fortunate Almighty God has blessed us as much as He has. I have them call me Antoinette to let them know we are equals. I am no better than them, they are no better than me."

"But you are their future queen. There should be some respect in that."

"Is respect always given in words?" Antoinette laughed, brushing the short strands of dark hair away from Edward's brow. "Sometimes it is given in deed. The woman has too much work and little help, yet because she respects me, she insists on providing cloth for the wedding. I even begged to pay her, yet she will not accept any coin. You don't earn the people's devotion because of how you are born, Edward. You earn it from what you do."

She kissed him, the gentleness of her touch flooding his senses with more longing for her than what he had before. She was beautiful to him, he knew, but her heart was what made him love her. Wisest of women, she deserved to be Audlin's queen.

He cupped her face to his and held it, their breath mingling as he closed his eyes. "Noble heart," he called her. "You are a wondrous woman. How is it that a man such as I has someone like you?"

She kissed him again, her loving hands caressing the back of his head. "You are a good man, Edward Engel, and you deserve a good woman."

He rested his forehead on hers, his eyes remaining closed. It was hard not to frown at hearing her words. She called him a good man, yet in his heart he knew it wasn't true. He could be better. He should be better. She just didn't admit it.

"Edward!" He heard a gruff voice call from a distance and he turned. The king of Audlin, Arden VI, strode confidently from the throne room, the pomp and elegance of his robes matching the grandness of the crown on his head. His graying hair and beard shined white in the sunlight that streamed from the windows, and he approached the happy couple, clearing his throat after seeing he interrupted their moment alone.

"My lady," King Arden said, beaming with pride at his future daughter-in-law. "You look as elegant as ever. You remind me of my dear Queen Maria when she was young."

"Thank you, Your Majesty." Antoinette smiled, slightly bowing her head as custom.

The king smiled back and then turned to Edward. His face changed to show the usual fatherly glance-brows lowered, eyes staring, and mouth in a frown. "Have you finished packing?"

Edward shrugged, looking away. More than anything, he hated it when his father confronted him, telling him he had done something wrong or that he was expecting it to happen. He was reminded so many times when he was younger, the rash child of Arden and Maria that was meant to be more of a reckless warrior than politician and peacemaker. And when it was announced that Edward would become king, the doubts increased, especially with his father.

Though handsome like his predecessors-muscular frame, chiseled features, a face that every woman adored-Edward lacked the usual elegance of the other monarchs. While they were simple, reserved, and soft-spoken, he was complicated, loud, and blunt. They favored learning and books, philosophy and debate. He learned through doing, and though he was a decent student in school and the university, his real expertise was in the knightly sports. He was a soldier, a knight born and bred in his heart.

He was nothing like his older brother, Stephen, and nearly every day he was reminded of it.

"You leave at dawn for Hugellia!" King Arden shook his head. "Edward, you must manage your time better. The carriage should already be loaded. Have you even started?"

"We have servants for a reason, Father. It's what they're paid for," Edward mumbled under his breath, but Antoinette stepped in.

"Sire, forgive me," she replied with another bow. "Edward was helping me with wedding plans. We were discussing linens with the seamstress."

Arden gave her a look, but softened his face. Even he could not be angry with her. If only Edward had her charm. "I know you mean well, my dear," he replied, "but Edward must learn responsibility. I know better than to believe he has helped you with the planning." He turned back to his son. "This journey to Hugellia is your passage to manhood, Edward. You are eighteen years old and must be mature! Ever since your brother died, the responsibility of this family-this crown-is on you. No more games, Edward. No more fooling around. You will be going there on your own and must delegate the entire way. I won't be there to help you."

"I know how to get to Hugellia, Father," Edward said with a roll of his eyes. How long had he listened to these lectures? Didn't they know he wasn't stupid? He knew the way to the capital of his mother's homeland. He knew how to give orders to his bodyguard. Just because his parents wouldn't be there didn't mean he couldn't make decisions on his own.

"I know you know the way," Arden continued, "but you test my patience. It's not just the packing you've neglected. There is much to be done between now and sunrise. You must be more responsible!"

"I am," Edward huffed, his eyes lowering.

"Do not take that tone with me." Arden glared. "Your brother knew his responsibilities, Edward. It's time you start taking them seriously like he did. He didn't waste his time with fancies and knights. If it were he in your shoes, the wedding planning would've been done, the carriage would be packed, and he would be in the throne room, observing, so he'd know how to act like a king!"

Edward said nothing as he pressed his lips shut, looking away.

Arden shook his head. "Sometimes I wonder, Edward..." he muttered under his breath. "I don't know why I bother. At least get your packing done. The servants are busy enough as it is." He turned, heading back to the throne room, his heavy feet stomping the floors as he walked off.

Antoinette watched as the king slammed the door to the throne room, the sound of it echoing through the hallway. Edward shuddered, closing his eyes for a moment. "I'm sorry," he whispered to her.

She gave his hand a gentle squeeze. "It's alright."

"No, it's not," he replied as he turned. "I need to get packing." He hurried to his room, down the staircase with Antoinette trailing behind.

"I'll help you," she called to him. He stopped, facing her with a frustrated look.

"You don't have to. Go and rest. I can do this on my own."

"I know you can," she said, offering him a comforting grin, "but you're going to be gone for nearly four months after tomorrow. I want to spend as much time with you as I can get."

Her words warmed his heart. How did she do it? Every time his spirit felt heavy, even a sentence from her lips could lift it. It was a gift from Almighty God, he believed, and she used it often. He exhaled, taking her by the hand and leading her towards his room.

When they entered, he found a few servants busy rummaging through tunics, debating with themselves on what to pack and keep there. Poor souls; they looked so flustered and tired. When Edward entered, they all stopped and looked, bowing low before returning to their work.

"Your Majesty," they said in unison.

Edward nodded in thanks. "I appreciate your help," he said, making them stop once more. "You are dismissed. I can take it from here."

They lowered their heads, not saying a word as they exited toward other duties.

Both Edward and Antoinette began with going through the tunics first. There were so many of them, some of which neither one of them had seen. Edward shook his head as he lifted one near the window for better light. "When did I get this?" he asked, showing it to Antoinette. "Can I even fit in it?"

It was small, fit for a child it seemed, but Antoinette laughed as he tossed it to her. "You wore it when you were younger. Do you not remember?"

Edward shook his head. "Apparently not."

"We were fifteen. You and I raced in the gardens and stopped at the willow tree." She held the tunic close to her heart, her head tilted and her face glowing. "You bent down and kissed me. It was our first kiss."

Edward smiled, yet secretly felt terrible he didn't remember wearing it. Did it matter what he wore? He only remembered her. Her hair was up that day, all messy and unkempt from all the running they had done. Her rosy cheeks and beaded brow were radiant; the out of breath laugh she gave made his heart flutter so much he thought it would stop. And he remembered the kiss-quick and secret as if it were forbidden, yet slow and sensual the second time. It was the day he realized how in love with her he was and how he wanted to be with her forever.

"I remember it well," he said, taking the tunic back and folding it into a drawer. "I don't think I'll ever get rid of this."

He shut the drawer and turned to another pile. He rummaged through the clothes, taking some of the colorful ones and hanging them back up in the armoire. Some of the earthy toned ones were given to Antoinette to fold into the suitcase, the clothes appearing more fit for travel and wear. When he got to the bottom of the pile, he held up an ornamented one and stopped, frowning at its sight.

Antoinette stopped and approached him, fingering the bottom of the tunic with her fingers. "That was Stephen's?"

Edward nodded, saying nothing.

"I remember this," Antoinette said quietly, brushing the beads. "It was a gift for his birthday."

"A week before he died," Edward muttered, gently folding it and taking it to the drawer. He opened it, placing the tunic on top of his. He closed the drawer, placing his hands on the chest and lowering his head with a sigh.

Antoinette followed, her hand gently rubbing his shoulder.

"Two years," Edward said as he stood. "Two years since Stephen died, yet my father and mother still grieve. Why can't they move on?"

"If you lost a son, could you?" she asked.

"I'd have to," Edward replied, his heart feeling heavy. "Death leaves us no choice. We can't go back and change things. We can't bring my brother back."

He turned and headed towards the window, crossing his arms and gazing out into the distance. The western horizon glowed dimly with hues of sunset's glory. The mountains that surrounded the city sprayed the expanse in gray and green, and the lushness of the valley where the palace and city of Reigal stood showed a beauty that seemed to never end. It was such a beautiful land Stephen could have ruled in peace.

He felt gentle hands wrap around his chest, a soft kiss gracing his shoulder. He felt Antoinette's cheek press against his back and she embraced him. His heart felt like melting when she was near, and his hands clasped hers in front.

"I know you're hurt," she said to him.

"Over what?"

She nuzzled her cheek against the softness of his shirt. "Your father's comparisons."

"It doesn't help," Edward said quietly.

"He loves you."

"But he doesn't believe in me." Edward lowered his head. Who was he kidding? He barely believed in himself. "He knows I'm not Stephen, yet he expects me to be."

"Do you want to be him?"

The question took Edward by surprise. Was that Antoinette's way of saying his father was right? He felt a heaviness in his gut that made him feel sick. Why should he be surprised at her musings? Stephen was perfect, the golden child of the family. Edward was the runt. If he could be half the man his brother was, he would be worthy of the crown he'd wear as king.

Edward bit his lip as he spoke. "Yes," he answered. "I wish I could be him. But I'm not."

She said nothing at first, making him wonder what was going through her mind as she stepped away from his backside and came to his front. She stood there, her arms remaining around his waist, the dimming sunlight catching in her hair as she blocked the window from his view.

"Do you remember when we first met?" she began, straightening a wrinkle near his collar. "At our countries' celebration party, when we were thirteen?"

"Of course," he replied.

"When my parents and I journeyed to Reigal," she began, "I heard all about your brother. They ranted and raved about how he would be the perfect match for me."

Edward scoffed. Of course her parents would say such a thing. They didn't exactly approve of him at the time.

"Anyway," Antoinette continued, noticing Edward's hurt look, "I went to the party and eventually met Stephen. I thought he was a nice boy and polite, but I knew he wasn't for me."

She touched his chin to face her. "And then I met you. You were so different."

"So I've been told," Edward mumbled.

She smiled, shaking her head. "Different isn't always bad," she explained. "Do you know why I fell in love with you, Edward, and not your brother?"

He shook his head, his gaze lowering to the finger she put on his chest. She drew a small heart in the center, putting her hand over it when she was finished. "It was this," she replied. "You love deep, Edward Engel. It wasn't your face or your charm that won me over. It was your heart."

He couldn't hide the smile that wanted to burst from his lips.

"Your brother was a good man," she said. "But I don't want you to be him. He didn't have the passion that drives you or the sensitivity that makes you understand when others cannot. He was a scholar, you are a knight. You protect while others run away, your courage being your strength. Your brother wasn't as strong-he was afraid to take risks and make the hard decisions you have been trained to face. Since Stephen died, you've been trying to change yourself so you could please your father. Don't. Be the man I know you are. That, in turn, will make you the king you're meant to be."

"But what if I fail?" he asked.

"You won't." She smiled. "I believe in you."

Edward wrapped his arms around her. *I wish I had the faith you did.*

All he could do was embrace her, holding her tight as she held him back. He breathed in her scent as he buried his face into her neck. "I don't deserve you, Antoinette," he stuttered.

"I know you miss him and I know you blame yourself," she said, stroking his hair. "But your brother's death wasn't your fault. It was a training accident. Nothing could have prevented that."

If she only knew. Edward held her close, never wanting to let go, yet knowing he probably should. How did he, out of all the men in the world, get a woman who loved him so *blindly*? She had no reason to love him as much as she did, yet she loved him with all that she had. He was her world, just as she was his.

But he knew the truth. He knew she deserved better.

"I love you," he said as he kissed her and then pulled away. He took her by the hand, leading her to the other piles of tunics. "We still have a lot to do. Come, let us finish."

He was ready.

The sun barely peaked over the horizon as Edward patted the nose of the chestnut horse he would ride to Hugellia. It would be a long journey. First, they would head north towards the port city of Circh and turn west at the pass through the Gazing Heights. The mountains were smaller and easily navigated through, and soon they would come across some hills and make their way to the villages.

From there, they would travel to the border, and after a journey through the grasslands and plains of the countryside, they would arrive at the city of Kettensburg where Edward would stay with his mother's family and receive whatever gifts or advice they would give him. He would also renew the treaty of peace between their two lands-a treaty that was expected since the families had intermarried for generations-and then he would return for his wedding with Antoinette.

Antoinette prepared for her own journey home, days' worth of riding in a carriage towards her forested homeland in the east. She would leave towards the afternoon, however. There was still much planning to be done and she had yet to choose a dress for the wedding.

As Edward's guards for the journey readied their horses and gear, he said good-bye to his mother and father first. The king and queen stood proud and tall as he embraced them both. "My sweet Edward," Maria, his mother, began as she kissed his cheek. "Say hello to my brothers for me, and to Uncle Aldaric and Cousin Emmerich. They shall be glad of seeing you."

He kissed her back. "I will."

"Have a safe journey," she said, and he moved to his father next.

He embraced him, but the touch was not as warm as his mother's. "Don't forget the treaty when you return."

"I won't," Edward murmured as he stepped away.

The king and queen took their leave as they went back into the palace, returning to their duties. Their servants followed, but Antoinette remained. Edward approached her, cupping her face with his hands and pressing his forehead to hers.

"Come with me," he whispered.

She chuckled as she put her hands to his wrists, stroking them. "You know I can't. It's not allowed, plus it's not proper."

"Is it wrong to want your company?" he asked.

She shook her head. "I think you want more than my company."

"Perhaps." Edward laughed. "But I wouldn't act on it. Not yet, anyways."

She kissed him, softly and gently. "It'll give you something to look forward to, then."

He smiled, the sweetness of her breath lingering on his lips. "It does, Mrs. Engel." He kissed her again, closing his eyes and imagining his wedding day was already there.

"I'm not Mrs. Engel yet, my love," she said, "and you're stalling. You should already be on the road. It is a two week journey to Hugellia."

"Not yet," he whispered, pressing his lips to her again. Already the knights were starting to stare, some of them snickering. He didn't care.

"Yes, now." She pulled away gently, stroking his cheek. "You must go."

He frowned, but nodded. It was a long journey he had ahead of him. The sooner he left the more daylight he would have to travel by. He embraced her one last time. "I love you."

She hugged him tightly, a few tears falling from her face. "I love you, too. I will pray for you. Be safe, Edward, and when you get to Kettensburg, *don't* forget to ask Emmerich to be in the wedding. You need a best man."

Edward nodded slowly. "I will," he replied as he stepped away. The knights horsed and lined up beside the roadway. Edward turned one last time to look at his beloved before getting on his steed at the front. She wiped more tears this time and he looked away, her sadness too much to bear for his own weak heart.

He snapped the reins and the horse moved forward, the knights following. Down the palace road he went and past the marbled gate towards the main path that led up the valley and into the mountain passes. Edward turned one last time before leaving the city and looked towards his home. Antoinette was still there, watching and waiting outside the palace.

Good-bye, my love, he thought to himself before leading his men through the mountains.

Chapter 2: The Rock is Thrown

The journey was long and dull.

For over a week the prince and his guards had trekked through rock and hill on long, narrow passes that opened through the mountains. The ride was uneventful, yet pleasant, and aside from a few clouds and wind, each moment was filled with warmth and sun. The men could not have hoped for better weather, and the days were full of peace and quiet for the prince and his seven guards until they neared the border.

During that time a great storm arose. Winds whipped their faces and rain stung their skin like needles. Lightning lit the evening sky as if it were daylight, and more than once there was a close call where a horse or knight was nearly struck. The village they had stayed in was well behind them and not another Audlinian town lay nearby.

They rode on for hours, Edward leading them north in hopes of finding a cave to shelter in. His search provided nothing but trees and grass, and the storm covered all. It continued, sometimes lessening, sometimes becoming worse. The men began to grumble, and Edward's heart fell at what he heard behind his back.

"We're lost."

"Don't go north. Head west!"

"Are you sure the prince knows what he's doing?"

"I hope I don't get struck by lightning."

Edward ignored them as best he could, but the words stung in the back of his mind. How could he lead a nation if he couldn't lead seven men through a storm? It was a test he knew Stephen could pass, his knowledge of weather undoubtedly becoming a blessing were he there. Edward knew nothing of weather patterns and predictions, however, only knowing what was happening now, and that helped him little. He rode on, ignoring his worrisome thoughts, hoping a plan would appear...or at least a barn for the night.

And then he saw it. There, in the distance, stood an iron gate. It was the border of the kingdom of Verloris in the north-solitary, mysterious, and unknown. Few ever visited the land and even fewer left. And Edward wasn't the only one who noticed it. The others did, too.

"Some say a witch rules this kingdom," said the prince's guard.

"I heard it was a troll who ruled, or maybe an evil sea monster!" said another.

"Whoever rules this darkness must not be trusted. We shouldn't be here. We should go back!"

Edward turned to them, desperate to prove himself to his men. He stood tall and erect, mimicking his confident father, and called them. "Do you all still believe in myths and legends? Do you really think such things as witches exist? If you all are such cowards, then you shouldn't be in my service!" He paused, wanting to smile at their sudden attention and silence. So this was what it was like to command. "We ride on to Verloris. There is no other shelter. We will depart when the storm passes."

The first guard, Sir Rikert, approached the prince. His graying blonde hair was wet from the rain, his facial stubble making him look more like a mountaineer than a knight. But his dark eyes told the story of a good, honest man, and he bowed his head in respect, speaking in a soft voice. "Sire, this place is forbidden by our people. Even your forefathers had no relations with them. I am not a coward, and I would fight for you wherever I could, but this place has an evil air about it, and the presence of gloom is strong. I advise we continue west."

"And what of the storm?"

"We ride it out," Rikert continued. "It poses risks, yes, but I would rather leave my fate to God and ride through thunder and rain in the nature He controls than rest comfortable in the halls of a devilled king. We should go back."

"A devilled king?" Edward laughed. "They are but stories and rumors. We have no reason to fear them. They have left us alone as we have left them alone."

"And for good reason," Rikert said. "They are not to be trusted. It is not wise, Sire, to journey into this land…"

"Do not question me, Sir Rikert!" said the prince angrily. He couldn't lose his leadership. Not now. "Remember that it is I, and not you, who is in charge. If you are so cowardly to enter such a realm as I see you are, then I bid you leave and return to your home!"

"I am a God-fearing man, Sire," said Rikert. "But I feel that if you enter this kingdom, certain destruction will come to pass. I beg you, do not enter those gates! Please, listen to wisdom!"

"I bid you leave, Mr. Rikert!"

An eerie silence followed as a crack of thunder could be heard. The other guards stared in wonder and disbelief at the thought of Sir Rikert, the most trusted knight in the king's service, was not only going against Edward's commands, but also being sent back to Audlin alone.

"Very well, Sire," Rikert said calmly amidst the stares. "I may return home without honor in your eyes, but I know that I have done right. I pray your decision does not bring too much trouble."

Rikert looked at the prince with pity and sorrow. He turned around slowly and, reining in his horse, rode away in the rain.

The prince turned to the rest of his men. He noticed that they looked frightened as they shivered in the cold downpour. "Do any more of you wish to join Mr. Rikert? Do I have any other dishonorable men in my service?" the prince asked.

A guard across from him squared his shoulders. "Sire, we are not cowards. Though tired and cold, we will follow you to death and beyond!"

The prince smiled. He was gaining back control. "Very well, Sir Ichabod. I thank you for your service."

The rest of the men did not seem as sure as Sir Ichabod, though many remained silent. One of the knights, Sir Marcus Peterson, looked back and watched Sir Rikert ride south towards the mountains. Deep in his heart, he felt like he should follow. Sir Rikert was a wise man and older. He wouldn't have spoken if it wasn't urgent. But it was Sir Peterson's first assignment as a knight. He was younger than Edward by two years, his career just beginning. He couldn't leave now and ruin it.

But his conscience still pricked him as Edward reassured the men the kingdom of Verloris must not be as bad as everyone said it was. He rode on with the others, forcing his doubts to the back of his mind, and followed the prince across the large, wide bridge to the gate.

The rain continued to pour as Edward and his men approached the iron bars of Verloris' edge. The country had many strongholds and castles built upon their lands, the one the men were approaching being the first. The city was called Cathal, and other than a few brave merchants who were desperate for coin, not a man from Audlin, Edeland, or even Hugellia had anything to do with them. The only exception was Braiden, a small kingdom of the southwest, and they would trade with anyone as long as it held a profit.

The gate was closed, but the prince stepped forward and knocked. Already he could hear his men shaking in the cold. They needed warmth. They needed shelter. He was doing them a favor by getting them out of the rain. Didn't Sir Rikert know the only way to ride out a storm was to escape it? Shelter was shelter. It didn't matter where it was at.

A gruff, much like an animal growl, was heard from the other side. Edward's attention snapped forward, and though he didn't want to admit it, his heart stopped for a moment.

"Who desires to enter the Verloris of Cathal?" the voice rumbled.

"I am Edward Engel, son of Arden and Maria, prince of Audlin," Edward began. "I come on peaceful grounds. My men and I were caught in the storm while journeying to Hugellia. We seek shelter for the night."

A pause came, and then the clicking of a lock. The door screeched open and they were greeted by a giant, burly man with no hair. His face had a hardened look, and though he was simply a gatekeeper, Edward imagined that if given a sword, the man would become a dangerous warrior.

"Enter, friend and neighbor," the gatekeeper said. "You are unfortunate that the king is not here, but you will be given food and quarter. I will take you to the lady. She will see to your needs."

"My humble thanks," Edward replied, bowing his head. "We are most grateful for your kindness."

The gatekeeper remained unfazed, his eyes void of emotion. He turned and began to walk towards the center of the town where a stone castle stood. Edward unhorsed, urging his men to follow, and they left their steeds with the stable master, being guided to the lady of the city.

Not an eye remained focused on the path that lay ahead. To the right, to the left, and behind the knights looked, wondrous and fearful of their new surroundings. Never had they seen such greatness, and such sorrow, in a land and people.

There was no wood-only stone. Grass was dried and withered, the trees barren and dead as though summer's light refused to give them life. The inhabitants of the city were as hard as the buildings they dwelt in, glaring at the knights and watching them as they passed by in the streets.

Sir Peterson gulped, his stomach already doing an uncomfortable flip. Did his eyes show the fear that echoed from his heart? He hoped not. A glance at the others showed they also felt the same concern as he, though they hid it better. He couldn't help but wonder if they thought the same thing he did.

If I'm really a friend, why do they look at me like the enemy?

Marcus turned his head away, focusing his eyes forward towards the castle. He whispered a tiny prayer of protection underneath his breath. If the city was as terrible as it looked, he could only imagine what the main castle was like.

The gate was lowered and the men followed the keeper into the castle. No one spoke during the journey inside its great walls. They were greeted by further silence. Guards, armored in chain and metal plates, stood at attention on every corner stop, looking ahead as if staring into a void. Furs ornamented the stone floors and tapestries depicting battle and glory hung from the walls. Dripping candles hung from the ceilings, but they provided little warmth or light. The inside was just as hard and cold as the outside, if not more.

The gatekeeper led them down two halls and up a flight of stairs to a large room. Inside were many beds and blankets with a single sliver of a window facing north. The keeper stopped at the door, holding a hand out for the knights to walk in. "Your quarters, fine knights of the prince," he said. "Food and drink will be served to you by our servants. Eat and rest now."

The knights did as they were told, filing in and finding a place to settle for the night. Edward followed until the keeper spoke. "Nay, Prince Edward," he said. "The lady provides special quarters for her honored guests. Your room is up the hall."

Marcus looked to Edward, his head slightly shaking no. It wasn't wise for the prince to be separated from his guards. They were in unknown territory-anything could happen-and since he was the only son of the king, his life was even more important.

But Edward nodded to the keeper, ignoring his guard's looks of objection. He was strong and needed to show his men he had no fear, but he also had to be diplomatic. It would insult the Verloris if he did not accept hospitality on their terms. He knew their culture little and did not want to provoke them, so he would follow without concern. His sword remained at his side, however, and there was not a man who couldn't be felled in a second when Edward Engel fought him.

"Of course, noble gatekeeper," Edward replied, eyeing his guards with a look that told them to remain silent. "I would not wish to upset the lady. Please, lead on."

The knights remained displeased, but nodded in agreement to the prince's wishes. Marcus remained at the front, his dark eyes lowering in shame as he watched the door shut and Edward disappear from view. He sat on the bed beside him in a huff, ignoring the confused yet casual murmurs of his fellow men. He bent his head in prayer, first asking forgiveness for not following Sir Rikert, the second for wisdom. And he had a feeling he wasn't the only one who would need it in that place. More than anyone, Edward would need it, too.

Edward was led to a grand room at the end of the hall. It was as big as a peasant's home, warm and welcoming. A great hearth stood at the center, its fire cackling gently and providing light. At the center was a bed built into the floor, piled with furs and silks and pillows with a sheer gold canopy hanging from the ceiling to cover it. A door that led to a balcony was on the left and a great table, already set with plates and knives and spoons, was on the right. A vat of wine was at the center, surrounded by golden goblets.

The keeper stopped as Edward walked in, eyeing his surroundings. "The lady will serve you dinner personally within the hour. For now, please rest and wait. Our servants will bring you fresh clothes to change in."

"That is not necessary," Edward politely interrupted. "I have brought my own clothing."

"The lady insists," the gatekeeper returned, almost perturbed. "She will see to your every need."

There was no need to upset the hosts. If they wanted to provide clothes, he would have to oblige. "Again, thank you."

Edward bowed his head. The keeper only grunted, turning and shutting the door.

Edward stepped forward, looking around. The room was beautiful and cozy, much like his room at home. He walked to the hearth, placing his hands forward to gather warmth. The tender flames shot heat towards him, taking the chill away from his body and bringing a smile to his face.

Sir Rikert worried for nothing, Edward thought to himself. *Still he rides in the rain while we rest in comfort. Didn't he know I can lead my own men? I know what I'm doing. I'll prove it to them all.*

The clothes were less than comfortable.

Edward fidgeted in the roughness of the cloth. It was of Verloris style and make, tight fitting and rigid, and more than anything he felt like one of the castle guards he saw only moments before. How did they wear such clothing, standing perfectly still and not being able to itch, scratch, or move? They were disciplined, surely-much more than he could be.

After the keeper returned with some servants and the clothes, he spoke of meeting with the lady. "She is the daughter of our king, regent of the fortress of Cathal," the man had said, "and one of the many caretakers of this abode. She will bring your dinner and meet with you in a moment."

That was fifteen minutes ago. Edward sat at the table, eyeing the setting before him and wondering what dinner he was to be served. Judging by the amount of furs on the bed, he knew it had to be some sort of boar or bear or other meat. That, he didn't mind. As long as it tasted good and was cooked well, he would be pleased, especially after the long journey in the rain.

His thoughts went to the door as the handle suddenly turned and creaked. He stood to his feet out of respect, planting his hands to his sides. In walked the gatekeeper, holding the door open. Servants soon brought food to the table, setting a platter of roasted pig and various vegetables, breads, and pastries around it. They quickly left, hurrying out of the room in an orderly line, and Edward waited. A minute passed until the keeper began to speak again.

"Presenting Her Royal Highness, Malina Serus, princess of Verloris," he said. A woman stepped forth, wearing a pleated gold dress that came together at the waist. She was fair, thin, and plain in form. Her face was as hard as the gatekeepers, yet surprisingly confident. Her raven hair flowed straight to her hips, a band across her forehead with a symbol of her people at the center. Braids with gold ribbons intertwined came down with her locks, and her gray eyes gazed to Edward, not as a simple guest, but as territory to conquer.

"Welcome, son of Arden and Maria." Her voice was as cold as her eyes. She stepped forth to the table across from him. "I am Malina, daughter of Calimus. I welcome you to Cathal."

She turned to the gatekeeper. "Leave us." The man nodded, stepping out and closing the door softly. Malina turned back to Edward, offering a slight smile. "Please sit, my prince. Eat and drink at my table."

Edward sat and she followed. "I thank you, Your Majesty," he replied. He took some food and put it to his plate as she poured them both something to drink.

"You look weary," she said, handing him the goblet. "My servant tells me you journey to Hugellia and were caught in the storm."

"It is true," Edward replied. "And forgive me for the inconvenience. I would not have stopped had the weather been better. I don't wish to intrude."

Malina smiled, taking a sip from her own goblet. "There is no need to apologize, my prince. All are welcome to the Verloris if they wish. It is a pleasure to host a neighbor we rarely hear from. Perhaps fate has brought you here for our lands to change our families' past relations."

"You have showed me nothing but kindness since I have arrived," Edward replied, taking a bite of food. "I will speak to my father about this, surely."

"You will be king one day," Malina said, looking at him in a way that made Edward shift in his seat. "Such decisions will remain with your reign, I hope."

"Yes, yes of course," Edward muttered. The woman continued to stare at him, and he wondered if she thought him handsome. Whatever her musings, it began to make him feel uncomfortable. He cleared his throat. "I will remember your kindness when I come to my throne."

Malina straightened herself in her seat. "Of course. I only wish I could say the same. My father's throne will go to my eldest sister. She is a foolish girl, but my father favors her. I hope she will listen to me when I speak for you."

"Whatever happens, happens," Edward replied. "We can only try."

"But you will be a good king," Malina continued. "I can see it in you. Your eyes dictate strength and power. Your people must fear you greatly."

"My people respect me," Edward cleared. "There is a difference."

"There is no difference." Malina paused, a smirk coming onto her face as she browsed his features. "I am glad my sister is not here. Had she met you, she would take you to husband and make you king of both our nations."

Now the conversation was becoming strange. Edward remained silent, looking towards his plate. "I'm glad I have not met her either. My fiancée would be displeased."

"Fiancée?"

That got her attention. Edward looked up, nodding. "Yes. Antoinette van Echt, princess of Edeland. We are to be married in a little over three months."

Malina paused at first, looking away, but then returned with her own confident glance. "A queen has been chosen quickly for the prince. You must be thrilled."

"We chose each other," Edward continued. "It was not arranged. I am in love with her, and she with me. And yes, I am more than thrilled."

Malina went back to her drink. "The lady of Edeland must be quite the beauty to steal a man such as yourself."

"Angelic," Edward replied. "There is no word to describe her features justly."

"Indeed." Malina lowered her brow. She stood up, straightening her dress and bowing her head. "If you will excuse me, Prince Edward," she began, stepping away from the table, "but I see you are weary, and I do not help much by interrupting your meal with my fancies. Forgive me. I will leave you to your rest and speak with you in the morning. If you need anything, my servants will be outside your door."

Edward bowed his head, smiling. That would teach her to flirt with him. He knew who he wanted. No one could change his mind. "Thank you, Your Majesty. May you have a pleasant rest."

"And you," she replied, rushing out the door.

Chapter 3: The Lady of Cathal

The rain continued through morning.

Edward huffed in frustration, crossing his arms as he glanced out the balcony window. The weather had only gotten worse since the night before, putting him another day behind in reaching Hugellia. Knowing his mother's family, it would send them in a panic, thinking something had gone wrong. He sighed, knowing there was nothing he could do but wait and speak to his men, hoping the family wouldn't notice if he was a day or two late.

The door knocked, quickly creaking open. In stepped the princess of Verloris, making Edward shudder. He remembered the awkwardness of the night before and had hoped to avoid her that morning by going to speak with his men. He had only awoken minutes ago and was still dressed in nightclothes. Despite the uncouthness, she did not seem bothered by his unkempt appearance, nor by the look of disapproval he gave when she approached him so freely.

"Are you hungry?" she asked, herself fresh and clean like she never needed sleep. "Breakfast has already been prepared. Your men are being served now. Will you join me in my quarters?"

Edward frowned, gathering his robe to his chest. "I am not dressed or ready."

"It matters not." Malina smiled. "A robe is suitable clothing for the morning meal. It flatters you."

"But it isn't proper." Edward tried to keep his tone polite but felt he was failing. Was the woman being too hospitable, or could she not take a hint? His loving speech about Antoinette ran her off the night before but clearly didn't keep her from coming back in the morning.

Her fingers moved to the long collar on his chest and she fumbled with the soft fabric. "It would be no one but us. You have no need for embarrassment."

He gently removed her hand and brought it to her side. She wasn't stopping and now he had to be blunt, rude or not. "I do not think it proper for a man pledged to be married to dine with a woman alone."

"You dined with me last night," Malina replied.

"Not in bedclothes."

"Does it matter what you wear?"

Edward secretly cursed her stubborn manner. "Your Majesty, I don't mean to be rude, and I am grateful for the hospitality you have shown me so far, but I insist we keep our acquaintanceship professional by no longer dining with each other alone."

She smiled, turning towards the door. "I understand. You wish to not ignore the men who travel with you. A quaint act of leadership. I will prepare a banquet in your honor instead. You and your men shall dine with the Verloris this afternoon at six."

Edward stood there, speechless. What was her game? He mentioned nothing of his men to her. Could she not see he addressed her forwardness? She was a mysterious woman, that one, and for once he didn't know what to think. One minute she was flirty, the next she was indifferent. Her constant changing made him feel uneasy.

Despite his personal protests, he could not decline the invitation. His father expected him to be diplomatic, and deep down inside, he knew Stephen would accept. If he was to be the king everyone wanted him to be, he had to change. Though he'd rather stay with his men and prepare for the journey to Hugellia, he had to accept Malina's offer to give his men dinner. He couldn't always think like a knight. He had to think like a king.

"Thank you, Your Majesty." He bowed politely, forcing the flowery words past his lips. "I will tell my men."

"I will see you then." She lingered at the door for a moment, gazing at him with a steady eye, until she turned and walked away.

"We're *what*?"

Sir Peterson couldn't hide the shock in his voice as he muttered his disapproval among the other knights. The prince seemed to not hear it, for as he spoke in the breakfast hall, he continued his declaration that they would stay one more day in Cathal until the rains stopped. "And," Edward continued, "the lady of Cathal, Princess Malina, has invited us to dine with her this evening at six. The dinner will be given in our honor, so I expect you to be at your best. You represent your country and king at this dinner and it is our duty to bring Audlin a good name to the Verloris."

After that he was gone, returning to his quarters to finish his own breakfast. Marcus crossed his arms, shaking his head in disbelief as he returned to the corner of the room near the window, eyeing the drips of water that slowly ran down the window sill above a gray backdrop of stone.

Sir Ichabod, guzzling a goblet of wine, approached.

"Not hungry, young sir?"

Marcus looked up at the older, huskier Ichabod. His dark hair was now thin and balding, but his muscles and large frame more than made up for what he lacked in good looks. The young knight shook his head, strands of near-black locks falling onto his lowered brow.

"I have no appetite to eat, thank you."

"And why not?" Ichabod stifled a small burp. "The food is the grandest I've ever tasted! We'd never see anything like this in Reigal."

Marcus frowned. "I'll pass."

"At least drink the wine."

"I don't drink."

"Then content yourself with rainwater!" Ichabod sneered, finishing his wine. "You do yourself no good by not resting when given the chance. Take my advice, from the learned to the learning: relax."

Marcus scoffed, looking back towards the rain. "I'll find no rest within stone. We are in the enemy's lands, Jacob. My hand stands ready by the bow."

Ichabod laughed, eyeing his now empty cup. "They are strange enemies to treat us so good, even offering us a dinner in our honor."

"Do not call them friends, yet," Marcus continued with a sigh. "They are a foul people with a history of war and vice. We should be leaving instead of partying."

"In the rain?"

"Yes, in the rain," Marcus repeated. "Water cannot damage the soul or body. These snakes of a people can!"

"*Sh!* Watch what you speak!" Ichabod lowered his voice, leaning in. "We have to tread carefully here, Marcus. The last thing we need to do is anger a monarch on our way to Hugellia."

"We risk angering our own monarch," Peterson murmured under his breath. "This Malina Edward described...I don't know. I just don't like the feel of this place or the people. This party of hers will come to no good, I'm afraid."

"I can see how a dinner party can be threatening." Ichabod snickered. "Heaven forbid we eat with them."

Marcus stopped leaning against the wall and stood erect, facing Ichabod in frustration. Though he was young and inexperienced, unlike the others, he seemed to be the only one that remained on his guard. "All I meant is we should be cautious. There is a reason this land is forbidden to us, Jacob. We shouldn't be here."

"Maybe you should tell the prince that," Ichabod returned. "Then again, you're starting to sound like Sir Rikert."

Marcus turned away, frowning. "It is not my place to question His Majesty's orders."

"Then shut up and drink!" Ichabod laughed as he grabbed another bottle to fill his cup. He offered it to the young knight, who only shook his head, turning his gaze back to the rain in silence.

The hours passed by like minutes.

Edward watched the fire kindle from a cushioned sofa across the room. His room was empty, silent, save the occasional rumble of thunder and the pitter-patter of rain on the window. His chin rested on his palm and his mind wandered as he waited for Malina's servants to lead him to dinner.

His thoughts drifted to the reaction of his men when he told them they would be staying in Cathal for another day. A few looked happy, glad for the extra day of rest and merriment. Most were indifferent, clearly following the wishes of their prince and future monarch, not wanting to be sent home like Sir Rikert for questioning orders. But there were a couple who looked at him in disappointment, even anger, and it was those faces that burned into his mind.

He saw Sir Fauler turn his eyes away in disgust, shaking his head. He saw the youngest knight, Sir Peterson, mutter something under his breath as he lowered his brow. Would Stephen have gotten the same reaction had he agreed to stay? What about his father?

Edward rubbed his forehead, the aches of worry already cramping his full mind. No matter how hard he tried to be the kingly prince he was supposed to be, there was always someone who disapproved. He didn't want to stay in Cathal any longer. He wanted to be in Hugellia more than anyone. But the storm was still strong, and he couldn't risk the men's health. And even more than that, they were at the mercy of a foreign ruler. One wrong move and a tone of disrespect could start a war, something his father would not be happy to participate in given his aging body.

More than anything, he wished Antoinette was there. He could use her encouragement, her faithful words that somehow always built him up when he felt torn down. He wanted to see her smile and her eyes that told him she trusted and believed in him. He wanted to sense that reassuring touch that made him feel like he was truly important.

A frown crept upon his face. The thought of simply leaving everyone else behind, forgetting Hugellia and running back to Reigal, came into his mind. He missed her so much at that moment, but she was far away. Was she thinking of him as he was thinking of her? Loneliness entered his heart, and it made his soul sink in despair.

His thoughts were interrupted by a knock on the door. He got up, almost pleased at the timing of it all. It forced the sense of loneliness to the back of his mind and allowed him to assume the princely façade that was coming back far too often.

Edward opened the door to find the gatekeeper standing before him. Edward had to laugh at the thought of seeing the man too many times to count. Why was he not at the gates as his job dictated him?

"Noble gatekeeper." Edward bowed his head in respect. "Is there something you need from me?"

The gatekeeper bowed in return, though his tough demeanor remained. "My lady bids me to announce you at the dinner. Are you ready to go?"

"I am," Edward said, following him out. The gatekeeper led him through the hall and down two flights of stairs to the banquet room. He said nothing, making Edward feel awkward at the lack of interaction. Back home, there would at least be simple pleasantries.

He thought he could start one. "Friend," Edward began politely as they continued to walk. "Do you have a name? I would wish to commend you to the lady."

"I am the lady's servant," the gatekeeper replied in a gruff.

"But you have a name, don't you? Something you are called by the lady?"

The answer remained the same. "I am the lady's servant."

Was it that he had no name, or was the man not allowed to say? It gave Edward an uncomfortable feeling. "Shall I call you Gatekeeper, then, since that is what you do?"

"I am not the gatekeeper," the man replied. "I am only the gatekeeper when the lady wishes it. I am the lady's servant."

By now Edward was intrigued. What was Verloris like? Were the people all "servants" as they were called, doing the bidding of the royal family? Did any of them have jobs, careers, or any choice in what they did?

"Did you have a regular gatekeeper?" Edward asked.

"The gatekeeper is whoever the lady wishes it to be," he replied. "The former gatekeeper fulfilled his duties as I have fulfilled mine."

"Forgive me for my intrusion," Edward continued, his curiosity rising. "I only wish to understand your culture, for it seems quite different from mine. Do your people have jobs…something they do with their lives?"

"They do the bidding of the lady and the royal family."

"Everyone here?"

"Mostly."

The monarchy sounded more like a dictatorship, but Edward kept his disapproval to himself. "Are there any who are not servants besides the royal family?"

"The Velori."

"And who are they?"

The gatekeeper stopped, looking at Edward with a glare. "It is better you not know, Your Majesty."

Edward gulped, hoping his sudden fear would not be so transparent. "I see," he replied, "and understand. You have a very curious culture…servant of the lady. Again, forgive me of the intrusion. I was only wishing to learn."

The gatekeeper grunted as he stopped in front of the banquet room. He put his fingers to the door handle and stood before Edward could enter. "I shall announce you to my lady. Your men have already been seated and shall stand upon your arrival. Your chair is next to my lady and you shall dine with her."

Edward frowned. "But my men…"

"Are at the tables in front of you," the gatekeeper interrupted. "Fear not, Your Majesty. The lady chooses to give them the honor they so deserve."

Edward nodded. He would have to play along.

The door opened to a vast room full of extravagance. Red and burgundy tapestries hung from the walls. Rich furs lined the stone floors and there was a large fire at the center gently blazing in the hearth. Long tables ornamented with cloths and red tassels stood in two great lines, stretching down from one end of the room to the other with a great oak table going across the front. Gold plates and goblets were set forth with royal musicians playing in the corners, loud and cacophonic. Women danced with tambourines and drums, many of the men enjoying the dance more than the music.

As Edward entered and the gatekeeper announced him, the music stopped and the dancers bowed. Malina, at the front table, was the first to rise, followed by Edward's men. She held a goblet draped in red silk above her head. "Welcome, Edward, son of Arden and Maria, to my table." She held out her arm to the empty seat beside her. "Come, take your place at my side."

It was an awkward position for him, and a part of him would rather sit with his men. Antoinette would not approve of him dining beside a woman so clearly smitten with him, and he did not approve of it either. But as he looked around the room and saw the same unhappy faces from before stare back at him, he consented. His men, all of them, needed a strong leader. They would expect him to be like Arden and Stephen. They would expect him to put his country first.

"Thank you, Your Majesty," Edward replied with a humble bow. The gatekeeper led him to the table. He was seated in a comfortable, cushioned chair; as he sat, the others followed. Malina set her goblet down and called for the dinner to be served.

"Honored sons of Audlin and Verloris," she began as they silently looked her way. "Guards of Cathal, knights of King Arden, and my lord, Prince Edward, I bid you all welcome in my father's name. Though you have been here but a day, I feel a friendship is already kindled. Eat, drink, and be happy, for..." She paused, adding a laugh that others followed. "Assuming the rains have stopped...tomorrow you journey to Hugellia. Enjoy your meal and drink your wine. Take your fill, for there is plenty to spare. What is ours is yours. Let the dinner begin!"

A cymbal was heard from one of the musicians, and instantly the sounds and dances of the night continued, even stronger than what they were as Edward entered. The great door at the end flew open, filling the room with servants caring plates and platters of succulent food and drink. Malina and Edward were served first, followed by the men, and in an instant there was much laughter and merriment.

But Malina was far from pleased. She turned to a servant who had just poured her wine, making a face of disgust at the cup in her hand. "Ergol!" Her voice made Edward cringe. It sounded so arrogant, so demeaning. The poor servant groveled to her, bowing.

"Yes, Your Majesty?"

She took the bottle from his hand, sneering at it. "I do not want this wine."

"It is our finest selection, Your Majesty, just like you requested."

Malina glowered, her eyes beading even further than what they normally were. "I do not want white wine. Bring the red."

"The red?" Ergol repeated.

"Yes." Malina turned to Edward sweetly, her face softening. "And hurry. His Majesty looks parched."

Ergol rushed away to retrieve the wine as Malina swayed to Edward at his seat. She bent forward, her hands resting upon his arm, her fingers aching to touch the skin underneath his sleeve. "I only serve the best to my honored guests," she cooed. "I trust the dinner meets your fancy?"

Edward cleared his throat, unsure of what to make of her forward advances. He had to be careful. "I am pleased with what you have done for me and my men, Your Majesty. Thank you. It is, indeed, an honor."

"An honor that is the greatest of pleasures." She smiled as Ergol brought her a newly opened bottle. She took it and poured the liquid, rich and red, into Edward's cup, followed by hers.

"It is aged a hundred years," she said, placing the bottle in front of them. "And is saved just for us. Royal wine fit for a royal prince and princess."

Edward took in a deep breath. He had never tasted wine, for his mother disapproved of it. She once witnessed a nobleman hit his wife, a dear friend of hers, while drunk and was abhorred by the man's behavior. She never allowed alcohol in her presence again.

He picked up the cup, offering Malina a fake smile for appeasement. He did not want to drink it, but as he watched Malina raise her goblet, expecting to drink with him, his thoughts betrayed him. Had he not seen his father share wine in a toast of friendship for a treaty with Braiden? When it came to building alliances, anything went.

"Drink, my prince," Malina said, touching the rim of her goblet to his. "And let us toast to a beautiful night."

"Of course," Edward stuttered, and put the goblet to his lips. The liquid burned his throat, and he was careful to drink it slowly so as not to choke him. The wine was far from bad. It actually tasted...good. Malina laughed, taking another drink, and Edward sported another smile. He still felt in control and wasn't dizzy. There was no sign of drunkenness. If his father could do it, surely he could. And he was strong, stronger than anyone would give him credit.

He drank again, feeling more like a king than a prince, and watched as his men laughed the night away.

Dishonorable pigs.

Already an hour had passed that seemed like a month. Marcus Peterson sat at the end of the table, furthest from

Edward and Malina, and sighed. Though food and drink were set before him, he ate little and drank even less. All hunger and thirst seemed to leave once he entered the banquet hall and watched his surroundings. What started as a simple dinner soon turned into a wild man's party. Singers sang songs that could only be described as vulgar. Wine poured freely from goblet to goblet, their cups seeming to be bottomless. Women barely clad danced near the men, enticing them to unearthly things in the dark. Even two of their most beautiful came to him when they saw him not eat.

"Not hungry, oh knight of the guard?" said the one with raven hair as she leaned forward, the scent of vanilla on her neck.

Marcus turned his head, careful not to look. She was beautiful, it was true, but he knew duty came before pleasure. She was not there to cheer him, but to deceive him.

"I am not hungry, thank you," he replied, crossing his arms.

Her sister in play, a tall, auburn-haired girl, laughed. "Shall I bring you more wine, then?"

"I have only drunk water," Marcus replied. "Perhaps there is another who is parched?"

The auburn-haired girl frowned while the raven-haired one laughed. "So young and feisty!" she said, leaning back on the table. She put a hand to his arm, feeling the hard muscle that suddenly tensed at her touch. "And strong, too," she whispered.

Marcus met her gaze with a glare. He yanked his arm away, lowering his brow.

She laughed, not intimidated. "You are anxious, knight of the guard." She took his hand in hers, pulling forward. "Come, let me soothe you."

He pulled his hand back. "My wife would not appreciate another woman pleading for my company in bed."

"You are married?" she asked, her smile widening further.

His eyes beaded. Was there no decency in this woman? "I am not married yet," he began sternly. "But one day I will be. And I made a promise that I would be honorable in mind and body for the woman I pledge myself to."

"And what if you never marry?"

"Then I shall be honorable in the sight of my God," Marcus sneered. "As should you be!"

Her face suddenly changed from flirty to angry, and had she been given the chance, Marcus would have received a slap then and there. But Sir Ichabod, already drunk with wine, tottered to Peterson's corner of the table and wrapped his arms around the young woman.

"I'll take up your offer if he refuses," he whispered in her ear.

The woman laughed alongside as she buried her fingers into what remained of his hair. The other woman soon joined, but Marcus stood, desperate to keep some honor for his fellow knights.

"I'm sure your wife would be pleased to see you now, Jacob."

"Is he waiting for a woman that will never come, too?" The raven-haired girl laughed, but Jacob waved his hand.

"Don't anger him too much, girls!" Jacob mocked as he nearly toppled over. "He might hit you with his arrows!"

"Like Cupid?" The girl laughed.

"Or a childish hunter," the other girl sneered back.

But Jacob ignored them as he staggered forward, sitting on the table, half way on Marcus's dinner plate. "Get me some more drinks," he said to the women. "Then we'll continue this conversation."

They slithered away as Marcus glared at them. Jacob coughed and cleared his throat, putting a hard grasp on the knight's shoulder.

"You are embarrassing the prince!" he sneered under his breath.

Marcus looked up towards Edward. He didn't look unhappy or angry. In fact, he looked quite merry. His wine goblet had already been filled once by Malina and more than that, he filled the goblet himself.

"I should take that as a compliment, Sir Ichabod," Marcus said, shuffling his shoulder away from Jacob's grip. "Especially by what I see tonight. Look around you. The knights of King Arden and his prince both drink the night away and waste it on flattery."

"You're an adult now," Jacob said, the stench of alcohol strong upon his breath. "It's time you started acting like one! What do you think the men do for entertainment while they're away from home?"

Marcus frowned. "I was hoping anything but this."

"Well, this is what we do. At least, this is what the *good* ones do." The women returned with more wine, and Jacob grabbed the goblet, guzzling until the liquid ran down his throat and onto his tunic. "Come, Marcus! Join us and be a man!"

Marcus shook his head, turning away. He would probably get in trouble for it. He'd probably even be sent away like Sir

Rikert. But he wouldn't get pulled down like the others. There was no room for shame with his humility.

"I suppose I shall remain a boy then, for I would rather have honor and dignity in the sight of God. Good night!" Marcus stood, heading towards the door. Jacob called his name, but the young knight paid him no heed.

Marcus turned to a servant, bowing humbly. "Forgive me. I am ill. I ask that I please be excused to my quarters for some rest. See to it that no one disturbs me except the other knights or the prince. Thank you." The servant nodded, opening the door.

Before leaving and returning to his bed, Marcus looked one last time at the revelry of the room. Drunkenness, lewdness, indecency...King Arden would cringe at the sight. What was even worse was Edward at the front and center, too busy with his own drinking that he couldn't notice what was going on around him.

God forgive you, he thought to himself, and turned and walked away.

Chapter 4: Prince Edward's Mistake

The room was a swirl about him.

How many drinks of wine had Edward had? He thought it was only a few, but perhaps it was more. It felt like more, at any rate. One moment he seemed fine and in control. The next he started feeling giddy, almost silly, and his mind moved as fast as the dancers around the table. Everything in front, behind, and beside became one giant blur.

I think I've had enough.

He pushed the wine goblet away from him, guessing three or four was his limit, wondering if he had far surpassed it. But as he stopped, he noticed the feeling didn't wear off. Instead, it seemed to linger, even worsen.

A part of him knew he should worry about it, but whether it was the wine or the wildness around him, he found himself not caring. He was at a party, after all, and this was what happened at parties. He might as well live it up.

"More wine, my prince?" Malina asked, interrupting his thoughts.

Edward shook his head, his stomach already burning from too much. "Many thanks, Your Majesty, but I am well-filled. I think if I drink any more drops, I shall burst like a balloon!" He suddenly laughed at the statement, as did she, thinking the statement funnier than what it actually was.

"Perhaps you *have* had too much." Malina laughed again, reclining in her chair. "As have I. Methinks we're both drunk!"

Edward chuckled as he steadied himself in his chair, his head suddenly dizzying more. "I believe you," he said, rubbing his forehead, "but is the room supposed to spin so much?"

"Only if you're not used to it."

Edward shrugged. So much for being the strong monarch. "I fear I have showed myself, then. I am not such a manly man, am I?"

"Nonsense!" The princess laughed as she flung her arm in the air. "The prince is only being modest. You are strong, handsome, and your men love you. One day the name of Edward will be the most powerful name in the land, and a thousand generations shall sing of your exploits in foreign halls!"

Edward smirked at the flattery, but knew it not to be true. Rather than debate her fancies, however, he longed for rest. His head refused to stop spinning, and for a moment he wondered if he might faint.

Malina noticed his silence and put a soft hand on his arm. "You do not feel well?"

He looked up, slightly annoyed. "I'm fine. I'm not sick, if that's what you think."

"But you are tired," she cooed, leaning closer. "As I am. Come." She got up from her seat, urging him to follow. "We shall return to our quarters and retire for the night."

"And the men?" Edward asked, staggering up.

She caught him by the arm, holding him steady. "They shall continue without us. Why should we spoil their fun?"

"My thanks, Your Majesty," Edward replied as he tried to take a step on his own. He wobbled, making Malina's grip tighter on his arm, and he nearly stumbled. Even the floors seemed to move opposite of the walls. Were he not careful, he could fall and be sick from the constant motion.

He was led out the door and back into the quiet hall. He took no notice of his men nor said his good-byes, and neither did they. The party was too loud, the wine too strong, and the women too enticing. But Edward had noticed none of it. Even the halls became a blur to him, and whether Malina led him up or down he didn't know. All he wanted was sleep and the hope of waking to feeling normal again.

"The rooms are dark," Edward muttered.

"As they are supposed to be," Malina answered kindly. "It is evening."

"How late?" Edward asked.

"I'm not sure," Malina replied. "It is before midnight, surely."

Edward stopped, the spinning almost becoming unbearable. He was tempted to lean forward, but Malina gently held him up with her hand against his chest. Her touch sent chills down his spine, the way she fingered his tunic. Only Antoinette had been allowed to come that close, and it worried him that Malina dared to cross a line she had been warned too many times about.

They stood there in the silence of the hall, looking at one another. Her eyes warmed to him, and she licked her lips as she looked to the floor. Her mind was on something, that much he knew, but the dizziness was too strong, the wine too potent. All energy to tell Malina something she wouldn't listen to anyway seemed to leave with his sense of balance.

"Let's keep moving," Edward said, urging forward. Malina complied, this time wrapping her arms around his waist to keep him steady.

Her embrace went unnoticed as Edward's mind became consumed with lying down. Were he to find a bed, then the spinning would stop. After a few minutes of silent walking, he was about to ask Malina if they were to his room yet, but as he opened his mouth to speak, she suddenly stopped in front of a door.

"We're here." She opened it, leading him into the room. He took no notice of his surroundings save the couch near the hearth and the fur blanket folded on the seat. She sat him on it, and he slouched to the arms of the chair, longing for rest. The dizziness continued, but slowly began to ease.

"I shall bring you some water," Malina replied, walking to the other side of the large, warm room. "The water will dilute the wine in your body. It shall speed the recovery process."

"Again, thank you," Edward said quietly as he closed his eyes, desperate to find stability.

Minutes passed like hours as he tried to regain his balance. Closing his eyes only made things worse, the dizziness fading and then coming back in waves. Soon it became gut-wrenching. He nearly fell forward, tumbling off the couch, before opening his eyes and catching himself at the edge of the seat. Water-he needed it quickly for the dizziness to stop. But as he waited, he found Malina never returned.

He lifted himself up slowly, trying to make out the room he was in to see if he could find her. He squinted, and for a moment the room came clear into view. He was not in the room that was declared to be his for the stay in Verloris. This room was much bigger, darker, and rearranged in a different way.

The couch was on the side, though the hearth was in the center. There was no table setting for dining. The balcony was there, yes, but it was much larger and grander than the one he had seen. In the center of the room was a sheer, white canopy that hung from the ceiling to the floor. Moonlight shone upon it, and Edward could see there was a large bed that was built into the floor with steps all around descending to it. In the midst of the canopy was a shadowy figure, feminine in form, standing in the center. It seemed to be looking at him, beckoning for him to follow.

Edward struggled himself up, wondering if he was in a dream or in reality. The line seemed too blurry now. He edged near the wall, bracing against it so he wouldn't fall over, and inched closer and closer to the canopy. He stopped as the figure suddenly tensed, silently waiting.

His fingers reached the canopy and pulled back the sheers. There stood Malina, her back to him, clad only in a gray, sleeveless nightgown. Her dark, curled hair flowed down her back, and her head peaked to the side as Edward stood before her. Her eyes met his in a seductive gaze, and she slowly let a strap fall off her shoulder.

Edward turned away, gulping, his mind moving faster than ever. Water was soon the last thing on his mind. He felt passion rise in his body and the adrenaline kicked in, but his reason became desperate to hold on. *I love Antoinette. I won't betray her.* He repeated the words to himself in his mind. But as Malina edged closer to him, and his dizziness worsened, he felt his guard slowly begin to crumble.

Malina wrapped her arms around his neck, her fingers twirling the short strands of his wavy hair. It sent a fire through him that burned, and he began to relish himself in the heat. She was becoming harder to resist, especially as his eyes roamed across the silk that was her only covering. "Oh

Edward," she whispered as her lips edged closer to his. "I could feel your desire rise since we left the banquet hall."

Her hands cupped his face and she kissed him slowly. Edward pulled away, nearly losing his balance, as he forced Antoinette's name to repeat in his head. "I..." He paused, the air catching in his lungs with every breath. "I'm sorry, Your Majesty. I'm afraid I have misled you or you must be confused."

"Confused?" She laughed, still toying with his hair. "Nay, my prince. I can read a man as well as a book. I see the loneliness of your heart. I see the fire of passion in your eyes. I see the longing to taste a woman's love on your lips. I am willing to give all of this to you now, and more."

The dizziness felt like consuming him. He fought it as hard as he could. "My...loneliness, my passion, my longing is for one woman, Your Majesty."

"And she is not here." Malina smirked.

"But she is in my heart..." Edward stuttered, suddenly feeling light-headed. He had to sit down. Fast. "I...I love her..." Suddenly he tumbled, the dizziness too much, and Malina caught him, laying him on the bed.

She followed him down, caressing his face. He felt her lips upon his neck, and suddenly he was too weak to object. His hands moved to her waist and began to tug at her gown. "Love me now, Edward," she whispered to him as his lips moved to her own. "And love your Antoinette later."

It was a good dream.

There he was, under the beloved willow tree of his family's gardens, holding Antoinette in his arms. She was laughing, he was loving her, and they were making new memories under the tree that was already filled with so many. Edward indulged himself in her beauty, her scent, her taste, as she did in his. Throughout the entire dream, all he could think of was one thing.

My wife. My beautiful, wonderful wife…

When the dream ended, he found himself slowly waking to a room barely lit by the morning sky. There was a noise from a bird or two, but their song seemed sad, long and quiet. Edward took in a deep breath and noticed his head still felt funny, but ignored it as he felt a soft hand gently caress his bare chest.

I guess it wasn't a dream after all. A slight smile came to his face as he felt soft skin come atop his and two small hands roam across his shoulders. Fingers made their way to his hair and soon he felt wet lips meeting his own. He started to give out a small laugh, to tell his wife how much he loved her, until he opened his eyes.

Antoinette was not there. Instead, another woman towered above him, and he knew her face.

Malina?

OH NO…

Edward gave a yell and darted up, nearly pushing the Verloris princess away from him. He landed on the steps, gathering the sheets to cover himself, and then quickly put his hand to his head. A sharp, horrible pain nearly doubled him over, and suddenly the memories of the night before began to come back.

Wine. The party. Dizziness. Malina leading him down the hall and into the bedroom. The memories were so cloudy and fogged from the wine that he began to wonder what really happened during the night. Did he follow her to the bed, or did she lead him? He remembered her kiss, but did he spurn it like he hoped? Vague flashes of the night eluded him more. He remembered the dizziness and the room spinning out of control. He remembered her disrobing, and her laugh, but there was little else.

He looked around the room, his breath coming in sporadic spurts and his heart racing. There were his clothes, spread about the bed. His body had a sticky feeling of sweat. And there was Malina, still lounging on the bed, suddenly finding the urge to get up and go to him.

"Hung-over?" she asked as she approached him, leaning forward. "Let me soothe your pain once more."

She moved to kiss him, but he backed away. "What *happened?*" he yelled, panic already settling in. "Why are we here like this?"

Malina laughed. "Do you not remember?"

The truth was he did. Although the memories were spotty, there were still enough to tell him he did the one thing he swore he would never do. He clutched his hair in his hands, desperate to keep himself from screaming. How would he explain this to Antoinette, to the men, to his father? He would never be trusted by anyone again.

"*Why did you do this to me?*" Edward demanded.

"Me?" Malina lowered her brow. "I didn't make you do anything you didn't want to do yourself! You drank the wine. You got drunk. You followed me to the bed. You made love to me. Everything we did was done with both you and I wanting it!"

Edward cringed. His head pained him terribly, but now his heart ached worse. He could not have made a more terrible mistake as he did now. "I didn't want this..." he muttered. "I didn't want this at all."

"Funny how men change their minds so quickly." Malina frowned as she inched beside him. She leaned towards his ear and whispered. "Last night you didn't want to stop."

Edward felt a twist in his gut that made him sick. Was it true? Had he really been that weak? Antoinette would hate him forever if she knew what he had done-he knew it. And she wouldn't be the only one...

"Oh, Edward," Malina soothed as she brushed a few sweaty strands from his brow. "Let the worries leave your mind. It is just you and I. Let us go back to each other's arms and comfort one another." She moved to put her arms around his waist, but he backed away.

"No!" he said sternly, quickly gathering his clothes from the bed floor. Malina sat on the steps, dumbfounded, her eyes beading. "I will not partake of this anymore!" Edward continued. "I have already betrayed the trust of the woman I love. I will not repeat it!" He fumbled the clothes as he put them on, his hands still shaking from the shock of the morning.

"Where are you going?" Malina asked, standing to her feet, the sheet clinging to her chest.

Edward stopped, still breathing hard as if running a marathon. He turned to the balcony and then back to Malina. "The weather is cleared and the rains have stopped. It's time for me to leave."

Malina's eyes darted to the window. The sky was still cloudy, yet the rains had stopped like Edward said. "But your stay has been so short!" Malina wailed as she clasped him, falling to his feet. "Do not leave just yet. Stay, my love! Do not deny me my heart's desire!"

He wriggled free from her embrace, stepping away towards the door. "I am sorry, Your Majesty, but I made a promise to my men that we would depart when the rains ended."

"But you are their prince! Tell them to wait a day more."

"I can't," he said, opening the door. "I shall leave as soon as possible. Have my horses ready and for the sake of all that is good, tell no one of what has happened between us!"

He hurried into the hallway, refusing to look back as he rushed into his room.

After Edward arrived, he ordered one of the servants to make him a bath. Within minutes it was ready, and as he dismissed them for privacy he shut the door, threw off his clothes, and began to wash. As he soaked in the warm water, beholding the body that was no longer pure, he scoffed. Tears threatened him, but he refused to let them fall, for all he could feel was anger instead of the sadness that buried deep within his heart.

His father was right. Antoinette was wrong. He was a complete and utter failure.

What would happen when they learned of what he had done? His father would be furious. Edward would be yelled at, screamed at, and probably even lashed for such a thing. And then there would be the endless lectures of how Stephen would've never fallen for such a trap. His mother would be hurt and would say little, but her silence would be deafening. There was nothing worse than a mother's disappointment.

And then there was Antoinette, his angel. Poor soul, she would be devastated. It would be a hurt even deeper than what his father and mother would feel combined. Hadn't they promised each other to save themselves for their wedding night? And there were no previous lovers for them both. They had planned to be their own one and only. From when they met as young teens to the days of their deaths they had promised themselves only to each other.

But only Antoinette could keep that promise now. Edward's lip quivered at the thought of her reaction when he would tell her. How would she take it? Would she be angry at first? Would she cry? And then there were the long term effects. Would she forgive him? Would she love him? Would she still be willing to marry him?

She always believed that he could be better than his brother. Out of everyone, she believed, and he just proved her wrong.

I can't tell her. Edward lifted himself up from the bath and dried off. As he dressed, the thoughts became clearer. He couldn't tell anyone about his one night with Malina. No one else knew, so no one else could tell, and if he kept silent, his father wouldn't be angry. His mother wouldn't be disappointed. And most importantly, he would still have Antoinette.

Out of everyone, he couldn't lose her. And hadn't he lied before? The many secrets of Edward Engel were long hidden, buried deep within a stone heart. There was enough room for one more, and in the end, the lies were worth keeping. They kept him from trouble and kept everyone else from hurts too deep to understand.

There was no other choice.

He dressed and readied himself, sending a messenger to tell his men to ready their horses and prepare for journeying to Hugellia. They would depart the castle at noon and would make great haste, for the van Ketten family could not be kept waiting any longer, and they must make good with the...*fortunate*...weather.

After a quick breakfast and finishing his packing, he gathered his things to meet his men at the gate with their horses. A group of servants took his things and went down to pack them onto his horse, and as he prepared to leave his room without a second good-bye, the lady of Cathal suddenly crossed his path.

She was dressed in an elaborate black gown, her hair neatly braided with silver sheer. She turned to the servant that was to escort Edward to the gate and replied, "I shall walk with the prince. Go; make sure his horse is ready."

Edward frowned as he watched the servant hurry to the gate. Malina tucked her hand into his arm, leading him down the hall and stairs behind the servant.

The kind silence between them became short-lived. "What are you doing?" Edward whispered sternly.

"That is a harsh tone for your lover, my prince."

Her smirk sent an angry chill through him. "You are not my lover, Your Majesty. One night of unbridled, drunken passion does not bind us."

"Does it? Or does it even matter?" Malina gave a soft laugh. "But I do not deny that our one night of 'drunken passion' gave me great pleasure."

Edward turned away. "Is this your way of increasing my guilt?"

"Guilt?" Malina asked, a surprise coming across her face. "There is no need for guilt in participating with that which is only natural. But if I may interrupt your self-loathing, may I tell you something?"

He turned back. "And what is that?"

"Stay with me. Just a little longer."

He faced forward in a fury, his words a whispering seethe. "Do you not understand me when I tell you I am pledged to be married? I have made a mistake and am sorry for it. Do not think I shall stay a day longer to continue!"

"Then leave, journey to Hugellia," she replied softly, her hand caressing his arm. "But stop by before returning home, so I may see you once again."

They arrived at the gate and it opened, revealing his knights already saddled and ready to leave. Edward surveyed them quickly, wanting to shake his head. Aside from Sir Peterson and Sir Ichabod, they looked tired, worn, or guilt-ridden, much like him. He wondered if they, too, did things that would haunt them until death.

Malina's tug brought him back to reality. He faced her and she whispered in his ear. "What do you say, my prince? Shall you come back after your journey to Hugellia?"

Edward bowed slowly and carefully, not wishing his men to see or hear what he had to say. "If I have my way about it, I shall never see you again," he replied, lifting his head and raising his voice for the usual pomp of the royal leave. "Thank you for your hospitality, Your Majesty. I bid you farewell."

With that, he quickly turned and mounted his horse, leading his men through the city and back into Audlinian country. Malina stood there at the gate, watching the men leave one by one. "Farewell, Edward Engel." She smiled to herself. "I shall see you sooner than you think."

Chapter 5: By the Fire

We're finally leaving.

Marcus followed the prince past the gates of Cathal in silence as they rode towards Kettensburg, his thoughts reminiscing of what had happened just hours before.

He had slept little through the night during their stay in Verloris. Between the sounds of music from the hall or the goading of laughter and debauchery from outside his door, any type of rest the knight could have had eluded him. He could think of nothing else but the lack of decency displayed by Edward and his men. Drunkenness, lewdness, improper relations with the women of the manor...Marcus could only imagine what was going on beyond the stone walls of his room.

By the time the night began to wane, the other knights showed themselves to their rooms. Some came early, their breath still reeking of drink, while others came late, barely coherent as they trudged in and collapsed onto their bunks. Still some others did not show until near morning, their clothes disheveled from staying in another room. Pretty soon it was quiet save the snores from the others, and as Marcus lay in his bed, watching the night turn to morning, he heard a light rumble of thunder in the distance. He sighed, waiting for the sound of rain. *Another day, stuck here,* he thought, turning his sight away from the clouds. *What else could go wrong?*

A loud knock was heard, waking the knights and causing a long line of groans and grumbles. Marcus hurried out of bed and opened the door, thinking something wrong. It wasn't like them to be woken with such abruptness. The gatekeeper stood before him, his demeanor seeming harsher than usual.

"Yes?" Marcus said. "What can we do for you?"

The gatekeeper remained stoic. "Your prince has requested your presence. You are to meet him at the front gate. Prepare your things for departure, for he expects to leave within the hour."

"So soon?" Marcus's eyes widened in surprise. Something must've happened-he was sure of it. Edward would never wish to rush out of a place unless he had to. "Is the prince well?"

"As well as expected," the gatekeeper said with clenched teeth. "Now go. You don't want to be late, little knight."

"I won't," Marcus replied, and watched as the gatekeeper grabbed the door and slammed it shut.

The other knights rubbed their eyes and foreheads, the sound of the slamming door adding to aches leftover from the night. Sir Ichabod grumbled as he groggily sat up. "Why'd you do that, Marcus? He was probably bringing breakfast! Call him back!" he said, stuffing a pillow to his ear.

But Marcus didn't care whether they complained to him or not. The prince wanted to leave, whatever the weather conditions, and that was not a good sign.

"Up! Up! Up!" he shouted as loud as he could, making the men grumble more. Blankets and pillows went flying to the floor as Marcus rushed them out of bed, pushing and shoving until they all were awake. "We leave within the hour. Pack your things! The prince has demanded it!"

"Forget the prince and the morning," Ichabod grumbled as he laid his head back down.

Marcus grabbed the knight by the collar, pulling him up. "Did you not hear the gatekeeper? Wake up!"

It took nearly twenty minutes for the knights to gather their things-a time too long, in Sir Peterson's opinion. But it was better to be late than to not show up at all. Within thirty they were out the door, making their way to the front gate to gather the horses, the eyes of the Verloris ever watchful as the knights passed through the streets.

Marcus kept a steady hand on the string of his bow shouldered on him. He noticed the gatekeeper, busy guarding the exit with a distinct glare, but in the corner of his eye Marcus could make out a shadow near the crevices of the walls moving swiftly towards them, disappearing once it caught Marcus's gaze. Whether it was a person, or the ill will of the land simply toying with him, he did not know. All he knew was that he wanted to leave quickly.

After they gathered the horses and had them saddled and fed with a quick breakfast of oats, the prince made his way down the steps. Marcus noticed the princess of Verloris, Malina, remained at the top by the door, waving to him. Edward, however, did not look back nor did he wave. The look about him was strange-a mixture of fear, anger, and confidence all in one.

Marcus handed Edward the reins of his horse when he approached. "We are ready, Your Majesty. Is there anything else we should do to prepare for the journey to Hugellia?"

Edward neither looked up nor turned. He grabbed the reins, rushing onto the horse. "No, Sir Peterson. I only want to rid myself of this place."

Edward rode past the gate, his knights quickly following. Marcus got onto his horse and waited for the other knights to pass in front of him. He kept his eye out for the mysterious shadow, still missing, and looked back at Malina before following the others out of Verloris. She waved to him, a warm yet frightening smile upon her face, and said, "Farewell, knight of the guard. Until we meet again."

But Marcus only scowled, urging his horse to move forward to follow the others. "Good riddance," he muttered under his breath, and meant it with all of his heart.

The knights rode on through the day, barely saying a word to each other. Rain started to pour again, though at a slower rate than before, but the prince would not stop and said barely a word as they rode on through the pass towards Kettensburg. Rocky mountain terrain soon became flatter and greener, and within a few hours the company began seeing the rolling grasslands of Hugellia in the distance.

By the time the sun began to set, the rain stopped and the prince called for a camp to be made in the grove beside the road. A fire was built and tents were set up, though slowly, for most of the men were still tired from the night before. A deer was shot and skinned for roasting, and as the meat cooked on a spit over the fire, the men gathered around and grumbled.

"A song shall cheer everyone's mood," Sir Fauler said. "Come, Ichabod! You know many-sing us one!"

Ichabod grumbled, putting a hand to his temple. "No songs. I still have a headache."

"No wonder, all the drinking you did last night," said another knight, his hand over his gut. He stifled a burp and moaned. "I'm surprised you had the stomach for it."

"Shut up, Waldern!" Sir Boscher replied, giving the knight a glare. "At least I know how to keep it down. A real man knows how to drink!"

"And a real man knows when to keep his trap shut!" Ichabod yelled, making his head ache all the more. "Be quiet, all of you!" he said as he took a rock and threw it at the fire, sending sparks flying towards the knights nearest to the pit.

Soon angry voices were heard. "You nearly caught me on fire!" exclaimed one.

"You?" shouted another. "That singed my ankle!"

"Ah, toughen up, you daisies!" Ichabod spat.

And that was when the camp began to fight. At first it started as shouting and insults, but soon there were blows. Knights began hitting and shoving and punching as if they were in a war of their own. Marcus, staying busy skinning the rest of the deer for fur, immediately hid the skinning knife underneath the carcass and stood. "Stop fighting!" he urged as he tried to pull one knight off another one. "Can you not see this is foolish? Stop this at once!"

Sir Boscher pushed Marcus away in anger. "'Stop fighting!' he says," Boscher mocked. "'Stop this at once!' says the man who is so perfect!" Boscher scoffed as he pushed Marcus hard, knocking him to the ground.

"You're all just tired and tense, Wilfred..." Marcus replied to Sir Boscher, holding a steady hand out as he stood back to his feet. "Please, just calm down..."

"Make me!" Boscher shouted, and lunged towards Marcus. Quick on his feet, Marcus leapt out of the way and dashed towards the front, kicking dirt towards Boscher's face to slow him in his tracks. Boscher yelled and clawed at his eyes, shouting curses towards Marcus as he ran to find the prince.

He didn't have to go far. Edward sat alone, hunched over and sitting on a log, looking up at the sky quietly. "Your Majesty..." Marcus panted. "The men are fighting each other. Please, I need help to get them to stop!"

Edward remained still. "What do you want me to do about it?" he asked.

"Something, anything!" Marcus replied. "They're angry and they're tired, probably from all that has happened the night before..."

"And what happened with them?" Edward turned, his brow going up.

Marcus frowned. "Don't you know? You were among them."

Edward sighed, facing the sky once more, as if he did not want to deal with the problem. Marcus, already burning with anger from days of apathy displayed by his kindred, stood face to face with Edward, no longer caring if it was disrespectful or not.

"The men are fighting each other," he seethed. "Now I don't care if they beat each other up. As far as I'm concerned they deserve it. But we are still in the wild and there are animals out there. If they don't stop shouting they'll draw every animal around towards them." Marcus paused, knowing what he was about to say could give him a lashing, but his anger was too strong. "You will one day be their king. Now stop sulking and start acting like one!"

Edward's brow lowered and he stood to his feet. He leaned forward towards Marcus and sneered. "Don't blame me for something you couldn't contain," he said, and taking the horn at his belt, he blew it towards the men.

"All of you!" Edward shouted as he grabbed hold of a few knights fighting. "I go for a moment to gather my thoughts and this is what I come back to? What is the meaning of this?"

The knights stopped, their bodies aching and bruised, as they slouched to the ground. "We...we're sorry, Your Majesty..."

"Sorry doesn't cut it," Edward scolded. "You are knights of Audlin and yet act like schoolchildren! Now why are you fighting?"

"I'll tell you why." Ichabod stood. "We're tired and wet and hungry. We traveled all day in the rain with barely a stop when we could've stayed another day in Verloris. We could've slept in warm beds. We could've had hot meals instead of waiting for hours for this venison to cook. We could've been treated like kings, but you rushed us out like cattle!"

"Bite your tongue, Jacob!" Sir Fauler replied. "I am glad to be rid of that place. I will have no fond memory of my being there."

"Here, here!" said Marcus as the rest of the knights grumbled.

Sir Boscher stood with his arms crossed. "I'm not fond of Verloris," he replied. "Yet I'm not fond of being wet and cold in the wild, either. We left in such a rush that we were unable to take all our supplies. Why did we leave so quickly?"

The men cheered at Boscher's questioning, but Edward tightened his lips. He would not answer the men, but only shook his head. "It was of our best interest to leave, and take what you will from that. We shall not turn back and we shall not return to that wicked place. We ride on into Hugellia. For now, eat and rest, and for the sake of all that is good, be quiet, lest you want the wild animals to be aware of you!"

The men frowned, not pleased with the answer, but returned to their place at the fire. Edward turned to go back to the spot he was at before. As he passed Marcus, the knight whispered to him, "Thank you, Your Majesty. I appreciate the assistance."

Edward nodded. "The men are tired and weary. Let them rest."

"Yes, Your Majesty."

"And since you are clearly so wide awake and alert," Edward replied, "you can take the night watch. *All of it.*"

Marcus knew he would get in trouble sooner or later for his words. He nodded, accepting the punishment, as Edward stomped off. "Very well," he replied, and returned to skinning the deer.

Chapter 6: Going Home

Antoinette rested her eyes, the gentle swaying of the carriage she was riding making her want to fall asleep. Rain patted the tree leaves in a steady drizzle, the rhythm of the drops mixing with bird songs in the distance. It was a peaceful sound, one she didn't want to end, but she knew from previous journeys that she was only a few minutes from home.

The calm before the storm... she found herself musing as she laid her head against the carriage seat.

She had been traveling for days, leaving after Edward had gone to Hugellia, and while Edward headed north and west to seal an already-signed treaty, Antoinette headed south and east, returning to her home town of Staalberg, the capital of Edeland, for her mother had requested it.

It was a strange feeling leaving Reigal, the city she had grown to love so fondly. Not that she didn't enjoy the trees and greenery of Edeland, for she always did, but it was the people that tugged her heart towards the west. Not just Edward, the obvious reason, but others as well.

King Arden, though he treated Edward more like a student than a son, was a stoic man, harsh and strong like there was always someone to protect. But deep down inside he had a soft heart, one that loved deep, and it was something Antoinette had glanced in him more than once. Already he called Antoinette the daughter he never had, and he doted on her much more than her own father ever did.

Queen Maria, opposite of her husband, never raised her voice in anger but had a joy that was contagious to anyone who met her. Life was precious and worth being happy about, she had always said. Whether noble or pauper, everyone she spoke with had a feeling they were important, that they mattered no matter who they were. It was a trait Antoinette hoped she could continue as Audlin's future queen.

Even Stephen, though he was gone, was such a kind boy that Antoinette was honored to call him her friend. He was quiet and shy with a head in the books, but she found in his company a sort of loyalty that told her he would always be willing to call her family.

I want to go home...

A pang of guilt entered Antoinette's heart. Was it wrong for her to view the Engels as her family and Audlin as her home?

I wish Edward didn't go to Hugellia. The wedding would've been sooner and we'd both be in Reigal right now.

The carriage stopped and Antoinette opened her eyes. She turned to the window to see the familiar wood and brick that was the van Echt royal palace, a few guards standing by the door at their post. A lone figure was with them, shivering in the cool air, dripping wet but a grin on her face.

Antoinette smiled as she saw her younger sister suddenly jump from the steps and run towards her. Without waiting for the escort to open the carriage door, Antoinette hurried out, nearly tripping over her skirt as she rushed forward, embracing the girl in the middle of the rain.

She's the only home I have here.

"You're late!" Bernette laughed as she pulled her dark locks behind her ear, her hair sticking to her fingers and her hat all bent from being soaked.

"I'm sorry." Antoinette grinned as she ushered her sister towards the palace doors. "The rain slowed my travels. It was muddy by the Edellwood."

"Excuses, excuses," Bernette said as they entered the palace. "I know you didn't want to leave your *fiancé* so soon."

Antoinette gave a chuckle at seeing Bernette's smirk. Her sister always was such a tease. "How long were you standing in the rain, Bernie? You're soaking wet."

"Not long." Bernette looked down at the small puddles her dress was leaving on the floors. Newly waxed wood, now extra shiny. She shrugged her shoulders as Antoinette followed her gaze down and her smile began to fade.

"It was going to be waxed again, anyways. At least that's what Mother said."

Mother. She was always upset about something.

Antoinette bit her lip as she ushered her sister in, forgetting the puddle-mess and leading her down the hallway to the main living room and the hearth. She placed her in front of the fire, pulling a small cushioned bench for her to sit on. "You need to dry off," she muttered, her voice shaking. "I don't want you to catch cold."

"I'll be fine," Bernette added, but Antoinette ignored her sister's insistence and handed her some blankets from the back closet. "Here," she said, placing them in her lap. "Now dry yourself off."

Bernette complied, knowing not to question. It was in Antoinette's nature to take care of others, even when they didn't want it. The curse of being the oldest of four children...

"Are Mother and Father home?" Antoinette asked as Bernette handed her one blanket, damp.

"Yeah," Bernie replied. "Father's upstairs doing business with his financial advisors. Mother is in the drawing room working on her needlepoint."

"I expected they were out. From Mother's letter, she sounded like she needed me here."

"You know how she is," Bernette muttered. "Always melodramatic. I think she just wanted you home so she could boss someone else besides me."

Antoinette put the damp blanket in a basket beside her. There was more truth in Bernie's words than she wanted to admit. "What of Caspar and Robert?"

"Our brothers are where they always are," Bernette said as she flung the blanket across her shoulders, snuggling tight into it. "Following father in their own little world of kings and princes and business."

"It sounds like nothing's changed in a month." Antoinette sighed, noticing Bernette still had the sopping hat on her head. *Silly Bernie*, she thought. *That'll make you sick quicker than anything.*

"You're still soaked," Antoinette said, changing the subject. "Maybe I should take you upstairs. You need to change into something dry. And let's get this hat off you."

Antoinette reached to take the hat off, but Bernette quickly grabbed it, pressing it hard against her head. She wouldn't take it off.

"Bernie," Antoinette stammered. "Take the hat off. You've got to get your head dry!"

"I like the hat," Bernette whined. "It's not that wet and besides, it's keeping my head warm."

Antoinette rubbed the bridge of her nose. She knew what was going on.

"How bad is it?" she asked.

"Well, this hat isn't my favorite," Bernette began. "Personally, I like the red one better…"

Antoinette frowned and quickly snatched the hat off. Bernette gave a quick "Hey!" but wasn't fast enough. Antoinette tossed the hat to the basket and placed her hands atop her sister's head.

Dark locks lay flat against a lighter scalp, the subtle image of a circle starting to show towards the crown of her head.

"Oh Bernie…" Antoinette whispered as she kissed her sister's head. "Your hair is still falling out?"

Bernette became quiet as she crossed her arms, staring at the fire. "No more than usual. It's nothing. Hair always falls out more when it's autumn."

"It's not autumn yet," Antoinette replied. "And this has been going on for a while."

"What's new?" Bernie muttered.

Antoinette moved to the side of the bench, sitting beside her sister and taking her hand in hers. "Does Mother know about this?"

Bernette kept her eyes on the hearth, the images of flickering flames mirrored in her eyes. "Of course she does.

She lets me hear about it every day. Why do you think I wear the hats all the time? She wants to keep it hidden, even from you."

Antoinette wrapped her arms around her sister, holding her close. Bernette was only sixteen and yet her health was already beginning to fail. When it wasn't the coughing, it was the fatigue. When it wasn't her sour stomach, it was her hair falling out in clumps.

The doctor's said there was nothing they could do but order her herbs and medicine. They had given hope she would grow out of it when she reached adulthood, but Antoinette worried it wasn't illness making her sister's body fall apart.

"Don't worry," Antoinette whispered, pressing Bernie's wet forehead against her own. "We'll just go upstairs and get you dried off. I want you to tell me all about your day today."

Bernette gave a weak smile which quickly faded as footsteps suddenly pounded into the room.

"Why are there puddles on my floor?" a voice screeched from the halls. "Clean this at once!"

Antoinette frowned as she held her sister's forehead to hers. *Mother.*

"I can't believe what filth this house is in!" Queen Susanna exclaimed as she stomped into the room, but then stopped and gave a slight gasp.

"Antoinette?" she asked in surprise as both Antoinette and Bernie looked up. "I didn't expect to see you so soon."

Antoinette stood quietly in the drawing room, her eyes gazing out the window towards a bird bath in a garden. Two little birds, sparrows by the looks of them, huddled together on the edge of the marble, hiding underneath a branch so as not to get soaked by the rain.

But then a great hawk came sweeping from behind them. Her great wings fluttered, shaking the leaves around her. The sparrows' protection was gone and the rain soon pelted their feathers as the hawk lorded over them on the bath. Defeated, they knew they could not stand their ground, so they flew away.

Antoinette let out a sigh. *I know how they feel,* she thought.

When the queen had come in earlier, she took her hand to Bernie, pulling her off the bench and urging her towards the hall. "Change your clothes and do your hair!" she barked. "Look at your sister-she looks beautiful, and she's been traveling for days! There is no excuse for you!"

Antoinette frowned, thinking of her mother's words to Bernette. *She was standing in the rain waiting for me,* she thought with a sneer. *Unlike you.*

That was twenty minutes ago. Queen Susanna had followed Bernette up the stairs once she saw her daughter stop and ask if Antoinette could come. "She's tired," the queen had said, but Antoinette knew the real reason. The queen was controlling, especially of Bernie. No matter what the poor girl did, she never looked good enough.

At least not to Mother.

The door opened and in walked the queen, her red and black dress full and perfectly pressed as if it were meant for a doll. Antoinette wondered if the king had been forced to press it for her. Heaven knew the servants were worked enough as it was. "Antoinette," she said, opening her arms and embracing her eldest. "I thought you weren't going to arrive until next week."

Antoinette barely returned the embrace. She wanted to see Bernette. "I got your letter. I came back like you requested."

"Letter?" the queen mused. "I thought I'd only sent plans for the wedding. But then again, it was written so long ago I must've forgotten." She flung her hand in the air and rolled her eyes like the idea was a trifle. "It doesn't matter. What matters is that you're here! Tell me, how are the wedding plans?"

"Going as expected," Antoinette replied.

"And you chose the cream silk table cloths, yes?" the queen asked. "Please tell me you did. Only a peasant would choose that cotton drabble."

Antoinette held her breath. "I chose the cotton."

"And why did you do that?" The queen's voice rose. "You are royalty, child! Act like it! A queen should never be caught with anything less than silk!"

Antoinette sighed. Everything was a fight with her mother- even the tedious things. "The cotton wrinkles less and is not as expensive. I don't want to work the servants any more than what they already have to do."

"Foolish girl," the queen muttered as she shook her head. "I knew I should have planned this myself. We shall return to Reigal in the morning to straighten this inconvenience."

"Tomorrow?" Antoinette's eyes widened. "But I just got back!"

"And your wedding will be sooner than you think," the queen replied. "If you'd stop wasting so much time making poor decisions, the planning would've been done already!"

Antoinette remained silent, looking towards the ground. If she wanted an argument, she would continue her disagreement, but her thoughts remained on her sister. She wasn't in the mood to fight with her mother. She wanted to make sure Bernette was alright.

"Can Bernie come?" Antoinette asked, interrupting her thoughts. "I mean for tomorrow?"

"Why should she come?" the queen asked. "She's doing none of the planning. It's already in trouble enough."

"I just thought...well...she needs to try on her bridesmaid dress," Antoinette replied. "And frankly, I want to spend some time with her before I leave for good."

The queen gave a sigh and nodded. "Very well. I suppose we should have her fitted sooner than later. I'm sure we'll have to get a bigger size at the rate she gains-which, if my eyes do not deceive me, we may have to do for you as well. Have you gained weight?"

Antoinette lowered her brow, saying nothing for a moment. After seeing Mother's expectant look, however, she relented. "I'll start packing," Antoinette replied, lowering her head. "I'll make sure we're ready in the morning."

"Don't forget to help your sister. Make sure she packs her hats, or at least fix her hair so it will be presentable!" the queen said with a smile. "We must look our best when seeing the Engel family."

"Of course."

Antoinette started to walk out of the room, her eyes on the floor and head bent like a servant's. But before she could leave, she heard her mother call one last time. "I am glad you're home, dearest. I hope you visit often after you're married."

Only to see Bernie, she thought, but replied with, "I will, Mother," and turned and walked away.

By the time she had reached the stairs she hurried her pace, her feet making stomping noises as she clamored up towards Bernette's room. It didn't take her long to get there, and when she entered the small and comfortable chambers she found her sister in an all too familiar position: sitting near the window reading, her hair down and straight and purposely unkempt.

"Dear me." Antoinette chuckled, making Bernie look up. "What would Mother think of you? Every hair is not in place and you are reading! Such an abomination."

"Heaven forbid I do anything for the benefit of my mind." Bernie smirked as she closed the book and set it upon the nightstand. "After all, what good is astronomy? Everyone knows that the art of manicures is more important."

They both laughed as Antoinette flopped onto Bernette's bed, stretching out and giving a yawn. "Mother says we are to go to Reigal tomorrow. I'm guessing it'll be early in the morning."

Bernie's brow rose. "What did you do? Say the wedding dinner was going to be eaten off of pewter plates instead of china?"

"Worse." Antoinette sighed. "I told her about the cotton linens."

Bernette shook her head. "We're doomed."

"Not as doomed as I'm going to be when we actually get to Reigal," Antoinette replied. "I didn't tell her about the dress I picked out before I left. It's made of taffeta instead of silk."

"Great. I was hoping to grow up first before the world ended."

Antoinette laughed. Even through all the put downs and demands of their mother, Bernie still kept her sense of humor.

"At least it's just us going," Bernette said, laying her head back in the chair and stretching her legs. "I thought I'd go mad with her constantly onto me this week. Clean this, fix that, why don't you look more like me instead of your father, blah blah blah."

Antoinette frowned, sitting up. "She's going too, Bernie."

Bernette's head shot up, her eyes glaring. "*What?* No!"

"I'm sorry," Antoinette said. "She wants to do the planning herself. Who am I to stop her?"

"It's your wedding! Shouldn't it be your decision on what you have?"

"You and I know that's not going to happen."

"Well if it was my wedding, I wouldn't let her do it," Bernette huffed. "I'd tell her to fly off and mind her own business."

"Bernie!" Antoinette scolded. "You shouldn't take that tone. She's our mother. We should respect that."

"I don't respect her," Bernette replied coldly, "and I don't care what she thinks."

Antoinette sighed, rubbing her brow. Barely a month had she been gone and already her sister was starting her own private mutiny at home.

"You shouldn't say things like that," Antoinette said softly. "She means well with what she says, and she loves you. She just doesn't know how to show it properly."

"*Hmph*," Bernette snorted, grabbing the astronomy book and forcing it open to whatever page she could claw at first. "If she's been using her nice words on me, I'd hate to see it when she's cross. You know what she told me a few days ago? That I looked like a walking corpse. All because she thinks I'm too pale!"

Antoinette bit her lip, ready for the stories to fly. Bernette was often long-winded when the mood suited her, and when she was in the mood, she let the words soar out of her like a hurricane wind.

"Right after you left, she scolded me like I was a child because I laughed at the cup of tea I spilled. 'Only a tavern wench laughs at such a thing', she said. And then she decided to remind me on how to properly sip tea for an hour."

"Bernie…" Antoinette tried to cut in, but was interrupted as soon as she tried.

"And then, she tells me I eat too much!" Bernette's face turned red in frustration. "I eat barely a plate of dinner and she screams at me. Do you know she told the servants to give me half of what she gets for dinner? You know what a bird pecking eater Mother is! And all she says is, 'You need to be skinnier. I can't believe what a cow you've become.'"

Antoinette bent her head, knowing the feeling too well. How many times had mother sent her to her room with a lighter dinner on account of gaining a pound or two?

Bernette paused, her breathing already becoming hard. Antoinette sat up as if to rush to her sister's side and calm her, but Bernette held her hand up. "I'm fine," she seethed. "I just worked myself up, that's all."

"And a lot of good it did you." Antoinette frowned.

"It may make it hard to breathe, but it certainly makes my mind feel better."

Antoinette sighed, putting a warm hand on her sister's. Bernette looked up away from the book, a sad expression upon her face. "I'm sorry, Antoinette. I just don't know how much more I can take. I feel smothered, like I'm locked in a cage and a lion is just pacing around me."

"It'll get better in time." Antoinette smiled, her best attempt at encouragement.

"But it won't," Bernette replied, her voice shaking. "Don't you see? She was worse with you gone. What's she going to be like when you're gone for good?"

Antoinette remained silent, not wanting to know the answer.

"You're lucky you can escape," Bernette muttered. "What am I to do when you're gone? I don't have any support without you."

Bernette closed the book in her lap, tossing it back to the table. She was no longer in the mood to read, it seemed. She gathered her knees to her chest, resting her chin and lowering her eyes to the floor. Her eyes became wet, yet no tears came, doubtless from them all being spent from the nights before.

It was then Antoinette began to understand, or at least, she thought she did. It was strange that Mother didn't remember sending a letter to bring her back home. Mother always remembered the details, no matter how small or trivial.

"Bernie," Antoinette said softly. "Did you send the letter to bring me back home?"

Bernette looked away. "I don't know what you're talking about."

Tried as she may, her sister couldn't fool everyone, especially her. "Be truthful, Bernie. For me."

"Does it matter?" Bernette mumbled as she pressed her face to her knees, her voice becoming muffled. "You're going to be leaving again, anyways."

"Oh Bernie, I'm so sorry…" Antoinette felt her voice catch as she saw a tear fall from the corner of her sister's hidden face. Had she not spent many sleepless nights in her bedroom, praying for the day she would no longer be under her parents' roof? Had she not cried herself to sleep, mentally replaying the hurtful words spoken to her by her mother until she thought she would go mad? Had she not rejoiced in the fact that Edward proposed to her so soon, providing her a home that was far away from the pit that was Staalberg?

But in her dark days she had a sister to turn to. In her tears, she had a shoulder to cry on. And when she felt weak, she somehow found the strength to support her younger sister so that the dark days seemed lighter than what they actually were. But who would her sister have now? She was at an age where she needed strength and encouragement, and she certainly wasn't going to get it from their head-in-the-clouds brothers or ignorant father.

"I'll arrange for you to come and stay with Edward and me," Antoinette said, clasping Bernette's hand firmly. "I'll ask that you be a handmaiden to the court. Surely Mother would allow that."

Bernette lifted her head, her eyes red and swollen but now dry. "We both know that won't happen. She barely lets me out of the house because she's so ashamed of me. I doubt she wants to parade her balding, cow-like daughter to the Reigal court."

"I won't ask for it," Antoinette seethed. "I'll *demand* it from her."

Bernette scoffed. "Good luck with that," she said as she sat up and rose from the chair. "I guess it doesn't matter anyways. She'll only let us go if someone else takes us from her."

Antoinette bent her head, feeling shame or guilt or a combination of the two. How could such a happy moment like a wedding turn into something so dreaded at the same time?

"But you know what? Maybe I'll get lucky." Bernette chuckled, her façade returning quickly like it always did. "You had ol' Eddie boy wrapped around your finger by the time you were my age, so who's to say I can't find me someone, too? Tall, dark, handsome, you know?"

Antoinette looked up, her eyes looking straight into Bernie's. Behind the smirked face, the casual stance, and the raised brow was a girl who crafted carefully every lie she told. Her face and body may have shown confidence, but her eyes reeked of doubt. Antoinette knew this. She had seen it in her own face once, when she was younger. But Bernette was never one to believe so easily that good things could happen. She had seen too much of the bad to make her think there was any good in the world.

But that didn't mean Antoinette couldn't have faith for her anyways. "You know what?" she said, forcing a smile. "I think you're right. I think out of everyone, you're going to get the best, and things are going to be so good for you later on that you won't even bother remembering all of this as a past."

Bernette chuckled as she pulled out a suitcase from her closet, beginning her packing. "I was only joking, Antoinette. Just trying to lighten the mood, you know?"

There was a pause, and Antoinette cleared her throat. "I was being serious," she replied.

Bernette's smirk disappeared, her eyes turning away towards her dresser. For a moment she said nothing, but as Bernette placed her hands on the drawer handles she gave Antoinette a quick glance and smile before returning to her packing.

"Thanks," she said quietly, and continued to pack in silence until the door swung open and in walked Mother.

"Remember to pack your corsets, girls!" she said quickly as she stomped in. "We must look our very best!"

Bernette stepped away from the drawer as Queen Susanna began pulling the corsets out from the back of the dresser, flinging them into the air.

"This one isn't big enough!" she huffed. "Too small...too ugly...not enough hold. We need to go shopping and get you a bigger corset, Bernette!"

Bernie could only groan as Antoinette stood and began to help go through the corsets.

Chapter 7: The Hunt

When morning came, the knights were ready for their travels ahead. A quiet night of rest and a stomach full of meat made even the grumpiest of the men content and hardy. They tore down the camp and saddled the horses before the morning sun peaked above the trees. All felt much better than the night before save the prince and Sir Peterson, who quietly and sluggishly gathered their things, void of any sleep.

Though Sir Peterson had a good reason to be tired after an all-night watch, Edward had no reason at all. He had the driest and most comfortable of all the tents, and yet sleep still evaded him. No matter how still he laid or how long he shut his eyes, all he could see was himself in Verloris, lying naked in a bed with Malina towering over him, a haunting laugh coming from her lips.

Though he tried to forget that fateful night, the memories continued to press on his mind. It was a feeling all too familiar, yet a feeling he had hoped he'd never feel again. *In time, I will forget*, he reminded himself as he gathered the reins to his horse. *I was able to forget before. I can do it again.*

On they rode out of the grove and onto the plains of Hugellia. Rock and dirt with a patch of green turned to yellow and gold grassland, and soon the road became so narrow that it started hiding in the ever-growing grass.

As Edward looked out upon his mother's homeland, he was reminded of his journeys there as a child. He remembered sitting in the back of the carriage with his brother, staring out the window and wondering how the land could be so lumpy and golden, like a batter of dough before being put into the oven to make bread. He thought of it as an odd looking land that had little chance of industry and commerce, but the ruling family of the land had proven otherwise.

Hugellia was a place with many hidden treasures. Fresh-water lakes could be found scattered across the northern side of the country while perfect pasture lands were found in the south and east. Small hills filled with iron and copper laid deep in the west, and with such a natural bounty of resources, the people of Hugellia were richer than all the surrounding countries combined.

"Have we arrived in Hugellia yet?" Sir Ichabod asked from behind, thankfully interrupting Edward's thoughts.

He nodded. "We have just passed the border. It is a day's ride to the city of Kettensburg."

"I'm glad of it, then!" Ichabod chuckled. "My rear is starting to go numb."

The others laughed, but Edward managed only a smile. He did not feel like laughing-not when he felt so tired.

"What's Kettensburg like?" Sir Peterson asked. "I've never been there."

"It's similar to Reigal," Edward replied. "Only the mountain does not raise the city. The city raises a mountain."

Marcus turned his head. "I'm not sure I understand, Your Majesty."

"The city is built like a giant box, with tall buildings on the outermost edges, but as you move further into the city the buildings grow taller, like a mountain. In the center, however, is like a little valley. There are flowers and trees and grass and a great lake lies there with a small island in the middle. The homes that are built around this lake are the grandest you have ever seen, made of marble brought forth from the mines in the west. The richest of nobles and the royal palace are there."

"It is the only city in Hugellia," Ichabod added. "Those who do not live in Kettensburg are either nomads or live in small villages. Out of the five million in the country, four and half million live in Kettensburg."

"It sounds magnificent," Marcus replied.

"It is a wondrous city," Edward said. "My mother still holds her homeland dear to her heart."

"And I shall hold it dear to mine when we get there!" Ichabod laughed. "I am in want of a warm bed and hearth."

"As am I," said a few others, and soon Edward began to hear chatter of the glories of Hugellia and how a Hugellian room was grander than any castle or palace in the entire world.

Will I find rest there? he asked himself, but then shook his head.

He would only find rest when he could forget the past.

It was midday when the company stopped for a break near a small forest by a lake. Some went to refill the water canteens, others tended to the horses. Sir Peterson busied himself with making a quick meal out of the remaining venison and rations they had. Edward wandered through the tree groves picking berries and checking them to see if they were safe to eat or not. He found that most of them were poisonous and tossed them to the ground. He already felt sick enough. There was no sense in making himself sicker.

His mind began to drift to Antoinette. He wondered where she was at the moment and what she was doing. Was she busy? Was she at rest? Was she thinking of him? Wherever she was, he was certain she was doing the latter.

Unsatisfied with the bundles of branches, he ventured deeper into the forest looking for better berries. Searching for the fruit reminded him of last summer when he and Antoinette went into the blueberry fields for some privacy and some lunch. They ate so many blueberries they both became sick, and poor Antoinette swore somehow they had gotten a hold of a poisonous berry to become so ill. She still hadn't eaten another blueberry since that trip, poor thing.

With his mind preoccupied, he reached for another bundle of berries without noticing the thorns sticking out. As he put his hand forth, he felt the back of his hand be scratched, and he instantly drew the hand to himself from the sharp pain. He gave a muffled curse as he checked his hand, rubbing the soreness and small trickle of blood away, but as the pain made him pause of his thinking with Antoinette, the pain also made him notice the sound of a low, rumbling purr coming from the tall brushes near the tree.

Edward froze, suddenly his mind coming to alert. He quickly gazed at his surroundings. How far had he wandered from the group? He didn't think it very far, but he heard no voices save his own ragged breathing.

"Is anyone out there?" he called, but there was no answer.

They've abandoned you...

No, no, they hadn't. They were out there where they were supposed to be, at the resting point. It was Edward's fault for wandering too far. He was stupid not to-

A snap of a branch was heard, interrupting his thoughts. The low, rumbling purr suddenly became louder and glowing, green eyes peaked from the leaves.

Edward felt his heart leap to his chest. Hadn't his mother told him stories of traveling to Kettensburg, how it was important to always stay in groups? "The grass lions are nothing to mess with, Edward. They killed my uncle, you know, and many other poor souls. Always they hunt for their next meal."

Edward stiffened his muscles as he reached for his sword. It was a grass lion, to be sure, though he had certainly never seen one before. If it was like any other animal he'd hunted before, a blade had no issue piercing the heart of one lion.

But after three other sets of eyes appeared in the brushes, Edward's confidence suddenly began to dip.

"Sir Ichabod?" he called out, this time his voice a little shaky. "Sir Peterson?"

Nothing came save the sound of snapping branches as the lions' heads rose from the cover of leaves.

"God, don't let me die here..." Edward pleaded, but he wondered if the Almighty truly heard him.

Your sins have found you...

"I didn't mean to..." It was a poor time for a confession, he was sure, but maybe there was some chance in a million he could still beg for mercy.

An eye for an eye, a tooth for a tooth, a life for a life...

"Have I not begged for forgiveness?"

He could not hear an answer because the first lion leapt towards him.

Adrenaline surged through his veins as instinct took over. He had been in mock battles and had hunted animals before, but this was the first time he had ever had to fight for his life. He swung his sword with power as he plunged the blade into the first lion's neck and it fell with a mangled cry. The second lion parried swiftly as it clawed Edward's shoulder, ripping his tunic and flesh. Edward gave a yell before he hacked at another lion to his left, felling it, but soon he was overwhelmed by the remaining two. He felt hard paws push him in the chest and knock him down, and soon another paw clawed the sword from his left hand.

No…please, not now…

But this was it. This was death at his doorstep, knocking and waiting for him to open.

He gave a final, sharp breath, readying to say his beloved's name on his lips before the lion's claw gashed his throat. As he gave the exhale he heard a sharp whizzing noise and the sound of two objects hitting the lions both in the heart. They fell to the ground, killed instantly, with Edward lying in the dirt, watching and wondering what had just happened.

Small arrows stuck out of the lions, and Edward felt like giving a shout of joy.

Marcus.

"Your Majesty!" Edward heard Sir Peterson's voice coming through the trees. The knight appeared, bow and arrow at the ready, and though he looked tired and worn, he was ready for battle and only lowered his aim when he saw that Edward was sitting up, surrounded by four dead lions.

"What happened?" Sir Peterson asked. "Are you hurt?"

Marcus offered his hand and lifted Edward to his feet, eyeing the gashed shoulder in concern. Edward shrugged, brushing himself off. "I'm fine, thanks to you. You came just in time. I...I think I would've been lunch had you not arrived."

Marcus lowered his brow in confusion. "I don't understand, Your Majesty. I've only just got here. I was out looking for you and heard you shout."

Edward shook his head. "Wait, you didn't kill these lions?"

"No. I thought you did."

"I only killed the first two," Edward said, looking towards the two lions with arrows in their chest. "Then who...?"

He bent down and pulled an arrow from one of the lions, studying it. The arrow was short, terribly sharp, and of a dark, silver color. His knights had nothing like it. Their arrows were long, more colorful and with a metal tip.

"Have you seen anything like this?" Edward asked, handing the arrow to Marcus.

Marcus took the arrow and fingered it, looking at it quietly. "Once, in Circh," he replied. "Some merchants came from the north with one of these, asking the woodworkers if they were familiar with such craft. They told them no and could not think of a bow the arrows could fit on. When we asked them where they got it, they said they found it in a field in Verloris."

Edward's heart stopped at the name. Verloris, Malina's home, the place he wanted to be furthest from that somehow seemed to keep haunting him.

"I don't know why one of these would be out here," Marcus replied, handing the arrow back to Edward. "Though we are still near the border. Then again..."

Marcus paused, and Edward knew what he was thinking.

"You believe we're being followed?" he asked quietly.

"I hope not," Marcus said. "But I am starting to wonder. Why else would these arrows just happen to save your life?"

Edward let out a sigh. Malina wouldn't let go of him so quickly, would she? But what reason would she have to follow him to Kettensburg, to his family, and what other reason would she have to keep him from death? If anything, his leaving her so coldly would make her want to kill him, not save his life.

"Did you see or hear anything suspicious during the night watch?" Edward asked.

"None," Marcus replied. "Nothing unusual."

"Then it is probably nothing." Edward hated to downplay it, but he didn't want Marcus to suspect anything. Malina had no reason to follow him. Malina had no reason to save him.

"What of the arrow? If the Verloris are following us..." Marcus said, but Edward held his hand up for silence.

"You said so yourself that this arrow is new technology. Perhaps those in Kettensburg would be more familiar with it," Edward replied casually, making Marcus frown. "It could have been a local hunter. There is a small village near if I remember correctly. It was likely one of them. The villagers of Hugellia have never been known for their sanguine nature. They are quite shy."

"We should ask them anyways, if only to put our minds at ease," Marcus said.

"We haven't the time. We need to get to the city," Edward said, tossing the arrow to the ground. *It's nothing. Surely it's nothing.* "Come. Let us gather our resources and leave this place. We need to get to the capital before they send a search party looking for us. We're already late as it is."

"But..."

"Just leave it, Sir Peterson."

Edward began to walk back towards the camp, but Marcus lowered his brow. As the prince continued on, he didn't notice Marcus shake his head in frustration, nor did he notice the eyes of a man watching him move on from the trees.

A hawk sat perched upon his hand with a small tube around its neck. A rolled up piece of parchment was gently placed into the tube, and the man in the tree whispered to the bird carefully.

"Tell Her Majesty that Edward is nearly to Kettensburg and is safe thus far," the man said. "Tell her she must move quickly. They are starting to notice."

He lifted the hawk into the air and the bird sped towards Verloris as the man jumped down from the tree.

Chapter 8: Arriving in Hugellia

Edward didn't remember the gates of Kettensburg towering so high into the heavens. Grant it, it had been a few years since he stepped foot into the city, but he couldn't help but wonder if the king of Hugellia had been spending some extra time building onto the wall. It wasn't thicker by any means, for war was something of a memory in their lands, but it was more…ornate.

Always wanting to show the wealth, Edward thought to himself as he and his knights trotted through the gates to the sounds of a herald announcing their entry. As they entered, the sounds of the town shifted to small cheers and welcomes, a few waves coming from the children running alongside the pebbled streets. If there was one thing the Hugellians were known for, it was their hospitality towards their friends, but if you were family, as Edward was, you were treated better than royalty.

It was the reason Hugellia was his favorite place to visit. The van Ketten family was the family who gave him the love and the praise he so richly craved when he was young.

Oh, how you have them fooled…

A pang of guilt suddenly hit him and he was reminded of Malina. He cleared his throat, wondering if his face showed any change of emotion as he worked the crowd in waving and smiling. Their faces remained unchanged. In fact, he could see them grow happier as he passed them in the streets.

Was it a terrible thing he had become so good at hiding his guilt?

The trek through the city and towards the royal palace did not take long. All roads, if you stayed on the main ones, led to the center of the city, and if you followed it just right, you would end up on the front steps of the van Ketten palace. And what a sight it was: pillars of the purest, brightest marble holding a building full of balconies and windows. It was like a home found in fairy tales or myths and legends, and one would expect the angels themselves to descend from the roof to welcome you with harps and song.

But on the steps no cherubs awaited them. Instead there stood the king of Hugellia. Aged and bent he was, yet regal all the same. The king, named Erick, was a tall man and handsome, especially in his younger days as it was rumored. Though many said Edward looked like his father, Arden, it was Maria who said her youngest son looked like King Erick. Their frames were nearly identical, and had Edward been alive to see his grandfather in his younger years, he would've sworn he saw his twin.

With the king were his three other children, all sons, two of which matched their father's proud demeanor. The younger two, Ulrich and Ambrose, stood with arms crossed and heads held high in pride. The eldest, a leaner, more studious looking man, stood on the right, with his hands clasped in front of him. The eldest son was named Aldaric, and if there was one who was humble and kind in Hugellia, it was him.

Behind them stood the wives and children of the princes, and some of the children were not really children, but adults with young families of their own. The van Ketten family was large and prosperous, Edward noted, and it seemed King Erick had no worry of his line ever ending.

"Welcome, my grandson!" King Erick bellowed in his deep, rumbling voice. "I am glad you have made it here safely. I was beginning to worry something happened to you in the wild!"

Edward embraced his grandfather with a nervous smile. "My apologies for the lateness, Grandfather. We were caught in a storm just north of the mountains."

"Aye, I believe it!" Erick replied. "We had such a storm the other day that it knocked some of our trees down into the streets. I even heard reports of some sheep being swallowed up by funnels from the sky. Thankfully that happened in the pasturelands instead of here, but still!"

Edward nodded, the king taking his arm and turning towards the rest of his family. "I'm sure it has been a year since your last visit, and maybe more. You must meet your newest cousins, Ed. Now you can put a face to the names you've seen in the letters!"

Edward was greeted with hugs and kisses all around, the warmth of the van Ketten family never feeling like it was too much. "Mother sends her greeting to all of you." Edward smiled, embracing them back. "She says to especially say hello to her brothers and to Cousin..." Edward looked around. "And to Cousin Emmerich."

Emmerich stepped forward, past the other cousins, and stood before him, his hands clasped firmly in the front like a gentleman's. For a moment the cousins simply stood facing each other in silence, but after a pause, Emmerich unclasped his hands and welcomed Edward with an embrace. Loose and somewhat cold, it seemed, and Edward returned the sentiment.

"Give Aunt Maria my greeting," Emmerich replied quietly, "and thank her for thinking of me."

Edward nodded as he watched Emmerich slowly walk away. Edward kept his gaze upon him, but as Emmerich faced his cousin again, this time at his father Aldaric's side, their eyes met only for a moment before Emmerich turned his head away.

He knows what you really are.

Edward ignored his thoughts, facing the king. "Come, Grandfather!" he said with his best attempt at a joyous voice. "Tell me of your days and adventures. I must have stories to give my mother when I return home!"

The king clasped his hand upon Edward's shoulder and laughed, telling him the first of many stories that afternoon.

Marcus sat at the dinner table, eyeing the stew laid before him. Already he had been served cheeses, fruit, salad, and bread, and by the time the stew came around, he felt like he would burst.

When they say they treat you like a king, they weren't joking!

Sir Ichabod seemed as if he were in Heaven. His stew had been eaten within minutes, and already he was waiting for the main course. "I hear it is roast veal and potatoes." He chuckled, licking his lips. "Oh, if all journeys ended like this one!"

Marcus smiled, forcing himself to take a bite of the stew though he felt like he was sure he couldn't. It was just the right flavor, the broth full of salty goodness that made his mouth yearn for more. He looked around, the men now smiling and forgetting their troubles in Verloris, and everyone around him was filled with laughter and song and cheer. It was a sight long missed, and for a brief moment he forgot the horrors of the journey there as well.

As he swallowed another bite, he turned to his left, eyeing the end of the table. There sat the king at the head, already now on the main course, and Edward to his right, laughing away as he finished some fruit. Two of the king's sons and their families laughed and dined along with them, but the eldest was missing.

Marcus looked around, turning to his right. There sat Aldaric and his wife alongside Edward's cousin Emmerich at the other end of the table. The seat opposite the king remained empty, for the queen had died years ago, yet a place setting and food was set anyways.

"Why are the king's eldest and his family eating at the other end of the table?" Marcus whispered to Ichabod, who sat beside him.

Ichabod glanced to his right quickly before taking a bite into the veal that had been placed before him. "Haven't you heard?"

"Heard what?" Marcus asked.

Ichabod sighed. "I see you keep up with palace gossip. If you had a wife, you would know such things." He took another bite of veal and shook his head. "Aldaric, the king's eldest, is only a half-brother to the king's other children."

Marcus raised his brows. "How so?"

"What do you mean how so?" Ichabod scoffed. "You really need a woman. Seems like you've got some things to learn."

"I mean why is he only their half-brother and not their full brother?" Marcus muttered.

Ichabod laughed, enjoying watching Sir Peterson squirm in discomfort. "It is a telling tale, I suppose. The queen, rest her soul, was married to the king's younger brother before she was married to the king. A great man he was, Sir Everard. A brilliant mind from what I heard, too. But one day the poor man was mauled by a grass lion while out on a hunting trip. Left his wife a widow with an infant son to raise. Sir Everard's brother, the king, took pity on her; at least that's what was said. Rumor was that he had always wanted her from the beginning and that was why he had never married at the time. It wasn't even a month after his brother's death that the king and the queen announced their betrothal. They married and the king took Aldaric as his own.

"But a year or so passed and soon the king had his own children with the queen. Two sons, whom you see here, and a daughter, our Queen Maria, Edward's mother. The king took preference to his own flesh and blood and Aldaric was sort of put on the side. The queen had asked King Erick to consider Aldaric for the throne since he was the eldest, but Erick would not have it. He told her he wanted his own son to become king after him, and after that there was a split in the family.

"The queen sided with Aldaric, for she always thought him better suited for the throne. The two sons sided with their father, for they both hoped to become king one day. The king's daughter, however, refused to take a side, yet she was very fond of Aldaric, for he had always defended her from their brothers' teasing."

"So that is why Queen Maria said to give Emmerich her greeting," Marcus replied. "Because of Aldaric."

"Emmerich is Aldaric's only child," Jacob continued. "Aldaric and his wife, Anna, had difficulty bearing children. Emmerich was the only child to survive past birth, so I suppose Queen Maria has a soft spot for him, especially since Emmerich was never granted a royal title like his cousins."

"Does Aldaric have a royal title?"

"His mother insisted he have one, so it was granted, but the king never used the title when addressing him, and after Emmerich was denied a title, Aldaric dropped his own. He did not want to cause any more division in the family, plus he wanted to stand by his son."

Marcus looked back over to Aldaric and his family. They ate quietly, yet looked peaceful, the pomp of the other family members far from their eyes. "How sad," Sir Peterson replied, "that such a difference was made."

"It's not all sad," Ichabod said after a gulp of drink. "Aldaric has done much for their kingdom. He is an ambassador, particularly to Edeland. Much of the extra wealth in Hugellia has come from trade brought about by good alliances."

"He is an asset then," Marcus said.

"Indeed. It is why the king still allows him into the palace," Ichabod replied. "And do not be surprised if you see Aldaric and his family at the royal wedding. It is Emmerich who introduced Prince Edward to Princess Antoinette."

Marcus smiled, glancing at Emmerich as he made quiet conversation with his mother. "The prince must be thankful for his kin. I'm glad he has family to turn to."

"It is fitting they're of the same age. I hear they are like brothers," Ichabod said. "If there was anyone like Prince Stephen, rest his soul, it is Emmerich van Ketten."

Marcus nodded, turning back to his right. Of Edward's brother Stephen, he knew very little, save the brothers looked alike yet acted as opposites. While Edward was more outgoing and action-oriented, Stephen was said to be more studious and quiet. Looking at Emmerich, Marcus could see a little of a resemblance. Though Emmerich's hair was not as black as Edward's, they shared similar facial features. But like Stephen, Emmerich seemed a quieter sort of fellow, and Marcus noticed the young man had a book tucked underneath the table.

But Marcus wasn't fooled. He had learned to read people-it was what made him a discerning man.

If they were like brothers, why weren't they together at the dinner table?

The night was late yet the party seemed like it would go until morning. Still the family ate and drank and were merry, the halls of Erick echoing with laughter and stories that could fill a hundred books if it were all written down. It brought a smile to Edward's face. Here, he was respected. Here, he was known. Here, he was loved.

You are fortunate they know nothing of your sins, but what if they did?

Edward didn't know the answer to that question, nor did he want to know it.

By the time the moonlight began shining through the windows, the king declared that he was weary and would retire for the night. He gave a gentle pat on the shoulder to Edward, urging him up out of his seat and saying the good prince needed his rest. Many stayed, including some of the knights to continue the feast until the morning, but the children had long been sent to bed, and many of the parents felt like doing the same.

The king, still holding Edward by the arm, walked to the other side of the table. "Emmerich!" he called, and immediately the young man stood at attention. "Show Edward to the guest room. I'm sure it will give you two some time to catch up."

"Yes, Your Majesty," Emmerich replied, and Edward felt a sharp pang in his stomach seeing such formality. Did they not share the same grandfather?

But then he remembered. No, they did not.

"Follow me." Emmerich turned to Edward, looking less than thrilled. Edward nodded, slowly following his lead and leaving the noise of the party behind them.

Emmerich led Edward quietly down a dark hall now lit by wall sconces and moonlight coming from the windows, the sounds of their boots echoing as they *clomp, clomp, clomped* on the hardwood floors. Emmerich said nothing and only looked ahead while Edward kept his eyes to the side, glancing out the window and viewing the lake and island in the distance.

"I see our old hiding place has remained undisturbed."

Emmerich quickened in his pace, but Edward remained slow, taking in the sites. "My father has asked the island be left as it were. It was Grandmother's favorite, so the king honored his request."

"We used to have so much fun playing there as children," Edward continued, trying to make the conversation less awkward than what it already was.

"We did," Emmerich replied solemnly.

"Do you still go there?"

Emmerich nodded. "Often."

"Does it look the same? Are the ruins of the old stone cottage still there?"

"Of course."

"I should like to see it again," Edward continued. "I once buried a toy horse there as a treasure. Perhaps it's still there to be dug up."

"So that's where my horse went," Emmerich muttered, and Edward let out a chuckle.

"I'm sorry, Cousin. I thought you knew about that."

"Well I do now, I suppose."

Edward noticed Emmerich's face remained stern. Why, *why* did he have to be escorted to his room by Emmerich? Why couldn't it have been his other cousins, like the brave and boisterous Dietrich or the always laughing Princess Sarah? Unless...

You need a best man.

Antoinette's request rung in Edward's ears. It seemed she had been one step ahead of him, as was his mother. Her greeting to him was supposed to be a reminder. He couldn't help but wonder if it was why Grandfather requested Emmerich to escort him.

But why did it have to be *him*?

He had to get it over with. Antoinette would want Emmerich in the wedding and so would his mother. This was one circumstance that he would not get what he wanted.

"Antoinette sends her greeting."

Emmerich's eye twitched. "Tell her I send her mine."

"I will," Edward started carefully, "but I think you should tell her in person. You are coming to the wedding, are you not?"

Emmerich paused, keeping his eyes ahead. "I don't know. I've been busy of late."

"That's not going to work, you know," Edward replied, and Emmerich gave him a quick, almost questionable glance. "Not that you aren't busy, of course. It's just...you know my mother and Antoinette. They insist you be there."

Emmerich returned his gaze to the front. "I will try to be there, then."

"Actually, I'm hoping you'll definitely be there," Edward stuttered. "I was hoping you'd be my best man."

Emmerich stopped, turning to Edward with a look that could best be described as an insulted fury. But instead of lashing out with words that undoubtedly wanted to fly, Emmerich retained his composure. It made Edward thankful the man had a rare temper, for if he didn't, he would surely be someone to fear.

"I thought one of Antoinette's brothers would be better suited than me," Emmerich replied, his words presented almost too eloquently. "It's her wedding after all. Usually the bride makes the party decisions."

"And she still is," Edward replied. "You being there would make her very happy, Emery."

Emmerich frowned at hearing the nickname those closest to him used, but it seemed to Edward that the mention of Antoinette being happy with Emmerich's attendance made his face sink even lower.

"You mean it would make *you* very happy." Emmerich's voice lowered and he turned, quickening his pace towards the guest room.

Edward trotted to keep up. "I didn't mean it that way, Cousin, and it has nothing to do with me. This is Antoinette's request, not mine."

"I don't know whether to be flattered or insulted by that," Emmerich muttered.

"I'm not going to pretend we are friends, Emmerich," Edward said, grabbing his arm and pulling him back to a stop. He let go as his cousin faced him with an icy glare. "But I cannot help at the choice she made, nor can I help who I fall in love with."

If words were like daggers, Edward was certain what he had spoken had pierced Emmerich's heart to the core. His anger softened to sorrow and instantly his gaze turned to the window in the distance. "Her happiness is all that matters," Emmerich whispered. "If she wishes it, I will be there."

"Thank you," Edward said quietly. He thought of putting a hand on Emmerich's shoulder, or maybe patting his back, but thought against it. There was still much bitterness between them, even after all the years apart.

Emmerich turned and began to quietly lead Edward down the hall again, but Edward noticed his pace was slower and his posture not as tall. It was the look of a defeated man, one who fought with fate and fate won.

You stole her from him. Edward's conscience pricked at his heart, and that sick feeling in his stomach returned. *You don't deserve Antoinette, but he did. And what would he think if he knew what you had done in Verloris?*

Worse yet, what would *she* think? Would Antoinette remain at his side?

The thought of Antoinette going to Emmerich was a feeling he couldn't shake, and he pushed the thought to the back of his mind, never wanting to think of it again.

Chapter 9: Doubts

"Do I have to wear this hairpiece?"

Bernette scratched the top of her head, making her scalp move. The poor girl looked like she had a wad of hair hanging off to the side, and even though her "shiner" (as she called it) was covered, she felt she looked sillier than what she wanted to. Antoinette chuckled at seeing Bernie's new "hat", but their mother quickly turned and gave a huff.

"Stop touching it, child! You must be presentable when seeing Queen Maria!"

Queen Susanna quickly took her hands to it, yanking hair this way and that until it made Bernette's head hurt. "Don't touch it anymore," she scolded. "We can't have a mess with this thing while seeing the royal family. Until the hair grows back, we have to keep this hidden."

Bernette crinkled her nose in frustration. "If it grows back, you mean. And at the rate you're pulling..."

Susanna pulled the hair harder, making Bernie give a yelp.

"Stop it this instant!" she seethed. "Now there. It's fixed. If you touch it again, I'm going to glue it to your head."

Bernette opened her mouth to say something, but Antoinette cleared her throat. "She'd really do it, Bernie."

"But it's so itchy," Bernie whined. "Are you sure this thing doesn't have lice in it?"

"Not another word," her mother said as she gave her "the look", which Bernie could best describe as a grumpy man having constipation.

Susanna spun to the front and straightened her dress so as not to have any wrinkles in the fabric. "Hurry, ladies," she said as Antoinette and Bernette followed behind.

When Susanna wasn't looking, however, Bernie snuck in a few extra scratches. "I swear she got this thing from a bear," she whispered to Antoinette, who only laughed some more.

"I'm surprised it hasn't given you a headache," Antoinette said quietly. "Just how heavy is that thing?"

"Like I said." Bernette shrugged. "Must be from a bear. A big, fat, fluffy one who never had a haircut."

The three entered the drawing room of Reigal Palace and Bernette was awed at how grand the room looked. Wooden floors, quite shiny (though not as shiny as Mother preferred it), with tall windows on the sides to let the sunlight shine through. White, plush sofas sat at the center of the room around a wooden table, and she could swear she saw the red drapes gently sway as she entered the room.

I can't believe Antoinette gets to live here...

Queen Maria stood and smiled, instantly embracing the three with her own warm welcome. "Susanna, you look ravishing!" Maria exclaimed, and Susanna began to tell a story of her beauty treatments that Maria would undoubtedly want to try. Maria, however, only nodded with a smile, giving a smirk to Antoinette as she embraced her. An inside joke, Bernette thought to herself, and she imagined conversations in which Antoinette told her all about how Mother really was.

"And Bernette," Maria said with a smile. She embraced the young girl warmly, making Bernette relish the touch. She had no memory of her mother ever hugging her like that.

"What a lovely young woman you are growing into," she said, and Bernette grinned. "Such a pretty face. It won't be long until the wedding bells shall ring for you!"

Bernette could almost hear her mother laughing in her mind. Pretty face? Sure. When she looked to see Mother's reaction, she only saw indifference. Mother neither smiled nor frowned, nor even offered a thank you.

And being the kind and gentle being that she was, Bernette decided to thank Maria for her.

"Thank you, Your Majesty," she said sweetly and with a curtsey. "My mother makes sure I am always following my beauty treatments. Not a day goes by that she doesn't remind me of them."

"So I've heard." Maria chuckled. "But if I may offer my own opinion, I don't think you need them. Both you and your sister have a natural beauty all your own."

Bernette couldn't help but grin. *Oh, I like you!*

"Well!" Susanna interrupted, stepping forward with flair. "Tell me of the wedding plans. We must have everything perfect for the big day!"

Maria gave Antoinette a glance as if knowing what was to come. She turned back to Susanna, folding her hands in front of her. "They've been going well. I believe everything is finished. Antoinette is a wonderful event planner..."

"Oh, of course!" Susanna exclaimed, making Antoinette sigh at her mother's constant flattery. "I'm afraid all of this is becoming a bit much for her, though. I just can't sit back and stay idle. I'm not built that way. We must get silk ordered for the tablecloths, and of course I'd like to check the fabric for the dresses. Those must be silk as well. Except for Bernie's-we need something that...stretches."

Bernette's brow lowered. "Did she just call me fat?" she muttered under her breath.

Antoinette could only smack herself in the forehead.

"Well, my Bernie's a growing girl after all," Susanna explained as even Queen Maria gave her a perplexed look. "I wouldn't be surprised if she's her father's height by Christmas."

"Dad's short. I'm already his height," Bernie replied, but Susanna pretended to ignore her.

"You needn't worry," Maria said. "I think the ladies will be just fine. The dresses that have been picked out already are more than fit for a queen."

"Splendid!" Susanna clapped in delight. "Now please, let us see them at once! You know how a mother worries. I just want to be sure!"

"My dearest Edward...how terribly I miss you," Bernette murmured over Antoinette's shoulder as she read the letter that was being written by candlelight. Antoinette smirked as she glanced at her sister and continued writing. "I long for the day I can see you again. Know that I think of you always and pray for your safe return to me."

Bernette cleared her throat and looked to Antoinette. "This is really sappy, you know that?"

Antoinette kept her eyes on the parchment and continued to write. "When you find the man of your dreams and write letters to him, I guarantee yours will be sappier than mine."

"Never. I'm not a romantic."

"Sure you aren't." Antoinette chuckled under her breath.

Bernette rolled her eyes as she continued reading the letter. "I am in Reigal with Mother and Bernie. We are discussing the wedding plans..."

Bernette paused, a smirk coming upon her face. "I beg you to return to me at once. Mother has been morbid to us all and she insists making my poor sister look like a gorilla with the hairpiece she is forced to wear. Also, she is driving your mother batty ordering her around. If you truly are a momma's boy, you would make haste! And don't forget to bring me back some chicken wings. I hear Hugellian barbeque is world-renowned!"

Antoinette tried to hide the laughter as she lowered her quill. "I didn't say that in the letter."

"I know," Bernie said, "but you should have. It's the truth, isn't it?"

"The poor man is already terrified of his mother-in-law, Bernie. Let's not scare him off."

"Oh, I'm sure he won't go anywhere. He knows Mother pretty well and still wants to marry you, after all. If that isn't true love, I don't know what is."

"Good point."

"So what's Hugellia like, anyways?" Bernie asked as she flopped herself onto Antoinette's bed, snuggling into the soft pillows and tossing her hairpiece to the ground.

"I'm not sure. I've never really been there, to be honest," Antoinette replied. "I remember Edward's cousin Emmerich telling me stories of the city, though. It's supposedly bigger than Reigal."

"Emmerich-he's the scrawny, boring fellow that used to visit us in the spring, right?"

"Yes. But be nice, Bernie." Antoinette turned and looked at her. "Emmerich is who you're walking down the aisle with."

Bernie's head shot up, her eyes wide. "Wait, *what*?"

"He's Edward's best man, silly. You didn't think you'd be walking by yourself now, did you?"

"Of course not," Bernette replied. "I just thought you'd hook me up with someone handsome!"

Antoinette frowned. "Emmerich's very handsome! He's a spitting image of Edward."

"They don't look a thing alike. Emmerich's a walking twig with a baby face."

"It's been four years since you've last seen him, Bernie. He's certainly not a twig anymore and that baby face has all grown up."

Bernie pursed her lips. "So he's fat now?"

Antoinette sighed. "No."

"Oh, come on! Isn't there another one of Edward's cousins you can have as best man?"

"Emery's in the wedding, Bernie." Antoinette returned to her letter. "I know him much better than you and I think you'll be surprised at how much you two will get along. He's a lot like you, you know."

"I think everyone would agree I'm not a twig, Antoinette."

Antoinette shook her head. "I meant in personality. He likes to read, you like to read. He likes boring stuff, you like boring stuff."

"I don't like boring stuff!"

"Sure you do. I caught you reading about how to build a Roman aqueduct on the ride here. What's the point of knowing something like that?"

"Architecture is a fascinating subject, thank you very much."

"Well unless you plan on building a city, I'd say it's rather boring."

Bernie crossed her arms and glared.

"Oh, don't be offended. I'm only teasing." Antoinette laughed. "Just don't write Emery off until you see him, at least. He's the most honorable, most humble man I know. There's not another heart like his."

"Well if he's so great, why aren't you marrying him?"

Antoinette paused in her writing. She often wondered about a possible match with Emery in her younger days. He was her greatest friend, someone she shared some of the most intimate, deepest conversations with when he and his parents spent time in Edeland. But he was nothing more than that. It was Edward who came crashing in with a declaration of love, and she took it.

"You have to have feelings for each other in order to make a relationship work, Bernie," Antoinette replied as she continued on with her letter. "Emery never saw me as more than a friend. You marry for love, not out of a necessity or because it sounds like a good match."

"Alright. I can see your point in that," Bernie said, hugging a pillow and resting her back against the wall. "But let's say he did like you...like, romantically I mean, and then you had to choose between him and Edward."

Antoinette turned to Bernie with her brow up.

"What?" Bernie asked. "I'm just asking hypothetically."

"It's a weird question."

"How is it weird?" Bernie asked. "I'm just asking 'if'. Besides, I thought the answer would be obvious to you."

"It is."

"Well?"

"I'd still choose Edward," Antoinette said, turning back to her letter. "I'd choose him over anyone else. I mean, he makes me feel so...so special. I still get butterflies in my stomach when he looks at me. My heart still races when he holds my hand."

"Alright, he makes you feel giddy," Bernie said. "So that's why you chose him? Because he gives you butterflies in your stomach?"

Antoinette sighed, rubbing her forehead. "I chose Edward because he has a good heart."

"But you just said Emmerich has a good heart, too. So what's the difference?"

"Edward is braver."

"So you want a man who has brawn over brains?"

"Edward's smart, too."

"And who's to say Emmerich isn't brave?"

"He's not a warrior."

"So you want a guy who can beat people up?"

"I never said that."

"So then why are you marrying Edward?"

Antoinette set the quill on the desk and turned back to her sister in frustration. "And why do you keep on questioning whether I love my fiancé or not?"

Bernette's eyes widened at Antoinette's sudden turn. It was rare for her sister to show any emotion that was perturbed. But after her face softened, Bernette cleared her throat. "It's just a question. No need to get upset about it. I know you love Edward. I just wanted to know why."

Antoinette returned to her letter but found any words she wanted to write had left her mind. Her sister's questions had befuddled her, making her mind feel like it had just been emptied.

But it wasn't the questions themselves that made Antoinette upset. It was the fact that Bernette had hit a nerve and it made Antoinette begin to doubt herself.

Why are you marrying Edward?

The answer was simple. It was because she loved him. Did she need a reason other than that?

But why do you love him?

He had a good heart. He was brave and he loved her.

Is that it? Is that all there is?

That's all that needed to be there. She knew what was in her heart; she *felt* it, and where her heart lead, she would follow.

"I think you're reading too many psychology books, Bernie," Antoinette muttered as she stared at the half-written page. "Love is simple. It's only complicated when you make it that way."

Bernette's voice was barely above a whisper as she spoke. "But if it were so simple, wouldn't we all understand it?"

"Only those of us who have experienced it would understand," Antoinette snapped back. "You don't know that feeling, Bernie. You just haven't experienced it yet."

Bernette frowned as she clutched the pillow tighter across her chest. "You're right. I don't know that feeling."

"Then you have no right to judge me by it, then."

"I wasn't judging you, Antoinette," Bernie replied solemnly. "And yeah, I know; I'm clueless when it comes to the warm and fuzzies. But I understand feelings. I know happiness and sadness and joy and pain. I know that feelings come and go and are so fleeting. If love is a feeling, then how do you know it'll last?"

Antoinette stood from her seat and approached the bed. "Because love is different. It has the power to last forever!"

"Feelings change so very often, Antoinette."

"I love Edward and Edward loves me. Why are you even questioning this?"

"And why are you getting so upset over a simple discussion? Unless you like Emmerich a little more than you're letting on."

"I don't! He's only a friend."

"Sounds like it's a little more than that."

"It's NOT!"

"But what if it is?"

Antoinette could feel her heart starting to race. She loved her sister more than anything in the world, but sometimes she could be so *infuriating*.

Especially if she's right.

She wasn't right. Was she?

But then Antoinette's thoughts began to churn. She remembered the letter Bernie forged to get her back to Staalberg. She remembered the teary conversation of not wanting her sister to move to Reigal and leave her alone with Mother.

The truth was simple: Bernette didn't want Antoinette to get married and leave.

"Bernie…" Antoinette rubbed the bridge of her nose, trying to calm herself down. "I know what you're doing. It's not going to work."

"What do you mean?"

"You're trying to make me question my decision to marry Edward so I'll cancel the wedding and go back to Staalberg with you," Antoinette said. "I know you don't want me to leave, Bernie. I don't want you to be left alone, either."

"Oh no. Don't you turn this back on me!" Bernie's eyes flared.

"It's ok, Bernie. I get it. And I told you-I'm going to find a way to get you to move here with me."

"Antoinette, this isn't about me!"

Antoinette put a warm hand on Bernie's shoulder, only for her sister to swat it away as she threw the pillow back to the bed and stormed off to the door.

"Bernie, it's alright to be upset."

"I'm not upset!"

"You clearly are, and I want you to know it's okay. You can be honest with me."

"Fine! You want me to be honest?" Bernie turned to her sister as she put her hand on the door knob. "I think you're marrying Edward just so you can get out of Mother's reach, too!"

Antoinette's mouth dropped and she gave a scoff. "I'm marrying Edward because I love him!"

"Oh, I'm sure you have the butterflies," Bernie sneered. "And I know I'm young. I know I don't have any experience. But at least I can look at all of this *rationally* and realize that anything based on a feeling is strong at first but then falls flat in the end!"

Antoinette felt like she had been punched in the gut. Air left her lungs and at first she couldn't speak. It took all of her strength just to mutter a response. "How...how could you say such a thing, Bernie?"

Bernie frowned, her eyes looking heavy. "I'm being honest, Antoinette, because you're my sister. I know you love Edward. I get that. But look at our own parents. They got married and probably loved each other more than anything when they were first together, but look at them now. They barely speak to each other, and when they do, it's a fight. They don't even sleep in the same rooms anymore. All because 'it's not like how it was when we were younger.'"

"Then what are you trying to say?"

"I'm saying love doesn't last," Bernie replied quietly. "It's not like how it is in the stories. People are shallow. They say they love you but they'll never show it."

"That won't happen to Edward and me," Antoinette said. "And it won't happen to you either, Bernie."

"Whatever," Bernette scoffed, but as she opened the door they found a guard standing there, readying to knock.

"Forgive me, Your Majesties," the guard stammered, giving a quick bow. "I was to inform you Sir Rikert has returned from the trip."

Antoinette stepped forward with a concerned look. "Only Sir Rikert? Is Edward with him?"

"No, Your Majesty," the guard replied. "The prince is not with him. Sir Rikert has informed me that he was dismissed by His Majesty and sent back to Reigal."

Antoinette lowered her brow. "Did he say why?"

"Because the prince wished to stay in Verloris," the guard continued. "Apparently there was a storm. Sir Rikert is speaking with the king and queen now if you wish to join them."

"Gladly," Antoinette replied, her heart already worried for her fiancé. She hurried down the stairs as Bernette remained quietly at the door and watched her go.

"I don't want you to leave," Bernette muttered under her breath as she held onto the door handle. "But I don't want you to get hurt, either."

By the time Antoinette had reached the throne room, Sir Rikert was nearly finished with his tale. As she walked in, staying towards the back, she could overhear the conversation coming to an end.

"So they stayed in Cathal?" the voice of King Arden spoke. He was slouched on his throne, rubbing his forehead as if fighting a migraine.

"Yes, Your Majesty," Sir Rikert replied. "At least, they were meaning to by the time I was dismissed. I was unable to know what happened after I left."

"At least they were out of that storm," Maria said.

"But look at where they stayed!" Arden muttered. "Sometimes I wonder where that boy's mind is! If Stephen were here, he'd…"

"Dear, you mustn't rile yourself up. Remember your blood pressure."

"I swear Edward's going to be the death of me."

"Don't say that, Arden. That isn't fair."

"It may not be fair, but it's true."

"Well I'm going to trust our son," Maria replied. "There was little choice in the matter. If I were in that storm, I'd stay in Cathal if that were the only choice."

"Let's just hope he isn't taken hostage." Arden sighed.

"Oh, Edward would never allow that. He'd fight his way out before they could get them. He's a talented swordsman, you know."

"He's also a foolish boy!"

Maria leaned back on her throne, her folded hands landing in her lap. "I don't know how you can say such cruelties, Arden, when our baby is out there all alone! I do hope he's made it to Hugellia safely. I worry so much over him."

"I assure Your Majesty that the prince is well looked after by the royal guard," Sir Rikert said. "Even without me, the company is well trained to defend the prince with their lives. Your son is in good hands."

"Thank you, noble knight," Maria said kindly. "You put my mind at ease."

Arden huffed as he stood from the throne. "My apologies, Sir Rikert, that my son so ignorantly dismissed you. I hereby reinstate you to the royal guard and put you into my service. I'm sorry for the inconvenience this has brought to you and I promise I will deal with my son about this once he returns. I will set the matter straight!"

"There is no need to apologize, Your Majesty," Sir Rikert said with a bow. "I only wished to keep you informed."

"Which you have," Arden replied. "We'll await word from Edward that he's arrived in Hugellia, but if there is no word received by the end of next week, we shall speak with the Verloris in Cathal."

"Yes, Your Majesty," Sir Rikert replied.

"Very well, then," Arden said as he stepped off the throne. "I will grant myself leave. You are free to return home to your family. I shall speak with you again in the morning."

"Of course." Sir Rikert bowed again, and Arden left the throne room, Maria trailing quickly behind.

Antoinette hurried to Sir Rikert as he was turning to leave as well. "Samuel! Samuel, wait!"

Sir Rikert turned and bowed. "Lady Antoinette," he said.

"I only caught the end of your conversation with Arden and Maria. Is Edward alright?"

The knight nodded. "Yes. Last I saw him, he was doing well."

Antoinette breathed a sigh of relief but soon gasped as she got a good look at Rikert's appearance. The poor man looked so tired, so worn. His cloak was already tattered and damp, doubtless for traveling so long in the rain.

"Oh Samuel, I'm so sorry you had to travel back all this way," she replied. "What made Edward send you home?"

Rikert sighed. Antoinette wondered if the man was bitter being sent away so quickly and without question, but whatever emotion he had on his face, it was not anger. Rather, it was sadness, as if the man felt guilty for leaving.

"I advised him not to enter Cathal. I did not deem it wise."

And clearly Edward didn't listen. Antoinette crossed her arms in thought. She knew little of Cathal-in fact, she had never heard of it-and wondered if Edward knew the same.

"Why was he advised to not enter Cathal?" Antoinette asked. "Is it dangerous there? Will Edward be safe?"

Samuel frowned as he looked at Antoinette. "I hope he is safe, Your Majesty. The Verloris are no allies of Audlin, nor of Edeland, nor of Hugellia. They are allies with no one but themselves. They are not known to be the friendliest of peoples."

This was an answer Antoinette didn't want to hear. She wanted Edward safe. She wanted him to return to her alive and well so they could be married and live together in happiness. "Oh Samuel, I fear for him. Should we go to Cathal and see if he's still there?"

"Let us wait on word from Kettensburg," Rikert replied, a gentle smile coming upon his face. "Fret not, Lady Antoinette. When I said the prince is in good hands, I meant it. He is safest with the royal guard."

Antoinette bowed her head, rubbing her teary eyes. Arden and Maria may have been reassured, but Antoinette wasn't.

She prayed silently that Edward was alright. She didn't know what she would do if she were to ever lose him.

"Has there been any word?" Antoinette asked as she looked out the window, patiently waiting for the courier to arrive.

Bernette shook her head as she lounged on a couch, hairpiece flopped onto her head and a book in front of her face. "Not that I know of. Then again, I'm not checking much. It's not like I ever get any letters."

"I'm serious, Bernie." Antoinette frowned. "I'm starting to worry. It's been nearly two weeks since Sir Rikert's return and yet there has been no word on Edward's arrival. I hope nothing has happened to him."

"I'm sure he's fine," Bernie replied. "Hugellia's a long ways off. Even if he was on time, you still might not have heard from him."

"I know." Antoinette sighed. "I just worry for him."

"Trust me. Ol' Eddie boy's fine. Just stop fretting and enjoy the peace and quiet while we have it. Mother won't be long on getting her hair done."

"I'm sorry, Bernie. I just can't help it. You know how I am," Antoinette said as she sat upon the chair across from her sister, her back straight and tall with her hands clasped nervously in her lap. "The road to Hugellia is long and dangerous, and this Cathal place...I'm unsure about it."

"Well, they were caught in a storm," Bernie said. "It was either risk getting struck by lightning or take shelter. Take your pick, you know?"

"Cathal must have been a terrible place for Sir Rikert to choose the storm over shelter. Do you know anything about Verloris, Bernie? From your studies?"

"Not much to tell," Bernie said, turning the page in her book. "Edeland doesn't have much to do with them since they're so far away. The Verloris have more of a history with Hugellia than anything. They had a big war a few hundred years ago that nearly wiped both countries out. Hugellia won and Verloris became isolationist. I heard they have a king and he's got two girls. It's a strict society. They don't exactly score high on the moral scale."

"What do you mean?"

"Little freedom. Fights to the death. Corruption. You know the deal."

Antoinette shook her head. "It sounds terrible."

"Hence why no one goes there for vacations," Bernie said. "But that's all I know-and that's coming from a history book. Who knows what it's like now."

"You don't think..." Antoinette paused, putting a hand to her lips. "You don't think they'd try to hurt Edward, do you? Like hold him for ransom or something like that?"

Bernie lowered her book and shook her head. "Like I said-they had more to do with Hugellia than the rest of us. Unless they were looking for a war, I doubt they'd do anything that stupid."

Antoinette wrung her hands together. Though Bernie seemed reassured, Antoinette still felt uneasy. Maybe it was because of the conversation she had with her sister regarding Edward and Emmerich. Maybe it was because Sir Rikert, one of King Arden's best knights, wasn't there to protect her beloved. Either way, she had a heavy feeling, one she felt in her heart and couldn't shake.

Bernette laid the book in her lap and lowered her brow. "Are you okay? You look like Mother just asked to spend the day with you."

"Hmm?" Antoinette looked up from her stupor.

Bernette frowned. "Gracious, you are worried, aren't you? Why on earth for?"

"I just...I don't know. I have a feeling."

"A feeling about what?"

"I don't know." Antoinette stood from the chair and returned to the window. "Like...something's happened to him. I hope he's not hurt."

"He's fine." Bernette rolled her eyes. "Besides, he's surrounded by all those big, beefy knights. You honestly think any of them would let even a hair get pulled from his head?"

"Well...no, but..."

"Besides, if you want something to worry about, worry about all those Hugellian ladies Eddie will probably be running into. I heard they're quite the lookers."

Antoinette crossed her arms and gave Bernie a scoff. "I'm not worried about that. Edward's loyal to me."

"He's a young man with urges. Don't be so sure."

Antoinette shook her head. "What is it with you hating men so much?"

"I don't hate them," Bernie replied with a chuckle. "I quite like them, actually. I just think they're all idiots."

"Some of them are intelligent, you know."

"If you call running around in a field, hitting each other with a bunch of sticks intelligent, then fine," Bernie replied. "It just proves women truly are smarter than men."

Antoinette gave a smirk but it quickly faded as she heard the courier arrive. As Bernie was going on about the superiority of female intelligence, Antoinette rushed out the door, ignoring her sister. Down the stairs the young woman went, nearly tripping over her dress. The courier quickly handed her the letter with a smile as Antoinette curtseyed, gasping for breath.

"A letter addressed to the Lady Antoinette," the courier replied as he handed her the letter. "And I'll just...*ehm*...give these others to the king."

"Thank you!" Antoinette fluttered between breaths as she tore the letter open, scanning it quickly. She breathed a sigh of relief as she recognized Edward's handwriting. He was safe, arriving in Kettensburg a few days late because of a storm, just like Sir Rikert had said.

The sound of Bernette's shuffling feet from behind caught Antoinette's attention. "Let me guess-Ol' Eddie's in Hugellia, right?" Bernie asked.

Antoinette nodded. "Yes. He arrived a few days late because of the storm."

"See? I told you there was nothing to worry about. Well-except those Hugellian ladies."

Antoinette ignored the last comment from her sister as she scanned the letter again. Edward sounded perfectly safe, content, happy. Though he didn't mention Verloris, he didn't act like anything else from the trip was amiss.

So why did that terrible feeling not go away?

Chapter 11: For the Love of Family

Emmerich had only been missing for a few hours, but it was enough to make Anna van Ketten sick with worry over her only child. Aldaric, busy planning a trip to meet with a representative, had been called away from his work by his frantic wife, desperate to know where their son had gone off to. He remained calm, for her sake, as Emmerich was a grown boy and had undoubtedly went off on an errand she didn't need to know of, but Anna wouldn't have it, so Aldaric reassured her he would find him and put her mind at ease.

At first Aldaric asked around to see if Emmerich was at his usual spots-the library, the archery range, even the monks' sanctum where he often volunteered to write down translated scrolls, just so he could learn the ancient languages. After all of his usual spots turned out empty, Aldaric went to the palace. Cousin Edward was still in town, busy seeing the sites and spending time with family. Surely Emmerich would be there.

But Edward was with his other cousins, the sons and daughters of the king's other children. Emmerich was never with them.

So there was only one place Emmerich could be.

It took a while for Aldaric to find a rowboat, but once he found one, he made his way to the island at the center of Kettensburg's lake, across from the royal palace where the centuries old cottage lay in ruins. It was an old playing ground where Aldaric, his wife, and his mother, the queen, had taken Emmerich when he was a boy. He was always fond of the ruins and the trees-the only place in Hugellia where history met with nature and one could find solitude when wanting to escape the world.

When Aldaric approached, he saw another rowboat perched on the shore and some footprints leading to the cottage ruins. He followed the prints through the trees and towards the stone walls overrun by ivy only to find his son sitting on the ground, his back leaning on a pillar, reading a book on cartography.

"You have your mother worried, you know," Aldaric said, making Emmerich look up in surprise. Aldaric approached the empty spot of dirt beside his son and slowly sat down upon it. He wasn't as limber as he was in his younger days, and he was starting to feel it at the age of fifty-two. Not that he would ever admit to feeling old.

"I told her I was going out for some air," Emmerich replied, folding a corner page in the book to save his spot where he left off. "I didn't mean to make her worry."

"I figured as such," Aldaric said, "and I tried to tell her. She worries all the same."

"She needn't worry. Believe me, I'm not going anywhere."

Aldaric gave a light chuckle before leaning back against the cold, hard wall of the ruins. "I was a bit surprised to find you out here. You aren't upset over anything, are you?"

Emmerich gave a shrug as he set the book down. It was true Emmerich often retreated to the island when he wanted some peace and quiet-either to cool off and recuperate or to just sit down and think without interruption.

"I was looking for my old toy horse. Apparently it was buried here," Emmerich began. "I never found it, though, so I just thought I'd read to pass the time."

"Toy horse?" Aldaric asked. "When did you have one of those?"

"I was six. You and Mom gave it to me for my birthday. I only had it a week before it went missing."

"And how did you know it was here?"

"Edward told me," Emmerich said with a frown. "This is where he said he buried it."

"Oh." Aldaric exhaled slowly. "And you never found it?"

"I probably never will. But it doesn't matter." Emmerich shrugged. "It's not like he hasn't stolen from me before."

Emmerich got up, gathering the book in his hand. "Mom is probably worried. I'll go back and let her know I was here."

Aldaric remained seated, letting out a sigh. Seventeen years he had known his son, enough to call him not only his child but his best friend. Did Emery not know he could share his frustrations with his father *no matter what*?

"You know, this wasn't the first place I looked for you," Aldaric said, making Emmerich stop and turn back. "I checked at the palace to see if you were with your cousins. You weren't."

"Why would I be with them?" Emmerich asked.

"It's not every day Edward visits from Reigal."

"And that would make me want to visit him or my cousins more?"

Aldaric frowned. It was no secret the children of the king's other sons were on less than friendly terms with Emmerich. His childhood was filled with accounts of teasing and threats and the occasional fights that would send him home with bruises and a black eye. It was something they learned to avoid since the king was blind to his children's cruelty. But Maria was always a good sister, never showing favoritism. She and Aldaric hoped to bring up Edward and Emmerich like brothers, especially after Stephen died.

"You should at least spend time with Edward. He'll be gone to Reigal soon, and after he marries, I doubt we shall see him as much."

Emmerich smirked. "That may not be such a bad thing-at least, the not seeing him part."

"You say that now, but you shouldn't," Aldaric replied quietly. "Edward is like you; he needs his family."

"Family is nothing but a bunch of relatives who bully and mistreat you," Emmerich said with a sneer. "Trust me. Edward fits in quite well with the others. He'll always have their support."

"You're still angry with him over what happened with Antoinette?"

Emmerich looked away towards a pile of rocks near the ruins. "That was years ago. It's in the past."

"It may be in the past, but it sounds like you're holding it well into the present," Aldaric said. "I know how much you cared for her and I also know what Edward did to you was wrong. He should've never lied. He should've never betrayed your trust. But what's happened has happened and you should learn to forgive."

Emmerich looked back up, his face hard with bitterness. "Why should I have to do anything? He's the one that made a mess of things."

"It's not easy, Emery, but forgiveness is the right thing to do," Aldaric said softly. "I understand your hurt better than anyone. Instead of letting one setback hold you down like this, you should learn to let it go."

"But it isn't fair."

"Life isn't fair, Son."

"It's 'fair' to those who don't deserve it."

"Perhaps," Aldaric said with a nod. "But that is the test of our character. How we handle the bad or the good shows what kind of men we are. Are we men of character? Of passion? Of principle? Of frivolous things?"

Aldaric stood and cupped his son's face with his hand, making Emmerich face his father in the eye. He lowered his hands and clasped the young man's shoulders, saying, "Life has been difficult for you, Emery. I won't deny it. But it has been difficult for many others as well. Instead of dwelling on what could have been, dwell on what can be. Your whole life is still ahead of you. You don't know what the future holds for you or for your cousins."

"So you're saying you don't envy Ulrich or Ambrose because King Erick loves them and doesn't love you?"

Aldaric paused, knowing Emery's words were meant well but hurt nonetheless. He never told about the many nights he laid awake, asking why his own father had died only to be replaced by a man who saw him as a burden. Aldaric swallowed hard and closed his eyes for a moment, remembering the hurt of the past. He opened his eyes and gave a weak smile. "I don't envy them, though I once did," he began. "I pity them now. Look at them, chasing after petty things and so unaware of the beauty of life. They care more of who is to be the next king than for the poor beggars in the street or the orphans asking for a meal. Either one of them may hold the title of king, but they will never be the king of the people's hearts.

"You envy Edward now because he has everything you want-family who loves him, a hopeful future, a lovely woman who will be his wife. But you do not see what he is already missing. The death of a brother is something not easily forgotten."

"He and Stephen didn't get along," Emmerich said coldly. "I doubt he misses him."

"Even the loss of an enemy can hurt, Emery. The loss of family is a pain far worse, a pain you have yet to experience."

Emmerich looked away. "I wouldn't miss the family if they were gone," he muttered under his breath. "And they certainly wouldn't miss me."

"You say that now, but time can change our minds," Aldaric said. "Besides, you'd miss your mother and me, wouldn't you? We're your family."

Emmerich gave a nod. "Of course I'd miss you. And Aunt Maria, to be honest, but that's it. I wouldn't miss the rest of them."

Aldaric put his hand on the back of Emmerich's head and caressed it like he did when his son was a little boy. Emery remained quiet, looking away, and Aldaric stopped. He was getting nowhere, he could tell. Emery was still holding on tightly to the past-the loss of Antoinette was something he was afraid Emmerich would never forgive Edward over.

But he was once like his son. He once hated Ulrich and Ambrose and King Erick with every fiber of his being. It wasn't until he grew up and saw how wretched his brothers and stepfather had become did he suddenly realize how much he pitied them.

He only hoped Emery would learn the same lesson.

"I suppose I can't talk you into spending time with Edward while he is here, can I?"

Emmerich shook his head. "It's doubtful."

"I won't force you then," Aldaric said sadly, removing his hand and walking towards the rowboat. "I will tell your mother where you've been. Are you planning on staying here longer or are you returning home?"

"I'd like to stay," Emmerich replied, returning to the pillar. "If just for an hour or so. It's more peaceful."

Aldaric stopped for a moment and nodded. "Very well. I will tell her to expect you at dinner time, then."

"Thank you."

"I'm leaving for the border in the morning," Aldaric continued as Emmerich sat down in his original spot. "I'm meeting with a representative of the Recu. Did you wish to join me?"

"I'll stay home and take care of Mom. We don't want her worrying over both of us," Emery said, turning back to his book.

Aldaric nodded, watching his son quietly for a moment. With a sigh, he turned away, returning to the boat.

Chapter 12: The One Who Should Be King

Three and a half weeks had Edward been in Hugellia, and never had he had so much *fun*. Hunting, fishing, feasting; it was almost enough to keep his mind preoccupied constantly with what he was *doing* instead of what he had *done*. The guilt lessened, his heart grew more at ease, and for a moment he was starting to think he would finally move on from that one slip up in Verloris.

His mood improved as he spent more time with his kin and less time with those who had unfortunately reminded him of the past. Most of his knights had been sent towards other duties (there was, after all, no need of them for protection while in Hugellia) and cousin Emmerich had been gone most of the time-where, he did not know, nor did he care. He heard a rumor that Emmerich's father had been away on business and had just got back, and he wondered if Emmerich had gone with him or stayed at home with his mother. Either way, the last three weeks had been grand. Never had his mind been more at ease.

I'm finally starting to forget.

Or he was getting so used to the guilt that it no longer plagued him like before.

That isn't such a bad thing, is it?

But after three and a half weeks, business had finally called. There was the treaty his father had wished him to have

King Erick sign, and Edward and his grandfather had put it off long enough. It was early in the morning, the beginning of the day before the mad rush of businessmen and councilmen would vie for the king's attention until he would go mad with boredom. Edward had hoped to be the first to see the king that day, not only to seem responsible and ambitious, but also to get the treaty out of the way so he could return to all the fun he was having.

Up the marble steps he walked, marveling at the beautiful weather that seemed to never end during his stay. He passed the rows of hallways that led to other rooms and stairs and headed towards the center of the palace, the throne room of the king, in which the ceiling reached multiple stories in height and where a great skylight stood at the top. Balconies from the other floors of the palace circled around a great gold and marble throne that sat in the center of the room. Servants stood towards the sides, ready to do the king's bidding, while musicians performed quietly in the back. As Edward entered, he made a mental note to redo his own throne room to be like his grandfather's when he became king.

Before he could gather the king's attention, he noticed his grandfather already had an audience. Edward frowned, for he never enjoyed waiting, and lowered his brow at who he saw was there.

Emmerich.

Fortunately for Edward, it was not Emmerich who was speaking, but his father, Aldaric. Emmerich, alongside his mother, stood in silence beside the stepson of the king, and as Edward approached alongside Lady Anna, Emmerich turned and glanced at him.

Edward glanced back, but said nothing. Emmerich only turned away.

"So you have met with the Recu, then?" the king had asked.

"Only with their emissary," Aldaric said as Edward began listening in on the conversation. "They are quite interested in making an alliance with us."

"A bold move for their new leader, no doubt."

"Or a smart one. I can arrange for you to meet with Chief Bohden, Your Majesty," Aldaric replied. "I recommend that you at least listen to his proposal."

The king rolled his eyes, clearly not interested. "The Recu are barbarians who care for nothing but hunting and the woods. What business would I want with them?"

"The Recu only wish to trade," Aldaric replied. "They are in need of grain and metals. Their climate is much colder than ours and they lack the resources we have."

"And what would they give us in return?" Erick asked. "Or am I supposed to be a charitable king?"

"They offer us furs and timber, Your Majesty."

The king laughed, and for a moment Edward noted it sounded like a scoff. "Our summers are too warm for furs and with plenty of wool, we do not need them in the winter. As for the timber, have we not an overabundance of stone? I would feel much safer living in a house of rock than a house of wood."

"They offer us friendship, Your Majesty," Aldaric pleaded, and Edward was surprised at the look of urgency in Aldaric's face. "The Recu have long been isolated and with their new chief, they are looking for allies. We cannot afford to look away."

"And why would we need more allies?" the king asked. "Have we not allies already?"

"There is strength in numbers," Aldaric said. "Braiden lies to the southwest and Verloris to the east. We are nearly surrounded by lands who may not have interests in our benefit."

"And yet you forget our closest ally, Audlin." The king looked to Edward, who let out a small gulp. He never enjoyed the political discussions of his predecessors, yet somehow he always got pulled into them. "Tell me, Edward. If Hugellia is attacked, will Audlin come to our aid?"

At least the question was easy. "Of course, Grandfather," Edward replied with a bow. "We would always come to the aid of our kin."

"You see? There is nothing to worry about then." The king smiled.

"Forgive me, Your Majesty, and forgive me, Prince Edward." Aldaric gave an apologetic look to Edward before returning to Erick. "The mountain passes block much of the border to Audlin. It would take them at least a week to muster to our aid. We need someone closer. The Recu are barely a day's ride…"

"You worry too much, Aldaric. Braiden has long been a trading partner with us and the Verloris have hidden in their own lands for as long as the world has turned. I worry not if either land attacked us, for if they did, our might would hold them off for months even if Audlin could not come. I doubt not the aid of my daughter's land, and I know we would render both Braiden and Verloris weak and wanting by the time we were through with them."

The king stood, the smile still upon his face. "And as for the Recu..." he began, stepping off the throne. "If they come to me with a better offer, I may be more inclined to listen."

But Aldaric would have none of it. "Forgive me, Your Majesty, but this is foolishness! The Recu may never offer another pact of friendship. Do not offend their new chief by slapping his hand away because he cannot give you fine commodities!"

"We have prospered without the Recu before, and we shall prosper even more without them!" the king replied, his voice raised. "If Bohden wishes to speak with me and beg for assistance, let him do so himself! For now I will not be insulted at his offerings of a poor man's trade. Do not think me so incapable of ruling my lands by telling me what is wisdom and what is folly, Aldaric, for you know nothing!"

Edward noticed Emmerich step forward and gently pull his father back by the arm. Aldaric looked livid, yet remained silent, and at the urging of his son, he simply bowed his head and replied, "Very well, Your Majesty. I will inform Chief Bohden of your wishes." Aldaric turned and stormed off, Anna quickly following after him and taking his hand into hers. Emmerich followed slowly, shaking his head after giving the king one final glance.

"Insolent boy," Erick muttered as he sat back down on the throne. He turned to Edward, who stood in silence. "Always he is trying to push his way on top and always I am having to push him back down."

Edward shrugged as he unrolled the treaty from its case. "I'm sure he means well. He makes a good point to be wary of your neighbors. I do not trust Braiden, especially after that skirmish we had with them a few years ago. I especially do not trust Verloris."

"We keep control over Braiden through trade and Verloris keeps to themselves. We respect that they have nothing to do with us, so we have nothing to do with them," Erick replied as Edward handed him the treaty. "Our lands have not had a war in over a century because of wise decisions made by myself and those who've come before me, and it will continue to stay that way when my own son becomes king."

"I do not doubt it," Edward replied warmly as he handed the king an inked quill to sign the treaty. "But if I may be so bold, Grandfather, I am glad to have you as an ally. You are a strong king and the lands respect you. I only hope to be half the man you are when I am older."

The king smiled as he signed the parchment and handed it back to Edward. "I am a strong king because I have been blessed from above," he replied. "I was meant to be king, and that is why I succeed. So will you, my boy. Life has not been kind to you, for I know you miss your brother, but fate has decided it was you who is to be king, and I know you will do your duties well."

Edward smiled back as he rolled the parchment up and returned it to its case. "Thank you, Grandfather."

He only hoped he was right.

Chapter 13: A Game of Lies

Edward was not one to have nightmares, but when he had them, they were so real that when he woke, he had to question whether what he saw had really been a dream at all.

Tonight's was no different, as if he were reliving a haunting memory that his mind just had to taunt him with.

He was atop of Malina, a thin sheet his only covering as his hands roamed every inch of her body, his lips claiming unconquered territory. She was practically *wheezing* in delight, and though in his mind he was screaming STOP IT, STOP IT, STOP IT, the sounds that came from her only fueled his drunken passion more. He knew he should stop, knew what he was doing was wrong and the ultimate act of betrayal towards the woman he loved.

But passion overruled reason. How could he deny his body's desire when everything just felt so, so *good?*

He could feel his muscles tense so hard they were starting to ache and he slowed his pace. He could feel even in Malina's hunger she was starting to tire out. His head rested in the crook of her neck as her hands draped across his back, and he simply breathed, his heart racing so fast he thought it'd never slow down.

As he laid there, still pressed against his lover and tangled in her embrace, he heard a whisper.

Liar.

His eyes darted open. He knew that voice so well that he was guaranteed never to forget it.

Malina paid no heed as she continued to caress him, whispering sweet nothings that bounced off uninterested ears. Edward looked up to find where the voice had come from, but he saw nothing unfamiliar-the windowed balcony, the fire cackling in the hearth, the furs on the floor that his clothes had been so casually thrown onto. He lowered his head and returned to Malina's neck, kissing it. Passion would erase that voice. Passion could make everything go away.

But as soon as his lips met her skin, the voice became louder.

I told you this day would come.

His head shot up only to find a pale, almost ghostly version of his brother Stephen standing right in front of him with a devilish grin.

It was then that Edward awoke.

He pushed himself out of bed, rubbing his eyes hard to make sure he was no longer trapped in his dreams. His heart was pounding, sweat was beading off of him, and his hands were starting to tremble. He fumbled for the wash basin on the nightstand beside him, splashing cool water onto his face in the hopes that it would calm his night terror.

Eight weeks had he been in Hugellia; eight weeks it had taken for him to think he had forgotten what he'd done only to be reminded that he was not only deceiving everyone, but deceiving himself.

Air seemed to have trouble going in as he gasped for breath, and he sat upon the bed, resting his face into his palms.

"Stop haunting me…" His voice shook as he begged into the night. "You were my brother. My friend. I didn't mean to…I didn't mean what happened…I…"

His stuttering in the darkness was drowned out by a single word repeating in his mind.

Liar.

Liar.

LIAR!

Edward dressed in whatever clothes were available and headed out the door. He needed air, needed an escape, needed *something* to clear his mind and bring it back to the peace it had just that morning when he was laughing and feasting with his cousins. The halls of Erick were empty save some guards standing watch as Edward stepped out of his room, and he grunted in frustration when he saw a guard turn to him, asking if he needed anything. Edward shook his head, trying to be polite, but wondered how he could tell someone all he wanted was to be alone, to shut up the past that stole sleep from him.

He played it coolly, saying something about the night sky being so clear that he couldn't help but take a walk and see its splendor. It was fancy wording, far from true, but it pleased the guard and he allowed Edward to pass freely. As the prince went down the hallway, he noticed the island in the distance across the lake and made a decision to spend the rest of the morning there. It had been years since he'd last been in the stone cottage ruins and he hoped its tranquility and peaceful shores would wash away the bad memories left in his mind.

The row to the island didn't take long, and Edward was marveled at how clear the night sky was. Every star in existence seemed to shine, and as he began to count them and figure which constellation was which, the memories of the nightmare began to fade. His heart rate began to slow back to normal.

When he reached the shore, he pulled the boat up the bank to keep from sailing away and made his way to the ruins. He used to love the place as a boy, imagining some great battle had raged in the city surrounding it and a lone warrior hid in the cottage, waiting for the right time to strike at his enemies and take back the city from within. Whether Edward's musings had any ring of truth to it, he didn't know, but as he approached the stone walls, fingering the ivy that had overgrown on it, he felt the nostalgia return. Warmth, happiness, peace. A childhood full of innocence and play that had no fear of the future or past.

He wished he could return to those days so, so badly.

His thoughts were soon interrupted at the snap of a twig. He turned sharply, instinct alarming his senses as he suddenly felt that feeling of being watched. At first he wondered if it was Stephen, somehow his spirit finding a way from the great beyond to come back and haunt him in reality because dreams were no longer enough. But after denying that such a thing could happen, his thoughts then turned to the arrows that pierced the grass lions on his way to Hugellia. Sir Peterson said the arrows were of Verloris make. Was Malina there, in Kettensburg? Edward shook the thought from his mind since it was so impossible. She would leave him alone. His mistake with her was in the past, never to be mentioned again.

His mind swirled with such possibilities of what the sound could be from, but within seconds he saw who had really snapped the twig, and when he saw him, a part of him wished it was Stephen's ghost or Malina instead.

It was Emmerich, a notebook of paper and a portable quill in his hand, stepping into the moonlight and looking just as perplexed as Edward to find him on an island in the middle of the night.

"What are you doing here?" Emmerich asked, his voice a sneer.

"Getting some air. I thought I'd take a walk since I'm too awake to sleep," Edward lied.

The lie seemed to be unsuccessful as Emmerich gave a sarcastic chuckle, shaking his head. "Your eyes are a little baggy for that."

Edward sighed, crossing his arms. "Fine. It's insomnia-call it what you want. I don't sleep well in the summer heat."

"Reigal is warmer than Kettensburg, Edward. If you're going to lie, at least make it creative."

"Who said I was lying?"

"I know you, Cousin. Since when do you ever tell the truth?"

Edward shrugged, knowing the reality in Emmerich's words but never wanting to admit it. "Believe what you want. I don't care. Why are you out at this time?"

"Charting the stars." Emmerich held the notebook up, revealing paper with dots and lines showing movements by time and constellation shifts. Edward frowned, wanting to knock the book from his hand and toss it to the water. Why did Emmerich have to be so annoyingly perfect? No insomnia. No haunting past. No father nagging him to be just like his dead brother.

Edward didn't even know what to say. He only gave a laugh and shook his head.

"You don't believe me?" Emmerich asked, holding the book out for Edward to take a look.

"No, no, I believe you," Edward said in disdain. "Only you would skip sleeping just to do something as boring as chart stars."

Emmerich frowned, making Edward secretly cheery. "It may be 'boring' to you, but learning has its advantages. Star charting is wonderful for learning the constellations, for navigating, for..."

"I was only teasing." Edward held his hand up.

"It was poor in taste, then," Emmerich scoffed.

An awkward silence passed between them, and Edward could see that Emmerich didn't want to leave the island yet. Doubtless he still had stars to chart and was waiting for Edward to say something about feeling tired and wanting to go back to the guest quarters. Edward didn't budge. He didn't want to go back to sleep, to his nightmares. He wanted the island to himself. Let Emmerich go back to his comfy bed in the city and sleep in whatever perfect slumber he deemed fit.

Edward wasn't about to leave. He just got there, but he knew how to get rid of his cousin.

"You know, Antoinette and I often sneak out in the middle of the night to go stargazing," Edward began, and at the mention of Antoinette's name, Emmerich's brow began to lower. "I mean, I'm not crazy about the stars, but she loves them. Loves sitting there in the moonlight, wrapped in each other's arms. She's got this thing where every time she sees a star twinkle, she kisses me. When it's a clear night like this, you can only imagine how many times we..."

Edward heard a snap and saw Emmerich's quill he had used to write with had suddenly broken in half, a small dribble of ink running down Emmerich's hand. Edward paused, desperately trying to keep a laugh from coming out of him, and shook his head.

"Oh Cousin, you broke your quill."

"It seems I have," Emmerich said as politely as he could muster through clenched teeth. He shook his hand to fling the excess ink off and gathered the pieces of the quill together inside his notebook. Already ink was splattered over his charts, ruining their usage.

"You should go get it fixed." Edward grinned. "You need to be more careful with your things, Emery. Looks like you have a habit of losing them."

Emmerich's face scrunched into a scowl as he slammed his notebook shut. "And it looks like you have a habit of showing yourself as a fool, Edward. One day everyone else will see it." He stomped off towards the shore where his boat lay tethered, clipping Edward's shoulder with his own on purpose.

Edward stood there, silent, a slight tinge of guilt creeping up for being so harsh on the cousin who had done no wrong to him.

He knows you're a liar. Liar. LIAR.

He pressed his eyes shut. Not only Stephen's voice threatened to haunt him, but Emmerich's as well.

His body sunk to the ground and he leaned against the cottage walls, resting himself in the cool light of the moon. A part of him thought he should chase after his cousin and apologize, but there was too much pride still left. The last thing he wanted to admit was his folly to the man who saw it in him the most. And wasn't that what Emmerich was waiting for? To see Edward admit how truly terrible he was so the family, the people, would despise him like he despised himself?

Another snap was heard and he opened his eyes. Perhaps Emmerich had come back, ready for a fight. But Edward knew Emmerich well enough that he was not one to strike unless provoked-*really* provoked. Perhaps it was another verbal quip to make him feel guilty?

If that was the case, Edward was better off ignoring it.

He shut his eyes, breathing in the cool night air, but after hearing a few crunches of leaves, and seeing a shadow darken the moonlight that had lightened his eyes, he paused. That feeling of being watched suddenly crept up again.

When he opened his eyes, he did not find his cousin. A barrel-chested man cloaked in gray and black stood in his place.

It took half a second for Edward to be on his feet and ready to defend himself. The cloaked man in front of him looked far from friendly, and Edward doubted even Emmerich would go so low as to dress as an assassin to scare his cousin. Edward looked around quickly, scanning the area. There were no other men like the one who stood before him, and as Edward opened his mouth to call for Emmerich, the barrel-chested man held up his hand for silence.

"Your kin has already left the island. He will not hear you."

Edward closed his mouth for only a moment. "Who are you?" he asked.

"I am Vacius," the man replied. "I am Velori."

Velori...Velori...where had he heard that name before? Edward's brow crinkled in thought. Doubtless the man was not a Hugellian. He did not have their accent, and though much of his face was hidden, his skin was far too pale for the typical Hugellian tone. He would not have been Audlinian. Edward would know his own people. Braidener, Edelandian, a Recu...

Verloris.

The memory came flooding back. On his way to the banquet given by Malina the night he was in Cathal, he and the gatekeeper had talked on their way to dinner and Edward had asked him about the people of Verloris. They were all called "servants" save one special group.

The Velori.

Edward felt his heart nearly stop. What was a Velori doing in Kettensburg and how had he remained unseen in the city?

"What do you want?" Edward asked.

"I want nothing, oh prince," Vacius replied. "I am here on behalf of the lady."

Malina. "So have you been following me on her request? Were you the one who killed the grass lions who attacked me?"

"Yes."

"Why?"

"The lady wished for you a safe journey," Vacius said. "I granted her request."

"Then why reveal yourself now? What purpose do you have in greeting?"

"The lady has a message for you."

"And what is that?"

"Return to Cathal."

Edward felt like laughing but stayed his tongue as the man's eyes beaded on him. It would be best not to provoke him, the prince thought, for anyone who could kill two grass lions in a second was skilled in the art of war making. It was time to be diplomatic and clever. Knowing Malina as well as Edward did, he would have to be extra careful.

"It isn't so simple for me to leave Kettensburg," Edward said, trying to sound eloquent. For a moment he wished Emmerich were there, just so his cousin could speak for him. He had always been better at that. "I cannot leave my family and friends here without reason. I'm on a diplomatic mission."

"And the king has signed the treaty," Vacius said. "What reason is there for you to remain?"

Edward paused, wondering how Vacius even knew about the treaty. "You are observant, Velori. Are all of you this way?"

"We see much, Your Majesty. It is our duty to know the world."

"Then tell me this," Edward continued. "What is the reason I must return to Cathal?"

"The lady wishes to speak with you."

"Then why did she not come herself?"

"She is not in a condition to travel."

"Unless she is gravely ill, I see no reason for her to remain in the shadows," Edward said. "If she wishes to speak with me, she need not send a messenger. Either speak with me in person or send a letter. You have wasted your travel time."

Edward got up to leave, but Vacius took him by the shoulder and led him back to the wall. The touch of the Velori, hard and cold like metal, sent a chill down Edward's bones that nearly made him shake.

"You...you dare stand in my way?" Edward found his voice sounded anything but threatening as he tried to seem strong. "I am not here on your bidding, Velori. If I wish to leave, I shall!"

He began to walk again only to be shoved harder into the wall, this time with Vacius standing over him.

"I am not your servant, prince. I am not even the lady's. I am only here because she has asked it."

"Then whose servant are you?" Edward gulped.

"I serve the Velori." Vacius removed his hand and took a step back. Edward felt his heart starting to race, fear starting to take hold.

"The lady has requested your presence. Whether you acquiesce her request is up to you."

"Why does she want to see me?" Edward asked. To draw him back to bed where he could relive his shame?

"It is not my place to speak her words for her," Vacius replied gravely. He pulled a sealed letter from behind his cloak, placing it into Edward's hand. "Read this. The lady's request is in the letter."

Edward fingered the parchment, unsure if he wanted to open it or not, but after a glare from the Velori, he hurriedly broke the wax seal and opened it, revealing a note in calligraphy.

He scanned it quickly, ignoring the typical pleasantries of "How are you?", "I miss you", and "My eyes long to see you again."

Would the woman leave him no peace? Edward pressed his lips shut, feeling the burn of anger. He told her he never wanted to see her again. *Never.*

His eyes scrolled to the bulk of the letter and his reading slowed. He read each word carefully, slowly, hoping it would amount to nothing.

His hopes would be dashed to pieces.

Do you remember our one night of passion? When we gave into our desires and became one?

A sick feeling came to his stomach. He wanted to forget what little memory he had of that night. He never wanted to remember it again.

Something else happened. Something wonderful. You gave me the one thing I have always wanted, but never could have until now.

And what was that? The chance to make a man fall? To make a man loathe himself and all that he was?

I am pregnant, Edward.

Edward stopped, re-reading the sentence once, twice…three times. He felt as if a burning rock was falling into his stomach. Malina? Pregnant?

No.

This child is ours. I have been with no other man save you.

No…

The doctors have confirmed my pregnancy. I should give birth around seven months from now.

NO!

Come back to me; make me your queen, for I have given you an heir.

"I don't believe you," Edward said firmly, his eyes beaded and his voice a snarl. He took the letter and wadded it in his hands, refusing to read any more. "I had no relations with her during my stay. *None.*"

"Do not insult me with your lies, spawn of the mountain lands!" Vacius spat. "You dare insult my people by denying your responsibilities?"

"I...I..." Edward found his voice leaving. *She can't be pregnant. It's a lie. It has to be a lie...*

"She has proof," Vacius replied. "In your haste to leave, you left behind a few personal items."

"I left nothing."

"You left your undergarment in her chambers, Your Majesty. You were far from secretive."

"An undergarment is no proof," Edward said. "You could have planted something similar."

"Then if you refuse the lady's request, I have no choice but to go to her father, the king. He will not take kindly to his daughter being abandoned by her lover during a time of need."

Edward put his hand to his forehead, already beading with sweat. "Don't...don't go to the king."

"Then will you speak with her? Will you go to Cathal?"

Edward swallowed hard, the lump in his throat refusing to go down.

I don't want to go. Malina isn't pregnant. She's lying. SHE'S LYING.

And yet he could not afford to have the king of Verloris involved. He would go to Edward's father, Arden. Everything would be out in the open, exposing all what Edward had done that night in Cathal.

The fire had to be contained before it could spread, but Edward did not want to burn.

There was no choice.

"Yes...yes. I will be there."

Vacius smiled, if Edward could call a twitch in the man's lips a grin. "You are expected as soon as possible. I recommend you leave in the daylight so as not to attract any more grass lions with your...nightly noises."

Vacius gave a quick turn and before Edward could blink, he disappeared into the shadows. He was gone, not a sound remaining.

Edward, his back to the wall of the cottage ruins, slid to the ground, his eyes staring blankly into the distance. Trees swayed gently in the summer breeze, lights bouncing off the dew of the leaves in the moonlight.

All the prince could feel was dread.

She can't be pregnant...she can't...

What if she was?

She isn't...I...I don't even remember the night I spent with her. I was drunk...we probably just kissed and nothing more, right?

But then Edward remembered the nightmare he had only hours before. What if it wasn't just a dream? What if it was a part of his memories?

No. No, that never happened.

But when he woke up that morning with Malina, he knew better.

Please...please don't let Malina be pregnant. Edward gathered his knees to his chest like a child frightened in the night. His whole body felt like ice was running through his veins instead of blood, and all he wanted to do was shiver.

The thought of Malina bearing his child convulsed him. What would he do if it were true? Should he abandon the child and pretend it never happened? His family would surely believe him over her. He could lie and say she had framed him. But then his child...his own flesh and blood...his little boy or little girl...

You're a father now...

No. It didn't matter. He didn't want children with Malina. It's not like he planned this.

You should accept your responsibility.

And that meant marrying Malina, bringing her to Audlin, raising their child as his heir.

And that would mean losing Antoinette.

He buried his face under wrapped arms, his forehead to his knees.

Chapter 13 – A Game of Lies

For the first time since his brother died, he cried.

Chapter 14: Leaving Hugellia

The sun was barely over the horizon when Edward left the island and returned to his room to pack. Normally he would not make such a rush of things-he still had to seem confident like nothing was amiss-but the thought of Malina's pregnancy put him in such a panic that no amount of pleasure or thinking could calm him. He had to get to Verloris fast, not only out of fear of Vacius going to the king of Verloris, but because Edward wanted to see if Malina's claims were really true.

Malina lies, doesn't she?

He threw his clothes into a small pack, not caring if they were folded or not. The trip wasn't supposed to be long anyways. In and out, containing the fire before it spread. Perhaps they could come to an arrangement-surely bribery did not work on only the greedy.

Then again, Malina had everything she ever needed. A few bits of coin would be nothing to her. What else was there to give?

As he gathered his things to take to his horse, he stopped at the door. He was in Kettensburg surrounded by family and his royal guard. He couldn't just sneak out alone into Cathal without anyone knowing. If ever there was a family that worried, it was the van Kettens, and as soon as they noticed Edward was gone, they'd be the first to send out a search party to find him. No, no-he couldn't go alone and risk the House of Hugellia finding out about his dealings with the

Verloris. They would never approve, and he was not about to lose the only family who still cared for him.

It was foolish to go into the wild alone anyways. His meeting with the grass lions proved that.

He would need to take someone from his guard with him, at least for protection on the journey. Someone brave, someone trustworthy, someone loyal. Most importantly, someone who could keep quiet. Someone who would obey without question.

Only one name came to mind: Marcus Peterson.

Edward went out to one of the guards standing out in the hallway. "Good sir!" he said, his voice forcibly cheery. "I wish you to do me a favor. Could you ask Sir Peterson from my guard if he'd accompany me on a hunting trip? It would be a shame to not spend some time in the natural beauty of Hugellia while I am here."

"I will tell him, Your Majesty," the guard replied.

Good, Edward thought. "Tell him to meet me at the city gate in an hour. He should pack for at least a week."

"It sounds like you are going on quite the hunt."

"I have a heart for the wild and a stomach for venison," Edward replied with a chuckle. "Now go, tell him!"

"Of course, Your Majesty."

Off the guard went to the knight's quarters while Edward went to King Erick to tell the same.

The king was in the middle of breakfast when he arrived unannounced.

"Ah! My grandson. Come in, come in!" Erick replied, his mouth full of egg. "What can I do for you?"

Edward came in haste, eyeing the food and wanting to taste yet forcing himself to abstain. He didn't ride well on a nervous stomach. "I wished to tell you I am leaving, Grandfather."

"So soon?" Erick replied, his eyes widening.

"Worry not!" Edward held his hand up and clasped the old man's shoulder. "I won't be gone long. The wild calls! I am going on a hunting trip for about a week. I will return when I'm finished."

"A week is an awfully long time, Edward," Erick said, his face sinking into a frown. "Rarely do we get to see you. Are you sure you wish to go?"

"You know me, Grandfather. I love adventure. While I am young and free, I wish to take it."

"That I know well." Erick sighed. "I grant you leave with a heavy heart that I am too old to join you."

"You shall be there with me in spirit." Edward smiled.

"Of course." Erick nodded, taking a sip of tea. "And how many are going with you?"

"One of my guards, Sir Peterson."

"I trust he is able to keep my daughter's precious child out of harm's way?"

"He is more than able. He is the greatest warrior in all of Audlin, a prodigy from Circh."

"That eases my mind then," Erick said. "Perhaps your other cousins would like to come along, though? At least you'd be able to spend time with them."

Edward frowned. He hadn't planned for this-his kin to tag along. They would only be in the way, questioning him, wondering why they were going to Cathal instead of a hunting trip like Edward had said. He needed an excuse, another lie to help hide the truth.

"I've a confession to make, Grandfather." Edward exhaled slowly, lowering his head. "This isn't just a hunting trip."

"No?" Erick asked.

"No," Edward repeated. "It is also a time of reflection."

Erick's brow rose in confusion. "I don't follow."

"My father wishes me to prepare for the kingship. He says I am reckless and rash and never take things seriously. Now that I am getting married, I need to become more serious. I want my time in the wild to be a time of self-study. What are my weaknesses and strengths, growing closer to God, just...finding myself. I need to do this, Grandfather. I need the time to myself to reflect on who I'm going to be."

"I see." Erick nodded. "I cannot scold you on that, Edward. You are wise to think of such things...though I wish you would've told me the truth sooner."

"I still plan on hunting." Edward smirked, feeling confident his lie seemed to be working. "I just won't be hunting all the time."

"Very well, then," Erick said. "I wish you a productive time. But please, do not forget to bring back some venison. You know how fond I am of it."

"Of course, Grandfather," Edward replied, and off he went to gather his things.

Marcus Peterson had little time to gather his belongings. Though the prince had told the guard he would be ready within the hour to leave for the hunting lands, time seemed to speed up, and Sir Peterson swore whatever hour he had been given to be ready somehow turned into a few minutes. His things packed and strapped to his shoulders, he rushed out the door towards his horse, ignoring the other knights as to why he had to leave so quickly.

"I've been requested by the prince to accompany him on a hunting trip," was the official answer Marcus gave to the guards as he left. Though deep in his mind, he wanted to say, *I have to leave now because Edward has a poor sense of planning and is the most procrastinating royal to walk this earth!*

But Marcus kept his opinions to himself. It wasn't his place to disobey Audlin's future king.

He found it odd that he was the only one to accompany Edward. Not that two men couldn't go on a hunting trip on their own, but after the incident with the grass lions, Marcus found it wise to have strength in numbers. It was strange that Edward, the one who was actually attacked, did not share this sentiment.

By the time Marcus reached his horse, Edward had already saddled and mounted. "You're late," Edward muttered as Marcus strapped his bags to the horse's saddle. "We have quite a journey ahead of us. We need an early start."

"My apologies, Your Majesty," Marcus replied, trying to catch his breath. "I only just received your message. I am ready now, though."

"Good."

Marcus got up onto the horse and took the reins. "Is there no one else coming?"

"No," Edward said as his horse started to trot towards the city gate. Marcus followed. "This is a trip that needs few, Sir Peterson. Besides, we won't be gone long."

"But what of the grass lions?"

"What of them?"

"Two may not be enough to fend off an attack."

"We'll be fine," Edward replied casually. "In fact, I dare say we will not see one grass lion on our trip."

Marcus didn't know what to think. It was foolishness to gallop into the wild with so optimistic an attitude. Though being positive never hurt, it was never wise to forget the dangers that lurked past the city gates. How could Edward forget so easily?

He followed the prince in silence past the city gate and into the grasslands of Hugellia.

A full two days had passed when Marcus began to wonder why they had not stopped to actually *hunt* during their hunting trip. Hours and hours had they been riding, Edward barely saying a word, and though Marcus was certainly a man willing to obey, he couldn't help but wonder if the trip they were taking was a hunting trip at all.

But when the landscape began to change, began to look more familiar, Marcus started to suspect the hunting trip was just a ruse. They were on the same path they had taken from Verloris.

When they stopped for a rest near a grove of trees, Marcus approached the prince, handing him a drink of water. "Is this where we are to hunt, Your Majesty?"

Edward was quiet at first, taking his drink as slowly as a man could. "No," he answered. "We are not to hunt here."

"We are going awfully far from Kettensburg to hunt," Marcus replied. "Where are these grounds, may I ask? Is the game better out here?"

Edward took another sip of water. He paused for a moment, staring off into the distance as if in thought. Marcus opened his mouth to ask something else, but before the words were uttered, Edward gave out a sigh.

"Can I trust you, Marcus?"

It was unusual for Edward to use his first name. In fact, Marcus tried to remember if he ever had. It gave him a heavy feeling in his heart, like a feeling of dread. He didn't know why.

"Yes," Marcus replied. "Yes, you can trust me."

"We aren't going on a hunting trip."

Marcus nodded, though in his mind he began to think of all the other places the prince would actually go. Back home to Reigal? Some random getaway trip? Neither possibility seemed true, judging by their surroundings. This was the same road they took from Verloris. It didn't take a smart man to figure out their real destination.

"Where are we going, then?" Marcus had to be sure. He had to hope he was wrong.

"We are going to Cathal."

Marcus was never a man to curse, but at that moment he let one slip in his mind.

"What reason is there to return to Verloris?" he asked.

Edward continued to stare into the distance. "They have requested it."

"Why?"

At first Edward said nothing. "They want to talk about an alliance."

"An alliance?"

"Yes. Perhaps a treaty."

Edward continued to stare into the distance, making Marcus wonder if Edward was telling all that was on his mind. "It's strange they would suddenly want a treaty of friendship. Did they mention why?"

"Only that Lady Malina requested it."

Malina? The witch of Cathal who clearly had no ounce of good in her body? "I find it strange she would request such a thing," Marcus replied. "I guess you gave a good impression."

Edward looked at Marcus for a moment, his brow lowered and his eyes almost…angry, if Marcus could describe them. But the look only lasted a second before Edward turned away.

"Speak of this to no one," Edward muttered. "It is only an attempt at an alliance. I doubt it will go as planned."

"Then why try if it won't succeed?"

Edward shrugged as he rose and returned to his horse. "Come," he replied. "We have had enough rest. It's still a long journey to Cathal and I'd rather be there sooner than later."

"But…"

"Please, Marcus. Just trust me and do not question."

Marcus gave a nod as he returned to his horse, his stomach feeling sick at the thought of having to return to Verloris, but his heart feeling near death at the thought of becoming allies with them.

Whatever the reason for the treaty, he could only hope the stay in Cathal would be as short as Edward seemed to think it would be.

Chapter 15: The Letter

"I SAID SUCK IT IN!"

Bernie cringed in pain as her mother pulled the corset strings tighter. Her chest burned, her bones ached, and even her muscles were starting to get sore from all the twisting and contorting her body had to do just to fit in the small bridesmaid dress.

All she could do was grin and bear the pain as Mother pressed her knee against Bernette's back for leverage.

"Work with me, child! How else will you fit in this dress?"

Bernie wanted to say she'd be able to fit in a dress that was made for someone her age and not a five year old, but the corset cut off too much air for her to talk. She only grunted with a purposely ugly frown, making Mother pull the strings harder.

"The dress isn't even made for her height, Mother. She needs a more...normal size," Antoinette said, biting her nail as she stood and watched. She had little trouble fitting into the wedding dress Mother had picked out, much to her disapproval, but Bernie's fitting was going less than ideal.

"This is just unacceptable!" Queen Susanna huffed, letting go of the strings and making Bernette gasp for air. The queen ripped the corset from her daughter's waist and threw it on the ground. "I didn't think it possible for you to gain more weight in the weeks we've been here, but I see you've proven me wrong! How hard is it to not stuff your face morning, noon, and night? Always snacking, aren't we, my pig?"

Bernette was still breathing hard, resting against a sofa, when her face suddenly turned red with fury. "You honestly think that all I ever do is *eat*?" she said, her voice nearing a yell. "If anything, I don't eat enough! You've got no problem making sure your daughters are starved!"

"It's all about control, Bernette, and you have none of it!" the queen snapped back. "Look at Antoinette! Not a problem with her fitting, and she's thin and beautiful!"

"Mother, no, that's not..." Antoinette put her hand out, trying to interrupt politely, but Susanna ignored it.

"You are FAT, you are STUPID, and I am ASHAMED to even be seen with you!" Susanna threw her hands up in the air while Bernie stood there, taking it with infuriated silence. "When I was your age, I was engaged to be married! When your sister was your age, she had prospects lining up for her hand! And look at you-*no one*. And no wonder, with the way you look! The only place you'll ever belong in is a home with all the other ugly spinsters!"

"Mother, please do not say such horrible things," Antoinette pleaded. "Bernie is still young. There's plenty of time to..."

"Do not interrupt me when I speak, Antoinette!"

Antoinette bowed her head in silence, but Bernie only clenched her fists in further fury.

"Why? Why do you not even try, Bernette?" Susanna asked. "Why must you shame your family this way?"

There was an edgy silence that filled the air for a second that allowed everyone to gather their wits. Bernette felt her anger rising. Her heart was pounding so hard in her chest that it hurt to breathe.

She couldn't stand back and take it. In fact, what she was about to do was the only thing she and her mother had in common: being opinionated.

"I am SICK of this!" Bernette shouted, standing up straight and glaring her mother down. "I'm sick of you yelling at me, sick of you calling me names! I am your daughter, not your doormat! What kind of mother treats her own child like you treat me?"

"A good and honest one!" Susanna glared back.

"Well if you're a good example of a mother, then no wonder the world is so messed up!"

"Bernie, let's not fight…" Antoinette pleaded again, stepping forward in between the two.

"No!" Bernette said, stepping in front of her. "You may not have the guts to tell the truth, but I do! You want to know what I really think, *Mother*? I think you're controlling, selfish, vain, and cruel! You have no right to…"

"*SILENCE!*" Susanna's voice boomed as she edged close to Bernie's face.

For a second Bernie didn't know what to think. The yell was so full of anger and hate that she felt her heart nearly stop in fear; images of a great temper rising from the queen suddenly paralyzing her thoughts.

"Mother, please, don't!" Antoinette stepped forward, teary-eyed, but Susanna ignored her.

"You *dare* disrespect me, child?" the queen seethed, turning back to Bernette. "I am your mother!"

"I don't care!" Bernette exclaimed, her voice shaking. "I'll never respect you!"

The fire in the queen's eyes was scorching, and for a moment even Bernette wondered if she went too far. Susanna beaded her eyes, lifting her hand as if to give her daughter yet another display of authority, until Antoinette stepped in front of her.

"Mother-your blood pressure. Please don't get yourself worked up. I worry over you enough as it is!"

Bernette stood firm, her fists clenched. She wanted so badly to lash out, to say to her sister, *What are you doing? You'll get in trouble, too,* but stayed her tongue. Antoinette rarely lied, but when she did, it was effective.

"Forgive Bernette for her foolishness, Mother. She respects you, and so do I," Antoinette said, her lip quivering as she put her hand on Susanna's shoulder. "She's learned her lesson. Now please, rest. I don't want you upsetting yourself."

However she did it, Antoinette's lie seemed to work as the queen lowered her hand. She sighed, rubbing her brow, muttering something about how "Bernette always makes my head ache."

Antoinette rubbed her mother's arm warmly and gave her a gentle smile. "I'll talk to Bernette. Just go and rest. I'll have the servants make you a cup of chamomile."

"Very well," Susanna said, but before leaving she gave one last glare to Bernette. "One more outburst like that, young lady, and I shall send you away from me! Perhaps when you are alone and miserable, you will learn how to respect others!"

The sooner, the better, Bernie thought, but after a quick look from Antoinette, she stayed her tongue.

It took a few minutes for Antoinette to get Mother settled and out of the room. While she waited for her sister, Bernette pursed her lips, her hands still shaking from the verbal terror Mother unleashed. She picked up the corset off the floor and tossed it across the room, flinging herself onto the sofa with an angry grunt.

When Antoinette arrived back, she rushed to her sister, wrapping her arms around her as carefully as she could. "You know you shouldn't talk back to her, Bernie," Antoinette said. "She's not in her right mind today. You only further her anger by talking back."

"I don't care," Bernie replied. "She's cruel, Antoinette, and you know it." She furrowed her brow in frustration. "One of these days I'm afraid she's going to burn down the palace just because we didn't wear the shoes she picked out!"

"She means well."

"No she doesn't," Bernie said. "She's just well at being mean."

"I'm sorry, Bernie." Antoinette sighed. "I don't know what to say."

"There's nothing you can say." Bernie's voice lowered to a whisper. "But at least you can escape it."

Antoinette frowned. "You will too. I'll get you out."

"Sure."

The wedding was coming up so quickly, and the thought of it filled Bernette's mind with dread. She was happy for her sister-she truly was. Edward was a decent man, if not a little cocky. But Mother was right that Bernette had no prospects. Who was she kidding? She doubted she'd ever have one. It was as if she was cursed to be alone. After all, what man would want a woman who was not only "fat" (as Mother called it), but who was going bald as well?

The thoughts swirling in Bernie's head made her heart feel heavy. She didn't want to be alone, stuck with Mother always hounding her with threats. It was Antoinette that made Mother stay her hand before Bernette could really be threatened. It was Antoinette that coerced Mother out of the room and calmed her down.

Bernie knew in her heart Mother wouldn't let her go to Reigal after Antoinette married. She would be ashamed of letting her "pig daughter" be seen in the queen's court. If Bernette couldn't leave, she would be separated from her sister forever.

And that was something Bernie did not want to think of.

A plan started to form in her mind. She knew it was wrong. She knew it would possibly hurt her sister if it worked. But for once in her life, Bernie wanted to be the selfish one. She was tired of how Mother treated her. She didn't want to be alone.

Bernette was quiet when Antoinette continued to encourage her, hopeful words being ignored as her mind went to work to formulate a plan and keep her sister from leaving.

She knew what she had to do. All she needed was paper, ink, a quill, and Emmerich van Ketten's address.

Emmerich was sitting at home, studying in his father's office when the door knocked. He looked up from the pages, his eyes starting to strain, and noticed his mother standing at the doorway with a sealed letter in her hands.

"Looks like you've got a note," Anna van Ketten said sweetly as she walked in.

"From who?" Emmerich asked, perplexed. He shut the book and held out his hand, Anna placing the letter in his palm.

"It says it's from Antoinette."

When Emmerich saw her name written in the corner, he felt his heart stop. As much as he welcomed to hear from her, he was confused as to why she was writing him now. Ever since her and Edward began their courtship, the words exchanged between them became scarce, almost non-existent.

"I don't understand," Emmerich said quietly as he broke the seal. "Why would she write me?"

"Maybe it's about the wedding," Anna replied. "You are in the party, aren't you?"

"Well, yes, but..." Emmerich unfolded the parchment to reveal a short note. He glanced at the writing-fanciful, beautiful, perfect-and he recognized her handwriting immediately.

"What does it say?" Anna asked, leaning over to get a peak.

Emmerich smirked, opening his mouth to read it aloud, but suddenly stopped as he glanced at the first sentence.

My dearest Emery,

I know the wedding is still weeks away, but I was wondering if you could come to Reigal early. I...I want to talk.

Emmerich felt his heart flutter. Talk? Talk about what? Dared he hope...

I want to talk about us.

He felt a sick feeling in his stomach. The good kind, the kind he felt when he first realized just how wonderful and special Antoinette was to him. He didn't want it to end.

I hate to ask you to travel, but it would mean the world to me if you came. There's so much on my mind and you've always been one to listen.

Emmerich smiled to himself. He'd travel the world if she asked him to.

Please keep this between us and especially don't tell Edward. I don't want him upset.

No need to worry about that one. Edward was gone again to who knows where else.

I miss you, Emery.

He guaranteed he missed her more.

Yours, Antoinette

"Well? What does it say?" Anna repeated again.

Emmerich set the letter upon his chest, exhaling slowly. "I need to pack."

"Pack? What on earth for?"

Emmerich folded the letter back and stuffed it into his book. He jumped out of the seat and raced to the door towards his room. "I need to get to Reigal."

Anna stood there, shaking her head. "Why?"

"Antoinette asked me to be there."

"Did she give a reason?"

Emmerich paused, wondering what to say. He knew his parents would disapprove of him running off to his cousin's fiancée, especially with the wedding so close, but he didn't care. He couldn't guarantee it, but from how she sounded, she was having doubts.

And that gave him more faith than ever before.

"I'm in the wedding party, remember?" Emmerich nearly laughed in delight. "This is what I get for being the Best Man!"

He barely took time to breathe before booking a passage to Reigal.

Bernette and Antoinette were sitting in the tea room when a servant arrived with the letter. Antoinette thanked him and took it, expecting it as word from Edward about what he was doing in Hugellia.

When she opened it, reading the contents of the parchment, however, her eyes widened in surprise.

"What is it?" Bernette asked.

"It's a letter from Emery," Antoinette replied. "He says he's coming to Reigal. Looking at the date, he should be here by tomorrow!"

"That's interesting," Bernette said, sipping her tea. "Did he say why he's coming?"

"Something about us talking."

"Hmm..." Bernie murmured as she placed her tea cup on the table. "Sounds like your old friend may have liked you a little more than you think. A bit convenient he wants to talk right before your wedding."

Antoinette set the letter down, rubbing her forehead. "It's probably nothing. He's in the wedding party. Maybe he's coming early to help."

"The wedding's not for another month," Bernie said. "What else is there to do?"

Antoinette sighed, shaking her head.

"Oh, don't be so flustered. Be flattered," Bernie said. "Besides, you actually may enjoy this conversation he wants to have with you."

"Maybe Queen Maria requested he come. She is his aunt, after all."

Bernette shook her head. "You're just denying the inevitable. I bet he's liked you all this time and never had the guts to admit it. Looks like he's finally found that bravery you said he lacked."

Antoinette gave Bernie an incredulous look as she pouted, throwing her head back and resting on the chair.

Bernette could only smile as she sipped her tea, happy that the first part of her plan was going so perfectly.

Chapter 16: Meeting with the Mistress

Why did it always have to rain when Edward arrived in Cathal?

He muttered a curse beneath his breath as he drew his cloak around his face, the rain whipping whatever exposed skin he had like slices of a knife gone wild. His skin crawled with the cold of the wind as it blew, and by the time they reached the gate, he almost welcomed the sight of Malina's castle in the distance.

"Who goes there?" called the gatekeeper, a different man from who Edward had seen before. He couldn't help but wonder what happened to the old gatekeeper.

"Edward Engel, son of King Arden of Audlin," he called out. He nodded to the knight beside him who bowed his head in greeting. "This is Sir Marcus Peterson of Circh, my guard. We were requested by Her Majesty, Malina."

"Of course," the gatekeeper nodded, his voice slithery like a snake's. He gave a long bow and smiled as he lowered the lever that opened the streets of Cathal to the two visitors.

Edward nodded in thanks and began to stride forward until being stopped by a barrel-chested man in front. Edward recognized him immediately-the messenger, Vacius.

"You will no longer need the horses," Vacius replied. "The lady has provided a coach for you so you need not travel in the rain."

Edward knew not to question the Velori. He dismounted the horse, urging for Marcus to do the same, and followed the man into the carriage.

The velvety-dark interior of the coach was a welcome comfort compared to riding on a horse for days. There was the scent of lavender in the seats soon drowned out by the smell of rain and worms as it whiffed through the door. Edward and Marcus sat across from the Velori as Vacius knocked on the driver's side, urging it to move towards the castle. There was a quick jolt at first, but then the three were set upon a steady stride towards Malina's home.

At first they were silent in their travels, with Marcus keeping his hands upon his lap, his fingers twitching as if wanting to hold a blade. Edward casually glanced out the window once or twice, trying to seem nonchalant about the matter. The ruse failed as Vacius gave a light chuckle.

"There is no need to be nervous, my prince."

Edward looked at Vacius. "I'm not nervous."

"Always lying, aren't we?" Vacius grinned. "You fail at that."

"I'm only weary from my travels," Edward replied. "I wish to rest. The sooner this is over, the better."

"This is far from over. It's just beginning."

Edward turned away, but Vacius' words made Marcus stare ahead in confusion.

The Velori noticed it immediately. "You needn't travel with company, Prince Edward."

Edward glanced at Sir Peterson as he glanced back, his face confused as if trying to figure out the cryptic messages between them. Signing a treaty would not require such informalities and taunts. Even a child would know that. It was foolish to think Sir Peterson would not.

"I needed protection in my travels. Too many grass lions in the fields, as you know."

"And you know that you are never truly alone," Vacius said.

Marcus' eyes widened. "The grass lions…" he muttered. "The arrows…did they come from him?" He turned to Edward.

Edward nodded quietly, not meeting his gaze.

"Do you even know why you are here, young knight?" Vacius asked, turning to Marcus.

Peterson beaded his eyes, but was interrupted by Edward before he could speak.

"Say nothing. I will talk."

"I did not ask you, my prince. I asked your servant." Vacius glared.

"I am not your puppet to be controlled. I am a monarch and am not subject to your whims. Remember that!"

Vacius gave another chuckle. "You have not told him the reason you are here, have you?"

Edward's face hardened. "Be quiet."

"Let me guess-you are here to sign a treaty?"

Marcus turned to Edward, the expression on his face changing with a sudden realization of horror. Edward only gritted his teeth, wanting to strike the Velori and smash his face into the seat.

"I said *be quiet*."

Vacius grinned. "Do you want to know why your prince is really here, Sir Knight?"

Marcus could only look ahead in wonder.

The carriage stopped in front of the castle and a footman put his hand to the door, opening it. The sound of rain hitting the streets seemed deafening compared to the silence in the carriage as Vacius' smile widened.

"You shall find out soon," Vacius said, giving a final glance to Edward before stepping out into the rain.

Edward felt his heart starting to pound in his chest. His secret was so close...so *close* to coming out, and in his mind he felt relieved that Vacius kept his silence. But then the realization came that maybe silence wasn't benefitting, as he looked upon Marcus and noticed he had not left the carriage yet.

"Why are we really here, Your Majesty?" he asked. His face looked worn, hurt, disappointed. It made Edward want to look away.

He opened the door nearest to himself and stepped out, following Vacius into the castle. Marcus only gave a huff of frustration, scrambling out of the carriage and hurrying to the prince's side.

"Your Majesty, are we in danger?" Marcus whispered as they were led to the door. "I understand if you wish to keep your business in Cathal a secret, but please, do not keep me in the dark if your life is in question here!"

"I asked you to trust me, Marcus," Edward whispered back as they stopped in front of the door. "And I repeat this request here and now. I cannot tell you our purpose here, and you must trust me that I know what I'm doing."

"Very well," Marcus replied, crossing his arms in defeat. "I will trust your judgment, but I ask that you trust mine. There is nothing I wouldn't do for you or your family, even if my life is forfeit. Please trust my allegiance, Sire. I would wish to help you in any way I could."

Edward lowered his head, feeling both touched and ashamed at such blind loyalty Sir Peterson would show him. Is that not what he wanted? Loyalty and respect that would be received simply because he was Edward Engel, crowned prince of Audlin?

You foolish knight. Do you not know you've bound yourself to a lie?

Edward pursed his lips together and nodded silently, turning back towards the door and following Vacius inside the hall. Marcus stood in the rain for a second, his face haggard and almost hurt, until he followed the prince inside.

The doors were shut, leaving a heavy echo in the air.

The journey through the halls of Malina's castle was all too familiar. The same sconces gave little light in the darkness, the same paintings depicting battle still threatened to haunt their viewer's dreams. The same echoes of footsteps on stone filled the silence of the area, making a lone man sound like a crowd in a room.

Edward felt his heart pound in his chest, his nerves getting the best of him. Not that he would ever admit to fear-fear was a weakness, a bane to any man that should stay hidden in the presence of enemies, but even Edward did not feel strong enough to hide his concern. He felt like an animal being hunted, the cage ready to snap shut and trap him from whatever freedom he had taken for granted.

Vacius stopped in front of a large door, interrupting Edward's thoughts. Edward recognized the room immediately, though he wished he hadn't. They stood before Malina's chambers, the same room he and the princess had...shared for one night.

"The lady awaits you, Your Majesty," Vacius said.

Edward nodded, his heart beating faster than ever. He turned to Marcus. "Wait for me out here. I'll be along shortly."

"Nay, my prince." Vacius held out his hand. Edward cocked his head to the side, eyeing him wearily. Vacius grinned. "The lady welcomes all to her chambers. Your guard shall accompany you."

"But..."

"I insist," Vacius said, his hand on the hilt of his sword, giving Edward no choice but to cooperate. He gave a nod, motioning for Marcus to follow, hoping and praying that Malina would not say too much on what Edward had done. Or that Marcus would truly be as loyal as he claimed.

The door was opened and there stood Malina by the hearth, clad in a red gown with her raven hair up and adorned in jewels. She had her hands on her stomach, gently caressing it, and turned when she heard the door creak.

"My darling!" she exclaimed, rushing to Edward. "How cold and wet you must be to travel in the rain. Tell me, was your journey from Kettensburg well? How was the weather there?"

She pined over him, fingering his tunic and brushing off the dust from his cloak, but he remained silent, his face stern, trying to get a look at her belly. She ignored him, continuing on with her fancies. "And what's this? A guest?" She turned to Marcus and smiled, her eyes looking at him hungrily. "I am glad to see you travel with your guard, Edward. You know how I worry for you when you are out in the wild."

She gave a playful smile, making Edward cringe, but instead of making conversation, his eyes went to her belly. He had to make sure she was really pregnant, had to see if what she was saying was truth or lie.

But when he saw that there was a bump, a slight roundness that never was there before, he felt his heart sink.

His face must have shown disappointment, for Malina approached him, her smile fading and turning into her cold, confident gaze. "I see you believe me now, dear Edward. Are you not happy at my announcement?"

Marcus looked confusedly towards Edward, but the prince ignored him. He didn't want this conversation in front of his knight. He didn't want this conversation in front of anyone.

"Dear, you must say something," Malina replied, putting a warm hand on his arm. "Your silence makes me think you aren't happy we are with child."

"*WHAT?*"

Malina turned as both she and Edward looked at Marcus, his face so full of horror and shock even he was surprised at his outburst. He cleared his throat, putting his hand on his chest in apology, but his face turned red with burning anger. "Your Majesty, forgive me for questioning any decision you make, but what madness is this? What does she mean she is with child? *With your child?*"

"Marcus, I shall explain it to you in due time. Just trust me…" Edward began, but Sir Peterson shook his head.

"I am trusting you, Your Majesty," Marcus replied. "But this, I do not trust." He pointed to Malina, making her eyes lower into a glare. "How do we know what you say is true, Lady Malina? Would you dare try to entangle His Majesty into your own twisted fantasy?"

Malina put her hand to her lips, stifling a laugh. "Oh, you poor dear. Did Edward not tell you of our little affair when you were here last? How we took to our bed and loved each other 'til the morn?"

Marcus's eyes widened and he turned to Edward. "No, her words must be false. Your Majesty?"

Edward closed his eyes, rubbing his brow. He wanted all of this to end, just to simply go away.

"No..." Marcus shook his head in disbelief. "No...she can't be true. What of your mother and father? What of Antoinette?"

"The Edelandian girl?" Malina laughed even more. "I think she needs to find herself another man."

"Malina, stop this. There is no need for taunts," Edward said, his voice firm.

Malina looked at him and smiled. "I wasn't taunting; just offering a quaint little suggestion."

"And how do we know what you're suggesting is the truth?" Marcus continued, approaching the princess with fiery eyes. "Forgive me for my abruptness, Your Majesty, but I cannot stand by and allow this insult to take place. What proof do we have that the child is truly Edward's? How do we know you didn't offer yourself to another man?"

Malina's face became hard and her voice rose. "You *dare* call me a liar, boy?"

"I only ask for proof, for His Majesty's sake!"

"And I ask what kind of *servant* addresses royalty without permission!"

Marcus lowered his brow. "A servant of Prince Edward, Your Majesty."

"Marcus," Edward put his hand on Sir Peterson's shoulder, clasping it. "I appreciate your honesty, but with respect I…"

But before Edward could finish, he heard Malina scream. "Vacius!" she cried. "VACIUS!"

The Velori, alongside three other guards, appeared and approached the princess. "Yes, my lady?" Vacius asked.

Malina gave a look of triumph as she looked to Sir Peterson. "It seems I have a rude guest in my midst, one who cannot hold his tongue. Cut it out when I give the word and then await my command."

"Your Majesty?" Marcus replied as his face hardened, but Edward gave a shout.

"YOU WILL DO NO SUCH THING!" he exclaimed, but Vacius took Marcus by the shoulders to lead him away. Edward pulled out his sword, ready to strike, but with three extra guards, now holding crossbows pointed to his face, he was outnumbered. Marcus went away in an angry silence, being led by Vacius to whatever dungeon would be his last home.

Edward was seething now as he and Malina were left alone. "Why?" he asked, his breath coming in pants from his heart pounding so hard. "Why would you do such a thing?"

"Respect should not have to be earned, Edward. It should be expected. Demanded, even," Malina replied.

Such a remark made Edward want to vomit. The saying was all too familiar. "No. No, you *cannot* hold one of my guards prisoner and torture him. I will *not* allow it."

"You are in my lands, Edward," Malina said. "What are you going to do to stop me? Send an army? Start a war? Oh, what a mighty king you'll be sending your people to die for one foolish boy who couldn't keep his mouth shut."

"He was right in his accusations," Edward seethed. "How do I not know you didn't whore your way into another man's arms when I was away? No matter what items of mine you may have, you never can prove the child is mine."

"No, you're right. I can't prove it," Malina replied coolly. "Just as you can't prove it *isn't* yours. But you're in a bind, Edward. You know this. I know this. You're someone who's about to take the throne of an entire nation and already you have a scandal."

"What do you mean?"

"Have you not learned about people, Edward?" Malina asked, taking a stroll about the room. "A woman has a powerful gift with them. We know how to read people, how to talk to them, interpret them, *manipulate* them. We know how to build them up or how to tear them down."

She gave a quick turn to face him. "Do you know what my words can do to you, Edward? Do you know how much power I already have over you?"

"None, from what I can tell."

"Darling, you're so silly when you're angry," Malina cooed. "Let us speak plainly then. You have impregnated a woman and are wanting to leave her and her child abandoned. Such a shame, you know. The careless father who leaves his family to rot. If he cannot take responsibility for his poor, innocent child, how can he be responsible with a nation?"

Edward remained silent, crossing his arms and eyeing the hearth.

"And then there's the secret he's been keeping from everyone he knows. No confession of his affair. No sorrow. No remorse. Just lies. So many, many lies. You are not an honest man, Edward Engel. It makes me wonder if you ever were. If even your knights could not trust you with the truth, then how can you expect your people to?

"And let us not forget dear Sir Peterson," she continued, heading back towards Edward. "You allowed a poor, young, promising life to be so violated, all because you could not lead him on the proper path, or because you could not negotiate for his release."

Edward's eyes beaded. "I can speak with your father on that."

Malina stepped to Edward's front, wrapping her arms around his waist. He tensed at her touch, giving her a glare as she leaned forward into him, expecting an embrace. "Edward...my sweet, handsome Edward," she soothed. "Who do you think my father will listen to? A prince who thinks he is a king or his darling little girl who wants her mocker's head on a stick?"

Edward left her embrace, turning his back to her. His heart was pounding so hard he could barely stand it. Anger-it surged through him like a torrent of rain in a hurricane, but who the anger was directed to was his greatest confusion. He burned with anger towards Malina, the woman who was clearly cleverer than any being he had met. He was angry with himself as well. Malina was right-he truly was in a bind.

Why…why did I not listen to Sir Rikert when he told me to turn back?

If he could go back in time, he would change it. He would change a lot of things.

"Then let us negotiate," Edward said through clenched teeth. "You clearly want something, Your Majesty, and clearly I am the one to give it. Let us bring forth our terms and come to a compromise where we can both leave each other in peace."

"I don't think you understand," Malina said. "There is no negotiation. What do you have that could possibly keep me away?"

"Money? Items? Land?" Edward asked. "What is it you really want, Malina? What can I give you that you would free my knight and leave me alone?"

Malina smirked as she approached him, running a cold, bony finger down his cheek. "I want you, Edward. And I have you."

He stopped her hand and removed it from his face. Never, *never* did he want to feel that touch again. "You will never have me, Malina. I'm pledged to be married to Antoinette. I intend to keep that promise."

Her smile faded and that look of triumph came upon her eyes. "Do you honestly think that sweet, pious woman of yours will stay with you if she knows you've been with another woman?"

Edward's brow lowered. "I'll tell her you're lying. She'll believe me over you, especially when you have no proof."

"I don't need proof, Edward." Malina smiled. "I only need to tell the truth. A little whisper of truth and your sweet little

Antoinette will start wondering whether you really have been faithful or not. She'll never trust you. Never fully confide in you. She may even leave you entirely."

"That's not true." Edward's voice rose.

"Oh, I think you know it is," Malina said. "A trustworthy man would tell his woman the truth. There would be no fear in your eyes if you were a trustworthy man."

Edward's heart suddenly sank at the realization. No matter what, he would lose Antoinette. No matter what, she would leave him.

I told you this day would come, said the voice of Stephen haunting his dreams.

His mind suddenly filled with visions of Antoinette, hurt and crying, learning of the truth. Doubtless she would go to Emmerich-go to the one man Edward did not want her to have.

Because you know he deserves her over you.

No. It's not fair!

Actually, for once it is.

"Here are my terms," Malina said, continuing her stroll. "There are two choices about you. The first is you ignore me, return to wherever it is you came from and pretend like none of this has ever happened. Of course, dear Sir Peterson will be mute…perhaps even dead if I have my way, and you'll have to explain to his family why his head rests on a pike above the Cathal gates. But I'll leave that up to you, as clearly you are a gifted speaker. You'll keep your precious Antoinette, but how long is anyone's guess as you and I both know gossip travels more quickly than the plague. News will arrive in Reigal of a child you fathered here in Cathal with me, and your new wife, alongside your family and friends, will begin to question every little lie you've ever told them. No one will trust you, no one will believe you, and no one will ever care for you again.

"Your second choice is this. Marry me, make me your queen, make our child your heir. I will tell the executioners to stay their hand, and your precious Sir Peterson will go free. His family will be thrilled he's alive and well, as will he be since his head will remain on his shoulders. Of course, you will lose your precious Antoinette, as I will not allow polygamy and I doubt she will want to share you, but take comfort in the fact that she will surely find love in the arms of another man, one who will be more faithful to her than you. Finally, your family and friends will be shocked at what you've done, but in time will applaud you for taking responsibility for your actions. Though you have 'made a mistake' as they would call it, you've proven yourself a king by accepting your responsibilities and putting others above yourself.

"Now, my prince," Malina said as she stopped in front of Edward. "What shall your choice be?"

Chapter 17: Edward's Choice

Marcus had never felt so much pain in his life.

How long he had been in the dungeon, he didn't know, but it felt like hours, maybe even days. He was bound to metal chains connecting to a stone wall, like a rabid prisoner on his way to the gallows. At first he tugged and pulled, trying to set himself free, but after the jailor arrived he had no strength left to struggle...no time to think of a way out. There were only beatings-hard, blunt blows to his abdomen and head, the feeling of air being knocked out of his lungs and the sounds of ribs undoubtedly cracking.

Marcus took it all in silence. He was prepared to die; his life was only worth a sacrifice to his country and king, but he worried for Edward. He worried what power the Lady of Cathal wielded over him now that she was bearing "his" child.

"Ye don't talk much," the jailor, his voice gruff and hoarse, said with a laugh. He struck Marcus across the mouth, the knight's lip splitting and his jaw radiating pain into his temple. "M'lady gave orders to cut out yer tongue when she says the word." He lifted a large pair of scissors, snipping them in front of Marcus' face. Marcus only looked at him, his eyes narrowed in steadfastness and muscles tensed.

"What? No last words? No begging for mercy?" The jailor shook his head, tossing the scissors to a table beside him with other instruments of torture. "Yer a strong lot, I'll give ye.

That's why I think ye'll be dead in the morn. The lady don't like ye strong lots. She puts an end to 'em quick!"

He kicked Marcus on the stomach and the knight gave a gasp as the air was pulled out of his lungs. He clutched his abdomen as best he could with the chains and doubled over, the pain and nausea nearly overwhelming him.

"I'll tell ye something else, too," the jailor continued. "I don't like ye strong lots, either. Ye think yer all high and mighty, sitting there an' looking tough." He gave another swift kick to Marcus' stomach, making him nearly make a cry, and spit in an empty corner. "I'll tell ye the truth, though. Every man has a breaking point, even the tough'uns. How long ye think yer going to last?"

Marcus remained quiet, pressing his lips tightly together.

"I see. Yer one of the stubborn ones." The jailor grinned. "Makes my job all the more fun."

Pain-searing and burning was how Marcus could best describe the jailor's "fun", if he could speak. Blow after blow he felt upon his body, his strength sapped of energy and his mind being overwhelmed by his senses. He tried not to yell, tried not to cry in the pain that plagued him, but even he wasn't strong enough to hold it in. His eyes became heavy, his breathing more spastic. He prayed to God for the pain to end, or at least the strength to withstand it. He didn't want to suffer and die as a coward.

More importantly, he didn't want Prince Edward to share the same fate.

We should have never come here...

"STOP IT!"

A familiar voice snapped Marcus back to reality as he opened his eyes, his vision blurry and tinted as he looked around to see where the voice had come from.

"Ye have no right to order me!" he heard the jailor say, but that familiar voice only scoffed.

"She has released him to me. Now be off before I skewer you myself!"

There was a sound of some arguing-something about needing proof and hearing from the lady. But after the crash of a body being thrown against the wall and a few sounds of beatings later, Marcus could hear the jailor whimper away, apologizing. "The keys..." He shook, the metal pieces clanging together. "Do what ye want with him, then."

"Be gone, jailor, 'til I have need of you," the familiar voice said. "Now go!"

The sound of feet shuffling away quickly disappeared into the distance.

A dark figure hovered over Marcus, and at first he thought it only a shadow, his imagination toying with him for being beaten so long. He felt hands grab his wrists and unbind them, the chains falling to the ground, and soon he was lifted up and set against the wall.

He felt a gentle tap against his cheek, another hand pressing against his shoulder to keep him steady.

"Marcus! Marcus, can you speak?" the voice said.

He tried to focus his sight as best he could in the dim light from the sconces, but the voice was recognized before the face. It was Edward kneeling before him, his face pale and ghostly and his eyes wide with fear.

"You…you shouldn't be here, Your Majesty." Marcus swallowed hard, tasting blood from his gashed lip. "I don't wish them to harm you."

Edward gave a sigh of relief. "They cannot harm me," he replied. "But I will not sit back and let them harm you. You're safe now. I'm taking you out of here."

"How did you…?"

"It doesn't matter. Now come! We must leave this place."

Marcus grabbed Edward's arm as he helped him up, leaning on the prince for support as his legs pained him to walk on his own. "Are we to leave Verloris?" Marcus asked.

Edward was quiet at first as he took hold of Marcus' arm and put it around his shoulder. "No," he replied. "Not yet."

"Wait, Your Majesty." Marcus stopped, reaching for the table beside him, grabbing onto its ledge and leaning onto it. "I am sorry for my abruptness. I know my questions have caused trouble for both you and me, but please honor my request. What Malina has said-about you, about the child-is it true?"

Edward gave a sigh as his eyes looked to the ground, a sadness glazing over him like a funeral pyre burning for a lost soul.

Marcus waited for a response in vain. "Your Majesty?"

Edward continued in his silence, making Marcus feel a tinge of anger. "Your Majesty, please…trust me. I have trusted you as my prince, my future king, and I have trusted you as an ally. I tell you now that I wish to trust you as my friend. Please-will you not let me aid you?"

Edward paused as if debating with himself on whether to answer or not. He nodded slowly, crossing his arms as he looked up at Marcus with a frown and said, "Yes. Yes, it's true."

"Why, Your Majesty?" Marcus asked. "Why did you do such a thing?"

"I did not wish this, Marcus. I didn't wish it at all."

"So it happened when we were last here?"

"Yes."

"Was it on the night of the party?"

"Yes."

"It was the drink then."

Edward nodded again, looking away. "Yes, and I was foolish to partake in it."

"So what do we do now?"

"Nothing."

Marcus blinked once…twice. Nothing? How could they do nothing?

"Your Majesty," Marcus began, "perhaps if we spoke to your father, the king, and…"

"No," Edward replied, shaking his head. "No, there is no need to now."

"No need to?" Marcus asked. "Your Majesty…what have you done?"

Edward looked up, his face haggard and worn. "For one, I've guaranteed your safety."

Footsteps echoed in the hallway. A sound of a metal door opening threatened to interrupt their conversation.

"No," Marcus continued, ignoring whoever was coming to them. "Your Majesty, do not forfeit your life for mine! What is it Malina has asked of you?"

"I am setting things to right," Edward replied as Vacius and the three guards appeared at the door.

"I don't understand…"

"There is no need to."

"But…"

"Your Majesty," Vacius interrupted as Edward turned to face him. "Your wife requests your presence."

Marcus' eyes widened. "Your wife?" he whispered as he looked to Edward in horror. "No, Your Majesty…no…"

"Tell her I will be there," Edward replied solemnly. "See to it that my guard gets proper medical attention. Bind his wounds. Have his cuts washed and cleaned. Provide him a room with food and drink so he can rest comfortably."

"Of course, Your Majesty." Vacius turned to the other three guards, pointing to Marcus. The three entered the jail and lifted the knight to his feet, but he only grunted and squirmed. He didn't want to go, didn't want to leave the prince behind.

"I do not need attention!" he replied to no avail. His strength was gone, beaten out of him it seemed, and pretty soon his struggling ceased. He would not escape with three other men holding him. There was no hope in that.

He turned to Edward before being ushered out of the jail. "Your Majesty, please, wait!"

"I will see you after you've rested, Sir Peterson," Edward replied. Before losing sight of the prince, Marcus turned his head one last time to look behind. He saw Edward face Vacius and say, "Make sure he receives the best of care."

"He will," Vacius replied. "The lady will keep her end of the deal as you have kept yours."

The next thing Marcus knew was being sent to a large, warm room where a doctor was waiting.

"Darling, what took you so long?"

Edward shut the door to his new chambers, Malina's chambers, quietly. It was in the middle of the night, he guessed, and already he was so tired, so worn. It wasn't the time that felt so heavy upon him, though. The events of the day-his secret coming out, his knight, his *friend*, beaten and nearly killed...

"Will you not answer your wife?"

The wedding. Edward closed his eyes, wanting to forget the memory of it. As soon as Marcus was dragged away and Malina offered her choices, Edward was given only a minute to decide what course he was to take, though in reality he needed only a second. As soon as he said he would marry Malina, she rushed him out the door and to a local judge to perform the ceremony. "A more proper engagement will be held later," she had said in her joy. "But I want you to myself *now*, Edward. You won't be able to change your mind."

He muttered his vows half-heartedly, barely hearing them in the fog of the moment. Whether it was shock or disappointment or anger or a mixture of the three, the entire ceremony felt like a blur. He didn't remember what she said to him or what he said to her. He only remembered thinking of

Antoinette, the woman who was now lost to him forever, and his heart broke. In fact, he thought it died.

When they kissed, sealing the marriage, he could only taste bile rising in his throat. He had taken a moment to look at his new wife-his bony, beading, snake of a woman he would now share his life with-and he could only feel dread.

If he could have screamed, shouted in anger at the world around him, he would. Instead, the pain echoed in his mind.

A cold touch, hands upon his chest, interrupted his thoughts. He felt the breath of Malina on his neck and he shuddered, closing his eyes and wanting to forget. "Are you ignoring me, Edward?"

He shook his head. "On the contrary. I'm thinking of you."

"Well," Malina cooed as she planted a kiss on his cheek. "Think not of your lusts, but act on them. Come, I have prepared a bath. Join me."

"I'd rather not," Edward replied as he freed himself from her embrace and stepped towards the balcony. He crossed his arms, staring at the outside world in its darkness, wanting to hide so all of his problems could not find him.

"Will you not love me, Edward?" Malina asked, stepping beside him. "If you are to ignore me every day of our marriage, then I can certainly..."

"Do you enjoy this?" Edward interrupted, facing her. "Do you enjoy feeling clever and gloating that you've won?"

"I don't enjoy it." Malina smiled. "I *relish* in it."

Edward frowned. "You sicken me," he said quietly.

"Well," Malina said, waving her finger in front of him. "An abusive husband already! Shall I teach you a lesson?"

Edward cleared his throat. "No. That would not be necessary."

"I will not take insolence from you Edward," Malina whispered as she touched his chin, squeezing it between her fingers and making him face her. "Remember that I can still make you suffer. You think you are so heroic because you saved one of your knights, but oh Darling...don't flatter yourself. You put him there in the first place and it was me who saved him by giving you mercy."

She kissed his lips slowly, sensually, but all he could feel was the bile overwhelm his taste. When she pulled away he swallowed hard to keep himself from gagging.

"I'm going to take a bath, but when I return I expect you to be...*nicer*," she said. "You're a man who will soon become a king, Edward. You really should stop thinking so much about yourself."

She left the room, shutting the door behind her, leaving him alone in her chambers.

For a moment he wanted to start taking things and throwing them, trashing the room and venting his anger that had been bottled up for so long now, but he stayed his hand, swallowing his pride, taking a deep breath to calm himself. She would not take kindly to his threats or tantrums. How did he not know she wouldn't punish Sir Peterson for his actions?

Edward let out a long, steady exhale as he went over to the table, eyeing the delicacies that had been laid before them from earlier. The food had grown cold-he had not the stomach to eat anything-but the wine and beer remained, and there was plenty.

The last time he drank he remembered little of his actions, his thoughts, his memories. He remembered barely a thing at all. Sure, it caused him trouble for drinking too much and getting carried away, but he was already in the deepest trouble he could be in. Things could not get any worse.

And it was so tempting just to forget. To forget the day, forget his marriage, forget the sorrows of his heart and mind.

Forget that you just shattered the heart of the woman you loved, and she doesn't even know it yet.

He grabbed the nearest bottle and opened it, taking a swift guzzle and ignoring the burn as it flowed down his throat. His mother would be furious, knowing how much he had bound himself to the bottle, but he didn't care. He wanted to forget. He wanted to drown his sorrows so they'd never rise again.

It didn't take long for the room to start spinning, for his thoughts to turn from sorrow to simply...nothing. It was maybe an hour when Malina returned, but he could only recognize a shadow and the cold hand that suddenly fell upon his cheek.

Chapter 18: A Bigger Mistake

Marcus had been treated quickly and efficiently after leaving the jailer's hall. While in the infirmary his wounds were cleaned and treated and his chest checked for anything further than a cracked rib or two. He was fortunate the jailer was weak and didn't give more damage than what he did. It was a rough beating, but not a damaging one, and it was expected Marcus would be back to normal in a few weeks.

He was now left alone in a room-his room, as they called it-with his thoughts and a warm hearth to keep the cold at bay. Though the doctors insisted he rest, he found himself wanting to walk the pain off rather than let it lay there and throb, so in his night tunic and pants he paced the room, the furs on the floor feeling prickly against his bare feet.

Edward-where was he at that moment? Marcus stood in front of the hearth, gazing down at the fire cackling beneath. With his wife? Had he married Malina already to save himself from a scandal?

He shook his head, not knowing what to think. Orders, he could follow. Even blind ones if they were for a noble cause. But being this in the dark...feeling this *lost*...he didn't know what to think.

There was nothing he could do but wait. Wait for Edward to reveal what on earth was going on or wait for something to happen, to force his hand into action.

He paced the room, feeling anxious, his mind wandering to thoughts of what could have happened or what would happen in the near future. If Edward was married to Malina now, his father would be furious and his mother upset. Antoinette...

Marcus closed his eyes, feeling a pain in his heart. Though he knew Antoinette very little, he always had a respect for her. She was so kind, so noble, so lovely. She did not deserve heartache like this.

Surely Edward knew his actions would hurt her, wouldn't he?

He wandered to the balcony and opened the door, the cold air meeting him and sending a chill to his bones. He covered his arms, desperate not to shiver, as he looked out the window into the kingdom. Darkness covered everything save a few lights in the streets. The sounds of wolves in the distance could be heard howling at the moon, but otherwise the city was silent. It was an eerie thought.

As he was about to go in and try to retire for the night, a small light from another window caught his eye. It was in another room across from him, also with a balcony, but much higher in the air than the middle room which Marcus occupied. He could make out a figure staggering about, a bottle in his hand, stepping about the room he was in.

The poor man's steps were swayed, however, and before he knew it, the bottle he once held in his hand slipped from his fingers and pummeled to the floor.

Marcus squinted to get a better look, to see who the crazy (and clearly drunk) man was. When his eyes adjusted to the darkness and he was able to see who the staggering man was, he froze and he felt a chill run down his spine.

Edward.

"Your Majesty!" Marcus shouted, desperate to get his attention, but the sound was not loud enough to carry. He rushed to the edge, grabbing the rails, shouting again and again to no avail. The distance was too far, the wind too strong...

Or Edward was too drunk yet again.

Marcus grunted in frustration, wanting to take every drop of alcohol and burn it for all the trouble it was causing the prince. He could only watch as Edward picked the bottle up, chugging it with fury. A woman soon entered the room, and Marcus could tell it was Malina.

"Don't throw your life away," Marcus muttered to the wind as he watched Malina sway about the room with confidence, approaching her new husband.

The world was spinning, a muffled blur that could barely be contained, and Edward didn't care.

He took another guzzle of drink-beer or wine, whatever it was-and laughed. How long he'd been drinking, he didn't know or care, but at least it no longer burned when he swallowed. He staggered about the room, giving a laugh after running into an end table and knocking over an empty goblet.

All he could think about was nothing. No hurt, no fear, no pain, no joy...just nothing. And he loved it.

The door opened and Malina had stepped in, her hair down and slightly damp from the bath but otherwise looking fresh and clean. She gave him a quizzical look when she first saw him, teetering around the sofa, but she laughed when she approached him, caressing his face.

"I see you've found the wine and beer, Darling," she said with a smirk. "Did you have to drink all of it?"

"Not all of it." Edward grinned as he lifted the bottle of wine in the air. Only a drop was left.

"You're drunk...very drunk."

"And you smell like orange juice."

Malina's smile turned to a frown as she gave him a nasty glare.

Edward chuckled. "You don't like orange juice?"

She said nothing, continuing her glare.

"Come now, orange juice tastes good!" He laughed, taking another swig. When he noticed her look did not change, he gave a sigh. "There I go-I've upset you. Tell me how to make it better so you don't look so gloooooooomy."

He fell upon the sofa, the bottle still in his hand, and sat there, waiting.

She gathered her skirt and walked to him, setting herself on his lap and putting her hands to his face. "So silly you are when you're out of your mind, Edward Engel. What would your father think if he saw you acting in such a way?"

Edward snorted. "He wouldn't be surprised."

"Oh?" She let her hands slide to his chest.

Edward inhaled deeply, taking another swig of wine, finishing the drop. "Not at all. The man hates me. He thinks of me as a waste."

"Why?"

"Because I'm not my brother."

Malina's eyes brightened. "You have a brother?"

"Had a brother. His name was Stephen." Edward frowned. "He died some years ago."

"I'm sorry to hear that," Malina cooed. "That must be hard for you, losing someone close."

"It was hard for my mother and father."

"And not you?"

Edward scoffed. "I got over it."

"How did he die?"

Edward paused, and for a moment he was quiet as he gripped the bottle in his hand. He pressed it to his lips, wanting to take a deeper drink than before, muttering a curse when he found the bottle empty. "He was pierced through the chest. It was an accident."

"Pierced through the chest?" Malina asked, her hands suddenly stopping.

"Yes, but I don't want to speak of it."

"Will you not tell me?"

"What's there to tell?" Edward replied. "He died, and here we are today." He held the empty bottle up. "Now tell me, have we more wine?"

"I can get as much as you'd like," Malina replied, leaning forward to him and kissing his lips. "Anything you want, I can give you."

Her kiss deepened and he followed her lead. Though the bottle remained at his side, his hands went around her, and for a moment they were lost in each other's passionate embrace. Between the kisses he heard her whisper in his ear. "Already you are *wild* for me, Edward. Already you have forgotten that wretch, Antoinette. Say you love me more than her, Edward. Say it!"

But at the mention of Antoinette's name he stopped.

The memories, the hauntings, the pain-they all seemed to come back. No matter how much the alcohol diluted his senses, somehow he could hear their voices scream at him and see their faces shouting their curses. He wondered if he should've drunk more.

Liar.

Thief.

Adulterer.

But before the last curse could be shouted at him, the one that Stephen would repeat to him over and over, he sat up, fleeing Malina's embrace.

"No!" he said, backing away. "I…I can't do this!"

He clutched his head, trying to drown out the voices, the faces, the guilt that had so plagued him in the past. He staggered away from the sofa with the bottle in his hand, Malina looking perplexed, yet angry.

"Edward? Come back here!" she demanded, but he paid her no heed.

He headed to the balcony, desperate for air, the cold wind hitting his face and snapping some of his senses alert. He took a swig from the empty bottle, and after it gave no relief, he threw it forward over the railing. He watched it go down-down into the deep, dark abyss of the night; down into the nothingness where only silence reigned supreme.

Liar, thief…

No, no…make it stop. He staggered around, trying to find more wine to dilute his memory.

Adulterer…

He glanced back down at the abyss beneath him where dark grass and shards of the bottle now laid. The drink helped him escape and now it was gone, shattered like his life and full of broken pieces.

He staggered about, searching for more wine to make him forget his haunting past, but as he moved forward, a bout of dizziness overtook him and his foot caught on a crack near the rail.

His reflexes were dulled and useless from the drink that numbed both mind and sense, and before he could register what was happening, he suddenly went flying forward, his bones about to become like the bottle shards.

He gave a startled gasp as he began to fall, but before his body could go over, he felt two hands grab him from behind and pull him back.

"What are you doing?"

He was thrown to the balcony's floor, water suddenly being dumped on his head. The coldness of the water mixed with the air suddenly brought him a moment of alertness through the haze, and he laid there, looking up and staring at Malina as she stood above him.

"Are you *mad*?" she seethed, bending down and slapping his face. "You dare leave my embrace to frolic in your own drunken stupor? Or did you honestly think you could be rid of me that easily?"

She grabbed his hands and pulled him up, and he was astonished at how strong she was despite her bony frame.

She pushed him back into the room, locking the door of the balcony and hiding the key near the mantle.

"*What were you thinking?*" she demanded again.

He fell upon the floor in front of the hearth, staring out into the distance. "I...I wanted them to stop..."

"Who's them?"

"I've hurt so many people..."

"Get over it," she snapped. "Your Antoinette is gone and better off without you."

"It wasn't just Antoinette..."

Suddenly her face softened, and she lowered herself onto the floor in front of him. "What do you mean?"

"Everyone. I lied to everyone."

"About us?"

"About so many things..."

Malina lowered her brow. "What things?"

He clutched his head, shutting his eyes and grimacing. "I'm so sorry. So very sorry."

"Sorry about what?" She paused, lifting his chin to face her. He opened his eyes. "Sorry about Antoinette?"

"Not just her."

"Sorry about Sir Peterson?"

"Not just him."

Malina paused, wrapping her arms around his neck. "About your brother?"

Suddenly Edward began to shiver, and he closed his eyes again, shaking his head. "I didn't mean to. I didn't mean to…"

"Edward, Darling," Malina soothed, cupping his face with her hands. "Tell me what really happened to Stephen."

When Edward awoke the next morning, he found himself lying in bed, his head aching and the light throbbing his eyes with pain. He sat up, nearly falling back down from the dizziness, and felt like he wanted to vomit. Regardless of the nausea or the coming headache, he wanted nothing more than to go back to sleep.

"Hung-over?" Malina's voice cooed from a distance, and Edward looked out, noticing her before him. She approached him, sitting on the bed, putting a hand onto his leg.

He sighed, rubbing his aching forehead. "Yes."

"I'm not surprised," Malina replied. "You drank too much for even me."

Edward looked around, noticing his clothes were still upon him, though they were different from what he had on before. "Did we…?"

"No." Malina frowned. "Though we came close. You spent most of the night throwing up. You didn't think I'd make you sleep in your own vomit, did you?"

Edward refused to answer the question. Knowing her, if she hated someone enough…

"I apologize," Edward said. "I didn't mean to display myself a fool. I don't remember anything."

"That does not surprise me. But I am in a forgiving mood."

She crawled into the bed with him, setting herself atop his body and covering her own with the sheet. "We never did finish what we started last night, Edward. Let us finish it now."

She bent to kiss him, but he gently pushed her away. "Please, Malina. When I say I have a headache, I really mean it."

"I don't care."

"You'd care if I started throwing up on you."

"Oh Edward, do you not get how this works?" Malina said, twirling his dark locks with her fingers. "If I say I want something, I get it. Do you understand?"

She set herself up. "Get me breakfast."

Edward sat up, perplexed. "What?"

"I said get me breakfast."

"You can do that yourself. You have help, don't you?"

"I have servants, yes," Malina replied. "But I want you to get them for me."

"I'm not *your* servant, Malina."

"Of course you are, Edward." She laughed, playing with his hair. "If I say love me, you love me. If I say get me breakfast, you get me breakfast. If I say cut off your hand, then you cut off your hand."

"You cannot make me do anything I don't want to do," Edward seethed. "I may be your...husband now, but it is nothing but a title. I will never love you. I will never care for you. I will always, *always* despise you for what you've done."

Malina put her hand to her lips and chuckled. "Oh silly, silly Edward. What a fool you really are. Did you honestly think I married you because I loved you?"

"Why else would you do this to me?"

"My father has a crown, Edward," Malina replied. "And so does my sister. But I was never given one. Do you know what a girl does when she doesn't get what she wants?"

Edward remained silent.

"She takes it anyway," Malina said, her face suddenly hardening. "So now I have one as your queen, and our child will have one as your heir. But me, Edward-I shall rule even over you."

"And how is that? I can make laws in my land to deny you any power of your own."

Malina smirked. "Liar."

Edward's eyes narrowed. "Don't call me that."

"Oh? And why not? Does it ring too familiar?" Malina replied. "Fine. Deny me any power. You know I'll take it anyways. One thief knows another, hmm?"

"Thief?" Edward asked under his breath, until suddenly the realization dawned on him. Her words…liar, thief…how did she know the meaning of those words to him?

His face must've shown his surprise as she kissed his mouth slowly. "Are you starting to remember the night before? About our little conversation?"

"No…"

"Oh, you liar." She giggled. "You thief. You adulterer…" She kissed him again, more passionately as she pushed him back onto the bed. She stopped, grabbing his hands, slamming them apart and holding them down.

He laid there silently in fear over her next word. He hoped she hadn't heard it. Prayed she would not know his greatest sin.

She smiled as she leaned forward, whispering in his ear. "*Murderer...*"

Edward could only lay there in shock as his eyes became wide.

"No..."

Malina smiled and began to sing as she bent down over him. "I know what happened to Stephen..."

He said nothing as she silenced him with her kiss.

Chapter 19: Emmerich's Arrival

It was about two in the afternoon when the guard arrived in the drawing room telling Queen Maria that a carriage from Hugellia was coming up the road. Antoinette was busy with needlepoint and Bernie had been reading a book, but at the sound of a visitor everyone dropped what they were doing and headed to the door.

Bernie could only smile as the ladies rushed to the front- some happy, some not so much. The carriage from Hugellia could only be one person: Emmerich van Ketten.

Bernie tried to remember the last time she saw young Emery. It had to have been four years ago, maybe five, when he was last in Staalberg with his parents negotiating some trade deal between his country and her own. She remembered the young man was always so polite and kind that she eventually found it annoying, but she was content with his visits nonetheless. It always made Antoinette happy to see him and the two would often go out on their own for walks and stay out talking for hours. Bernie tried to tag along once or twice, but after trailing behind and being ignored, she found herself staying in the library among her books where she belonged.

When she was younger and Emery visited more often, she was certain that her sister and the Hugellian would become an item. It didn't take any amount of skill to notice the man was clearly smitten with Antoinette, following her around like a puppy and looking at her with dreamy eyes. It was obvious, so painfully obvious that even Mother took notice and started keeping her daughters busy whenever Emmerich came over. For some reason, Mother never liked the poor man. She spoke poorly of his parents, too, though Bernie always thought them kind and gentle.

Bernie would never admit she was a little jealous of all the attention her sister received instead of her. Emmerich van Ketten was handsome, after all, despite his lean physique and lack of certain soldierly qualities his cousin was superior with. After a few conversations with him and noticing he had an inability to not mention Antoinette every ten seconds, however, Bernie decided to give up and not waste her time on something that was clearly never going to happen.

And so she decided to play matchmaker. At least for now, until the wedding could be delayed or possibly postponed indefinitely. Grant it, if Antoinette's relationship with Edward ended, a new one would probably begin with Emmerich, but Bernie wasn't worried about that for the moment. She would worry about that more when the time came-and if she was still living at home.

The carriage came to a stop and Maria rushed down the steps to greet her nephew. Queen Susanna followed slowly behind while Antoinette and Bernie remained at the top of the stairs.

"Nervous?" Bernie asked.

Antoinette had her arms crossed as she kept her gaze ahead. "Not at all. Should I be?"

"Of course not." Bernie chuckled. "He's just coming over to talk, right? Just think of it as seeing an old friend."

Antoinette gave Bernie a small glare. "I am seeing an old friend!"

"An old friend who's probably in love with you and is going to make a lavish confession," Bernie muttered with a smirk.

Antoinette rolled her eyes as she turned her sights back forward. "I highly doubt that."

"Oh, please. Everyone always falls in love with you."

"No they don't."

"Sure they do," Bernie replied. "But at least you don't have a creepy guy falling for you this time. Emmerich's a nice man. You already know he's a good match."

"Is there a reason why you're pushing this so much?"

Bernie's brow went up. She had to cover her trails, fast. She couldn't let Antoinette figure out her secret plan. "I'm not being pushy. I'm just teasing! Lighten up, Miss Tighty Pants."

There was a pause until Antoinette gave a snicker. "Miss Tighty Pants?"

Bernie chuckled alongside. "Well, I was going to say 'Miss I-Constantly-Worry-Over-Everything-Here-And-There', but I thought 'Tighty Pants' sounded better."

Antoinette laughed, making Bernie breathe a little easier. Crisis averted.

The carriage door opened and Bernette turned to watch, hoping that this part of the plan-one of the most important-would go smoothly. Emmerich was to open the door, come out looking perfect and wonderful, and Antoinette was going to get the smitten look in her eye.

But when the door opened and he stepped out, Antoinette remained neutral. No gasp in her breath, no smile fluttering her face, no rosy cheeks blushing when his eyes met hers.

She just stood there, waiting for him to eventually greet her, and watched.

Bernie looked at Emmerich and then back at her sister. Though it wasn't hard to realize Emmerich still had feelings for her sister-his gaze never left her even as he hugged his Aunt Maria-it seemed Antoinette had nothing of the sort. Was he just a friend to her? Did she not care that he was handsome *and* kind *and* basically would leash himself like a dog if she asked him to?

If only Antoinette wasn't so loyal to Edward…

Bernie pouted silently to herself at seeing her plan hit its first roadblock. Love was simple-find somebody cute who thinks you're cute back and bam! You're an item. As she watched Emmerich give a greeting to Queen Susanna, who met his glance coldly, Bernie noticed how different the young Hugellian was compared to the last time she saw him.

Of course, Emmerich hadn't lost any of his looks; in fact, he gained quite a bit. Light brown hair, thick and wavy that made her want to run her fingers through it. Clothing that fit smooth against his body; tight enough to show that he wasn't the skinny kid Bernie remembered him as, but loose enough to make anyone wonder just what did all those newly-formed muscles look like underneath all that cloth.

If Bernie could see that, why couldn't Antoinette?

She's hopeless.

"My sweet Emery! Was the journey well? How is Edward?" Queen Maria asked as her nephew was pulled into her embrace once more.

"The journey was well," he began, letting go and facing her. "We ran into a little rain in the mountain pass, but nothing we couldn't handle. And Edward is fine. Last I heard he was on a hunting trip. He should be back by now, though."

"Oh, I hope he stays careful in the wild with all those grass lions about!"

Bernie noticed Antoinette gave a concerned look at the mention of grass lions, but ignored it. "He'll be fine," Emmerich replied. "He didn't go alone."

"Well as long as he isn't by himself," Maria said.

But Emmerich was done with the conversation regarding Edward. His sights were set to Antoinette and he headed up the steps to meet her. He bowed his head, taking her hand in his and kissing it. "Lady Antoinette," he said, gazing into her eyes. "It is lovely to see you after such a long time. You look wonderful."

Antoinette gave a polite smile, but after noticing he still held her hand after kissing it, she quickly let it go and led him to Bernie. "Thank you, Emery. It's nice to see you again, too. Surely you remember my sister, Bernette?"

Bernie wanted to stick her tongue out at Antoinette for pushing Emmerich away so quickly, but kept her composure. "Hi again." Bernie gave a quick smile, hoping he'd take the hint to return to her sister and *woo* her like he was supposed to.

Instead, he took her hand in his and, bowing his head, kissed it. "It's been a long time since I've seen you, Lady Bernette," he said. "You have grown into a lovely young woman."

At first Bernie stood there, shocked that he would even compliment her, let alone kiss her hand without gagging and screaming and running away like so many others had *clearly* wanted to do, but she shook her head, gaining her composure.

She was wearing fake hair. She wasn't exactly skinny like her sister, either.

Of course the man was lying. Bernie knew how people thought, especially in regards to her. She had to give him credit, though, for trying to butter up to Antoinette by complimenting the sister. Clever man, indeed.

"Thanks," Bernie muttered, no longer meeting his warm smile. After a pause, he finally took the hint and went back to Antoinette.

"How have you been, Antoinette?" Emmerich asked.

She tilted her head shyly. "Busy, but well. And you?"

"I'm doing quite well, thank you."

So far so good, Bernie nodded to herself. *Small talk always leads to deeper conversations-*

"How is Edward?"

-until the brilliant eldest sister ruins it all by asking about her freaking fiancé…

Emmerich's smile suddenly faded. He looked disappointed, almost frustrated at the sound of Edward's name. Bernie noticed it quickly, studying his composure. Whatever emotion or feeling he had towards his cousin was quickly hidden, but that small blip of raw opinion showed in his eyes. Edward was a name Emmerich didn't like to hear. Why was that?

"Edward is well," Emmerich replied too quickly.

"Is he behaving in Hugellia?" Antoinette chuckled. "I hope he isn't causing too much trouble for the king."

Emmerich gave a forced grin. "No, no trouble at all."

No trouble for the king, Bernie mused. Trouble for Emmerich? Most definitely.

He was jealous of Edward.

"I miss him terribly," Antoinette continued. "He's been gone for so long."

Emmerich looked away. "I'm sure he'll be back soon."

"I hope so."

Emmerich became silent. Bernie could only imagine what was going through his mind. *I hope Edward takes his time. I hope he gets lost on the way back. I hope he's plagued with the runs during his travels so it'll take him forever to get home.*

She could only smirk at the thought.

"Come in, dear Emery! Let's not stay out in this wind!" Maria exclaimed as she clamored up the steps and took him by the arm. "You must be so tired from all that traveling. Come; let me get you a nice cup of tea and a meal."

"Thank you, Aunt Maria," he replied, his demeanor warming. He turned to Antoinette and Bernie. "Will you both join us?"

Before either of them could answer, Queen Susanna's voice came through. "Of course not!" she stammered. "They're busy with the wedding plans."

Wedding plans? Bernie wasn't about to go back to that torture. She'd choose dining with the lost puppy and his aunt over Mother nagging about linens any day. "Well, I'm not busy," Bernie replied, stepping forward. "I didn't even get to eat lunch! I'd be happy to join you."

"You've already eaten enough!" Mother hissed, pulling Bernie back. Emmerich gave Susanna a sharp look and Maria frowned.

"We have plenty of room," Maria began, but Susanna shook her head.

"They need to try on their dresses," Susanna said, giving a smile to the queen but ignoring Emmerich completely. He only lowered his brow.

"Good day, Queen Maria," Susanna replied, taking both daughters by the hand. "And good day to you, Emmerich."

Without another glance, she pulled them back into the palace and headed down the hall.

As the girls struggled to keep up with their mother, Susanna huffed as she stormed towards a back room. "The nerve of that boy!" she snarled under her breath. "I can't believe he has the gall to show his face here-before the wedding of all times!"

"Mother," Antoinette began, suddenly stopping and pulling everyone back. "Please. We shouldn't be rude. He's travelled a long way to get here and he's probably just wanting to help. You know how he is-always wanting to be there for everyone and do what he can."

Bernie's eyes widened. Maybe there was hope in the plan yet thanks to Mother. Perhaps her rudeness would make Antoinette feel sorry for him...

"Nonsense!" Susanna said. "The only thing that boy is interested in is taking you for himself and stopping everything we've worked so hard for!"

Bernie gulped. Apparently Mother noticed Emmerich's puppy dog look, too. *Drat...*

"He's not like that, Mother," Antoinette said. Oh, what a naïve sister Bernie had. "He'd never do such a thing. There's not a rude bone in his body."

"He's had his eye on you since you were children, Antoinette," Susanna said. "I didn't think you were so daft that you'd never notice it."

"We've only been friends. He respects that I am marrying Edward and hasn't said a thing in objection!"

"Yet." Susanna's brow lowered.

Bernette could only watch as her sister and mother went back and forth. As happy as she was that her plan had frustrated her mother, standing in a hallway watching an argument was not her idea of fun.

"If you two are going to go on about this, can I go?" Bernie whined.

"And go where?" Susanna asked.

"To eat lunch. I'm starving!"

"Always thinking of food, aren't we, my pig?" Susanna asked, making Bernie frown. "You shan't be leaving. I don't want you associating with Emmerich van Ketten, either."

"Why not?"

"Because..." Susanna paused, her face beginning to turn red. "Because he is beneath us!"

Antoinette gave a pout while Bernie widened her eyes. "That's a shallow thing to say, don't you think?" Bernie asked.

Susanna shook her head. "It's not shallow. It's the truth," she said. "That boy is worthless. I only put up with his family for the sake of your father and the trade that was brought in from Hugellia. You know them as kind and polite, but I know what they really are. I've known his family since infancy. They are the laughingstock of Hugellia and have no royal titles whatsoever. Emmerich's father is nothing but a dreamer who pretends to know how to run a country, but the king knows how foolish he really is! And don't get me started on Emmerich's mother. A peasant she was, cleaning gutters in the streets. If Aldaric van Ketten was any kind of a smart man, he would've married up instead of down! He had his chances of staying a noble, maybe even gaining a royal title, but he didn't take them. No, instead he married a poor harlot! She still smells like trash every time I see her."

"So you're punishing Emmerich because of his parents?" Antoinette asked, a look of disappointment on her face.

"That's pretty judgmental, even for you, Mother," Bernie muttered.

"Don't pretend to know them as well as I do." Susanna's eyes narrowed. "That boy may look and act like his father, but he's nothing but a peasant like his mother." She paused as she grabbed their hands again, starting to pull. "Now enough of this chatter. It is time we find something to keep you both busy!"

The sisters complied, following their mother, remaining silent in shame.

Marcus Peterson slept little during the night. After seeing Edward nearly falling off a balcony ledge, his mind had been put on alert. What made the prince so careless? Had it not been for Malina pulling Edward back into the room, the prince would be dead, but Marcus wondered just how bad it had gotten to make him so witless to stagger about on a balcony. Marcus was worried, very worried, and all throughout the night he could only think of one thing:

What was going to happen next?

Was Edward no longer sane? Could Edward not handle the responsibility that now fell before him? Was Edward being manipulated by Malina, being held captive by her claims? Or was Edward simply doing what he wanted to do? So many questions needed answering, and Marcus was lost in trying to figure it all out.

He had called on a Verloris guard to ask of the prince's whereabouts. He wanted to see him, to make sure he was alright and see if he needed anything. The guard only shook his head, saying the prince was resting in the princess' chambers and needn't be disturbed. That was five hours ago, and Marcus was left in his room feeling trapped, pacing the floor back and forth trying to plan his next move.

It wasn't long before he started to feel stir crazy, wanting to get out-*needing* to get out. He banged on the door of his room and the guard returned with a gruff, asking what the matter was this time.

"Please, honorable guard," Marcus begged. "I must check on His Majesty. We traveled so much the day before and I worry for his health. Please, I beseech you, let me check on him. I promise once I see him I shall let him be, as long as he is well. Will you grant me this request?"

The guard gave a sigh, but nodded. "Very well. I will ask the lady for you."

"Many thanks," Marcus said, and waited by the door.

Edward was slow to getting up after Malina had left. His head still ached and his stomach felt sick, but the effects of his binge drinking were the least of his concerns. What he was worried about most was how Malina knew about Stephen.

Did I tell her? Or did she somehow find proof?

No, she didn't have proof. He made sure that was well-hidden and never to be found by anyone.

But simply knowing that he told her, that he was so drunk he let his guard down yet *again*, this time digging him even further into the ground, made him feel wretched. Terrified. Whatever power he had to himself was now gone with the information she held over him.

Liar, thief, adulterer, murderer-she knew him better than anyone now. Better than his parents, his family and friends, Antoinette...

He sighed as he sat on the sofa, eyeing the waning flame that burned in the hearth. He rubbed his face and leaned back, feeling helpless...lost. He didn't know what to do anymore, didn't know how to feel.

The future, however, was known to him. He knew what to expect when he got home and that worried him even more.

If he could only return to his sleep…

A knock on the door was heard and Edward sat up, expecting Malina to enter and taunt him more with her victory. "Come in," he said, his voice cracked and heavy, as he turned and faced the entrance.

He was relieved to see it was Marcus Peterson-tired, a little bruised, but otherwise well.

"May I enter, Your Majesty?" Marcus asked, and Edward nodded.

"Yes, you may enter."

Marcus walked in, shutting the door behind him. The poor man looked like he hadn't slept at all the night before, and Edward felt a pang of guilt. Doubtless it was from the beatings he received, the pain from all the aches and bruises keeping him up in agony all night. Somehow Marcus still managed a smile. "I would've been here sooner, Your Majesty. Forgive me, but the guards wouldn't let me see you without permission from Malina. Are you well?"

Edward nodded slowly as he offered Marcus a seat in the chair beside him. "I have a headache, but otherwise I'm fine."

"You had me worried," Marcus said. "Terrified, actually. May I be so bold as to ask what you were doing on the balcony last night?"

"Balcony?" Edward asked. "I was on the balcony?"

Marcus' eyes widened. "Do you not remember?"

"Apparently not."

"You nearly fell to your death!"

Edward pressed his lips together in a frown, folding his hands and leaning forward. He had no recollection of the night before-not his conversations, nor his actions, nor his apparent brush with death. It made him feel sicker than before.

"What happened?" he asked.

"You had gone out onto the balcony. It looked like you had a bottle in your hand," Marcus replied. "You were swaying and threw the bottle over the railing. After you saw it fall, you staggered a bit and nearly fell yourself!" Marcus shook his head, rubbing his brow. "I tried shouting for you, to get your attention and to stop you, but you couldn't hear me. We were too far away from each other. I thought for sure you were going to perish until Malina grabbed you and pulled you back inside."

"Malina?" Edward asked.

"Yes," Marcus said. "I am not fond of that woman, Your Majesty, but I am thankful she saved your life!"

Just why did she save his life? Edward's eyes narrowed and he bent his head in thought.

"Your Majesty," Marcus continued after a pause, "were you drunk last night?"

At first Edward didn't answer. He didn't want to tell the truth. "No."

"Then what was in the bottle?"

"Wine, but it was Malina's, not mine."

"But surely it was. Why else would you have it?"

Edward gave a heavy scoff as he shook his head. "Why are you even questioning this?"

"Both my mother and grandparents were drunkards," Marcus replied quietly. "I know the influence of alcohol better than most."

"So what's your point?"

"My point is you don't have to lie to me."

Edward muttered a curse to himself, rubbing his eyes. Was this the fate he was resigned to now? His house of lies suddenly crumbling to the point that no matter what he said, no one believed him? He had heard it said that truth was freeing, like unshackling a caged man. But that wasn't truth. Truth was the shackle. Truth was what ruined everything and made lives crumble and shatter.

If he was truthful about Stephen, his father would kill him.

If he was truthful about Emmerich, his mother would be heartbroken.

If he was truthful about Malina, his fiancée would leave and never see him again.

How was truth freeing when it robbed him of the only good in life he had left?

"What do you want from me, Marcus?" Edward asked bitterly. "A confession? A story?"

"I don't want any of the sorts. I was just…"

"Then what is the point of you being here? Have you come to *gloat*? To *mock*? Are you happy to see me fall so low?"

Marcus' expression fell. "What? No, that's not…"

"THEN WHY ARE YOU EVEN HERE?"

"Because I was worried about you!" Marcus' voice neared a shout, and suddenly Edward's demeanor calmed, and he looked at him quizzically. "You nearly died last night, Your Majesty! Would you be so careless now, at such a time as this?"

"She should have just let me drink," Edward muttered under his breath as he shook his head. "No one cares for me, anyways."

"Don't say that. Don't ever say that. Where would we be if it weren't for you?"

"Better off."

"That's not true, Your Majesty."

"Stop it, Marcus..." Edward buried his face in his hands, immersing himself in the darkness of his palms. He wished his head would stop aching. He wished all the pain would go away. "You waste your loyalties on me. Your life was nearly ended because of my mistake."

"And yet I'm here, alive and well."

"Only because Malina had mercy."

"Or because you are selfless," Marcus replied. "I'm not stupid. I know Malina is incapable of mercy on her own. She had to gain something for me to be spared."

Edward knew what Marcus was implying, but he gave a sarcastic laugh. Yes, Edward's marriage to Malina saved Marcus. But even if the knight was not there, Edward would still be bound to his fate.

Because justice comes to all sinners, and I am the greatest sinner of all.

"Marcus, I am far from being as pious as you make me out to be," Edward replied solemnly. "I do not deserve such flattery. You waste your breath."

"Your Majesty..."

"Don't bother with the title any more, Marcus," Edward interrupted. "I think we both know the crown will no longer be mine once I get back to Reigal."

Marcus' brow furrowed. "What makes you think that?"

"Because I know my father, and I have failed him enough already."

"But, Your Majesty..."

"Just Edward, Marcus," Edward replied. "I'm in a foul mood as it is, so please-don't question me."

"Alright...Edward."

"Thank you."

Marcus looked nervously aside. He looked like he was at a loss of words, like he didn't know what to say. Edward didn't blame him. What else was there? To tell his sorry excuse of a prince that he was a failure, that he wished Stephen were alive because he would've made a wiser prince and heir?

"Edward?" Marcus asked. The prince looked up, ready for the accusations to fall.

"I'm proud of you."

What? Edward tilted his head, beading his eyes. What kind of madness was this?

"Proud? Why?" Edward asked.

"You didn't have to take responsibility for all of this. You could've lied and walked away from it all and pretend it didn't happen."

"I didn't have much choice, Marcus."

"You did have a choice," Marcus replied. "But you made the right one. It's not going to be easy and I know when we get back...a lot of things will be different. I just want you to know that I'm on your side. I'm not proud of what you did, Edward..."

"I'm not either," Edward whispered.

"I know," Marcus continued, "but I made an oath to stand by you, to protect you at all cost. I'm keeping that oath. Even through this."

A part of Edward wanted to lash out, wanted to tell him *you fool, you fool-don't you know that I had this coming? Get away before I pull you down to Hell with me.* But Edward remained quiet for a moment, unable to scold his loyal guard, his friend, and just nodded as he rested his lips on folded hands.

"I have done many terrible things, Marcus. I'm a liar. I'm a thief. I'm an adulterer..."

"Are you sorry for what you did?" Marcus asked.

"What?" Edward lifted his head.

"Are you sorry for what you did?"

Edward's answer was faster than his thoughts. "Of course."

"Then I don't care what you did," Marcus continued. "If you are sorry and you try to make things right, then I'll stand by you until the end."

Edward sighed as he gave a quivering smile. A fool, Marcus Peterson was, for remaining at his side, and Edward was never more thankful for it than now.

He could only hope the others would be so forgiving.

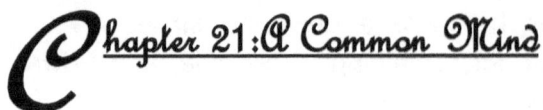

Bernie couldn't take it anymore.

Flowers. Cake. Frilly dresses. Mother freaking out over a wrinkle in the tablecloth.

If chaos was what it took to create a wedding, then she wanted to elope.

She sat on the sofa, watching as Mother picked and pricked at the wedding dress Antoinette was modeling for the seamstress. "Take it in here!" Mother would bark, pointing. "This must be perfect!"

For a moment, Bernie pictured herself as Antoinette in the dress. Mother would probably be sticking her with an iron poke, nagging about needing more fabric and elastic and wondering why her little pig couldn't keep her snout shut.

I'm so glad I'm single...

She thought of ways she could escape her confinement. It wasn't like she was being helpful to her sister just sitting there. She wanted to get out, breathe some air, find a corner where she could hide and catch up on her summer reading. Maybe she could fake illness, to start gagging on the floor like she was going to lose her breakfast? That would get Mother in a panic. She could also pretend to faint. That would warrant her being sent to her room to relax.

Oh, the options that were available. Fainting was a predictable one-it was, after all, getting warm in the room-but Bernie didn't want to be predictable. She wanted to cause a little bit of trouble at the same time, too.

It was time to start gagging. Desperate times and all.

"Mother..." She put her hand on her stomach and started to moan. "I don't feel so good."

Susanna turned, perturbed at her youngest daughter's interference. "What is it, child?"

"I think I'm going to throw up."

"Why on earth for?"

"I think I ate too much."

That would get her. Oh, that would get her good.

Bernie started to gag, and suddenly her Mother's eyes became wide. "I told you only to eat one egg!" she snapped. To see her mother in such a panic made Bernie want to fall to the floor and laugh, but she held it together. Composure was more important when escape became necessary.

Susanna rushed to find a pot nearby and Antoinette gave a concerned look to Bernie as she bent over, holding her stomach, moaning and gagging more than ever. "Bernie-are you alright?" Antoinette asked as she took her in her arms and cradled her.

"Get back!" Susanna shooed Antoinette's hand away and removed her from Bernie's side. "If it is the flu, you needn't be sick before the wedding! Get away!"

Antoinette complied hesitantly.

"Go to your room, child, and don't you dare get vomit on the dress!" Susanna said as she handed the pot to Bernie. Bernie clutched it, moaning some sort of thank you, and gagged into the pot and let a little spit drool onto it.

"Guard! Guard!" Susanna shouted, and instantly a man came forward into the room. Susanna pushed Bernie onto him and his eyes widened in concern as Bernie looked up at him, gagging on his uniform. "Take my daughter to her chambers. See to it that one of the maids look after her. If her illness worsens, notify me."

"Y...y...yes, Your Majesty," the guard mumbled, and he led Bernie by the shoulders towards the door.

Susanna rubbed her forehead as if feeling faint herself before giving a calming exhale. She returned to the seamstress and the dress, but before Bernie left, Antoinette met her gaze. Bernie gave a wink and waved, making Antoinette chuckle behind her hand.

As the door closed, Bernie straightened herself up and handed the pot to the guard and laughed. "Ugh. I thought I'd never escape. No need to take me to my room, good sir," she replied as she strode down the hall. "But if anyone asks, I'm in my room throwing up. Thanks!"

And off she skipped down the hall.

Already she was dreaming of what to do with her free time. Sketch on some paper. Day dream by the window. Sneak some pastries from the kitchen. Read a book on the heliocentric view of planet Earth.

Bernie smiled to herself. Controversial reading, that was. Mother would highly disapprove.

Oh, the choice was so simple...

She hurried down the hall and through the main corridor, past a long stretch of windows and into a room that was laid in white marble; one of the grandest rooms in the palace. It was said that Queen Maria was an avid reader-a trait she had learned from her eldest brother-and the room was built as proof of King Arden's love for her after their marriage.

Whatever the reason, Bernie was just glad it was built.

She went through the shelves of books, aisles and aisles of them, until she found the section on astronomy. There, tucked in the back, laid a book on heliocentricism, and she quickly snatched it up, feeling a guilty pleasure knowing she was able to read a book on astronomy.

Oh, Mother would disapprove indeed! Especially since the book was not on beauty or weight loss.

Bernie clutched it to her chest and walked over towards the windows. She figured a chair would at least be near so she could plop down and spend her new free time reading in peace and quiet. But as she approached the corner, she stopped, quickly hiding behind a bookshelf. There was a lone figure at the chess table, playing a solitary game in the sunlight.

It was Emmerich van Ketten.

Bernie paused as she watched him from a distance. He had a stack of books beside him, a mixture of topics from what she could tell, all of them looking well-worn and read. Doubtless he had been bored during his stay in Reigal. He had come to speak with Antoinette only to find that her mother kept her so busy no one would see her. That left the poor boy alone, nothing better to do than to wait his turn for a moment Antoinette wasn't being chauffeured.

It was an odd stroke of luck Bernette found herself receiving. Here, she had a chance to fix whatever was left of her plan. She could speak with Emmerich, feed a fib here or there and maybe even arrange for a meeting with him and Antoinette. Of course, that would mean giving Mother something to do in the meantime. Perhaps a rip in one of the tablecloths or Antoinette's veil somehow coming in contact with mustard would do the trick...

Bernie smirked at that last thought. She quietly stepped forward towards the chess table, admitting to wanting to strike up the conversation purely for rebellious purposes; to not only mess with Antoinette's upcoming wedding and delay it, but also to do something to spite Mother.

When she approached, he looked up and met her warm gaze. He stood, giving a smile and a slight bow. "Lady Bernette. Forgive me; I didn't notice you were here."

"I was just browsing through the library," Bernie began, noticing he dressed nice again. "Saw you over here, thought I'd say hi."

He smiled at her, a typical goofy grin one gives when seeing someone they barely know and not knowing what to say. "Hello," was the best he could come up with.

Obviously, the conversation was deflating faster than a balloon. She had to fix it quick. "Uhm...sorry if I interrupted anything. I didn't mean to walk in on you when you were playing with yourself."

His brows went up for a moment and her eyes went wide.

Bernie felt the redness rush to her face. She was a good conversationalist-always had been. Since when did she ever say something so *stupid*? She'd never done that before to anyone.

She wanted to melt, alright, at his look. Melt into a puddle and swim away to the nearest drain so she could hide from that moment forever.

"I mean...uh...I didn't mean to...uhm, you know...I meant the game...uhm..." Years of studying debate had led her to this moment. This bright, shining, clear moment of confidence. Oh, would Mother be proud.

"It's fine," he replied, giving her what she could only guess was a nervous grin. *Great*, she thought to herself as she bit her lip. *Now that you've freaked the guy out ...*

"I see you found a book," he said, nodding towards the astronomy book in her hand. Good. A change of subject. At least he knew how to save the dead conversation that turned awkward. "Do you enjoy reading?"

She gave a nod, suddenly feeling more terrified to speak than to move.

"What's your book about?"

"The heliocentric model of planetary orbits," she answered, and suddenly she felt like smacking herself. *Idiot! What is with you?* she scolded internally. *He's not going to know what that is! You should've lied and said it was about deer hunting or fencing or-*

"You think the Earth revolves around the Sun?"

Bernie paused from her thinking and gave him a perplexed look. "Wait-you...you actually know what I'm talking about?"

He nodded, giving her the same perplexed look. "I'm surprised I'm not the only one who's studied heliocentricism. There aren't many who like astronomy."

At first Bernie didn't know what to say. She'd always thought Edward and his family were a brawn over brains type of group, but apparently Emmerich was an exception. How had she not noticed this before? She never heard him talk about astronomy or anything remotely smart when she followed him and Antoinette on their walks.

Then again, she never went on many walks in the first place...

She gravitated towards the chair across from him, curious to finally find someone who shared a love and understanding of all things intellectual. "You've read about the theories challenging a geocentric view?" she asked.

Emmerich nodded as he sat down. "I've been charting the stars and planets just to see how they orbit. So much of it is elliptical..."

"I know, right?"

Emmerich laughed as he leaned back in his chair. "I admit you have made me glad I am not alone in my endeavors, Lady Bernette!" he said. "It is a pleasure to meet a fellow lover of science. You must have learned it from your sister. She has always loved gazing at the stars."

Bernie's smile nearly fell at the mention of Antoinette, but she remained steadfast. Who was she kidding, getting giddy at the mention of science? Of course he'd change the subject back to her sister. That's why she left the walks in the first place.

It was hard to hide the frown that wanted to come up.

"She got me started in it, I'll admit," Bernie muttered. "But she just likes to look at them. Me? I like to study them. See where they move, know what they are, guess what they could actually be like."

Emmerich nodded in agreement. "I understand. It is one thing to observe, but another thing to know. I take it you are fond of study and knowledge?"

"Definitely."

"Well then," Emmerich replied, rearranging his pieces on the board. "Would you like to play a game of chess with me? To pass the time until your mother finds you and drags you back to the wedding planning?"

Bernie sighed as she helped set up the pieces. "How did you guess?"

"I know your mother too well." Emmerich snickered. "I've been trying to find a moment to speak to Antoinette for days. It seems both you and she are constantly preoccupied."

"You have no idea."

"Actually, I do," Emmerich replied. "My family and I used to stay in Edeland during trading season, remember? We saw...quite a bit."

"I'm sure you did." Bernie smirked.

Emmerich laid out his hand, offering her the first move. She moved her pawn forward two spaces and he continued. "I hear Antoinette was called away on dress business today. I assume that's why you are here and she is not?"

He made his move, going forward with a fellow pawn, and Bernie counterattacked with her piece. "Actually, I was there with her. I faked a stomach flu so I could get out."

"Really?" Emmerich asked, surprised.

Bernie nodded with pride. "A woman has her ways."

"You must be a fine actress to fool your mother."

"I'm not a good actress by any means." Bernie shrugged. "I was just desperate to get out."

"I can only imagine."

Bernie watched as Emmerich moved a bishop forward, capturing one of her pawns. She crinkled her face, thinking of her move for a moment, and decided to move her queen. It was risky, but then again, she liked risk.

"Do you think she'll have any free time?" Emmerich asked as he made his move. "Antoinette, I mean."

"I'm sure she will eventually," Bernie replied. "Mother has to sleep, right?"

"Would you mind doing something for me, then? Tell her…I don't know. Tell her I'd like to meet with her so we can talk."

Bernie felt a flip in her stomach. She had to plan her moves carefully, as careful as moving a chess piece across the board. She had to make sure Antoinette was willing to talk, and of course she had to hide it all from Mother-not an easy task as the woman thought herself all-knowing. Most importantly, no one could suspect it was Bernie who sent the letter.

"What did you want to talk to her about, if you don't mind my nosiness?" Bernie asked.

"She sent me a letter," Emmerich answered, pausing for a moment before making his move. He slid a knight forward and captured a pawn. "She asked to speak with me about something personal."

"Personal, huh?"

"Yes," Emmerich replied. "Though, out of respect to her, she asked me to keep it private."

"So you're not even going to give me a hint?"

He chuckled. "I'm afraid I can't."

"Well, I guess I can't blame you for that." Bernie sighed, capturing his knight. "She has her way with people."

"She certainly does," Emmerich said, frowning. "It's why Edward loves her so much."

Bernie glanced up from the board. There was that look in his eye again, like a sadness that had been hiding yet no one knew to look for it. "You say that like it bothers you."

Emmerich stopped as he was moving his king, giving Bernette a quizzical glance. "It doesn't bother me."

Bernie watched as he finished his move. She quickly pushed her queen forward, eyeing his king. "That doesn't sound convincing."

"Why wouldn't it?"

"You know, when you first got here," Bernie began, watching him move his king away from her queen, "you seemed happy to see everyone, but every time someone mentioned Edward's name, you got this weird look in your eye. You got quiet."

Emmerich looked away, Bernette's queen moving forward. "Do you usually observe people so well?"

"I like psychology, too."

Emmerich gave a snicker. "Dear me. Remind me not to talk of my childhood, then."

He moved his king and rested his chin on his fist, watching her make a move on the board. "Edward is my cousin, Lady

Bernette. We grew up like brothers, but I'm afraid time has driven us apart. We're not as close as we once were."

"Why's that?"

"We grew to be different people. Different interests, different manners, different characteristics." Emmerich watched as Bernie's queen had him cornered. He exhaled slowly, conceding defeat. "But such is life. People change. Families grow apart."

"You seem close to your Aunt Maria and I'm guessing you like your parents."

Emmerich nodded sadly. "They are different from the rest of the family. Aunt Maria and my parents are kind and loving. The rest...well...let's just say they're kind to those who are like them."

Bernie wondered if he looked at his family like she looked at her own. Different. Hostile. *Why don't they accept me? Do they even care?* There was pity in her eyes as she captured his king. "I'm sorry to hear that. I like your Aunt Maria. Your parents were nice, too, when I met them."

"It matters not." Emmerich moved a pawn-a wasted turn, leaving his queen exposed and ready for capture. "I have no expectations my family and I will ever be close, but I have my parents and I have Aunt Maria. That is good enough."

"What happens when they're gone, though?"

Emmerich was silent for a moment, making Bernie wonder if she overstepped her boundaries. She didn't mean to make him sad. She didn't even mean to nearly beat him at chess. Why was it she just couldn't say anything right to him?

"I'll be alone, I guess," he replied quietly. He eyed her piece that stood beside his queen, and he glanced up. "You have me cornered. Aren't you going to move?"

She nodded, moving and overtaking his queen. "Checkmate."

He smiled warmly. "Good game. You have a clever mind, Lady Bernette. It was an honor to be bested by you."

They sat there in silence for a moment, and pretty soon Emmerich began rearranging the pieces back to their original places on the board. As he was moving the pieces, however, Bernie spoke. "It doesn't bother you that your family treats you so different?"

Emmerich shook his head. "No. In fact, I expect it. My father is not the king's son. We are only seen by our family because of my father's work in bringing more trade to Hugellia. When I'm older, if anything happens to my parents, I shall leave my family behind. I won't miss them and I doubt they would miss me."

"Do you really mean that?"

Emmerich nodded, giving his answer too quickly, she noticed. "Yes. I do."

Bernie continued to add pieces to her squares as Emmerich finished his. There was a silence between them, but Bernie noticed the look on his face. There was a lot of sadness in it, a lot of hurt, and she only guessed how much rejection he had experienced in his young life. Though she was far from being an expert on the van Ketten family, anyone who heard palace gossip knew the rift between the king of Hugellia and his stepson.

She tried to be optimistic despite the rumors. "Maybe you're wrong. Maybe your family really does love you, but they just don't know how to show it."

He looked up from the board. "Is this you using psychology on me?"

"Maybe." She grinned.

"Well." He exhaled, leaning back. "This should be pleasant."

"I'm only making conversation."

"Of course."

"Ugh," Bernie huffed. "You're worse than Antoinette."

Emmerich could only smile in return.

"Fine. I won't analyze you, but I will say this," Bernie said, placing her king and queen back on the board. "You talk pretty freely about your family squabbles."

"Squabbles?"

"Yeah," Bernie continued. "You've only just seen me after how many years and already you're telling me about how you're viewed in your family and how you view them."

Emmerich feigned indifference. "I'm just an open person, I guess. Is that a problem?"

"Not at all," Bernie replied. "But I don't think it's just because you're an open person. You weren't open with me about what the letter between you and Antoinette said and what you two are wanting to talk about. An open person wouldn't be able to keep that information tucked in."

"That's because your sister wanted it to be a private conversation."

"Sure. And that's a believable excuse. But do you know what else I think?"

Emmerich crossed his arms. "I'm afraid to ask."

Bernie smirked. "I think it bothers you that your family treats you so differently."

Emmerich shook his head. "It doesn't bother me at all. I don't care what they think."

"I think if you didn't care, you wouldn't be so open about it. Not to mention you wouldn't have brought it up with someone you barely know."

Emmerich said nothing as he rubbed the back of his neck. "You've read Hans Handel's *Chronicles of the Mind and Body*, I take it?"

"*A Study in Family Relationships*. All five volumes."

Emmerich snickered. "It figures. But I still say it doesn't bother me."

"Don't make me start quoting Handel's thoughts on denial."

Emmerich laughed. "I don't know whether to be intrigued by your mind or to be terrified by it."

Bernie's eyes widened. Did she say too much? Did she go too deep *again*? She sunk in her chair, feeling like a mouse, wanting to hide in a hole in the wall. She pressed her lips shut for a moment, looking away.

"I'm sorry. I don't mean to be so nosy."

"There is no need for apologies," Emmerich said, making her look up. "But, if I may be so bold as to use Handel's psychology on you, I think your observations of me reflect mutual understanding rather than nosiness."

Well, there it went. It figured he would be able to guess she looked at her family the same way he looked at his.

"Touché. I guess you can read me just as good. You just had to be smart, didn't you?" Bernie sighed.

"I'm far from intelligent," Emmerich said, "but reading Handel does make me feel a little knowledgeable."

Bernie grinned as he leaned forward, folding his hands. "It is nice to speak with someone who understands, though."

Bernie's smile widened and she was about to say something more, but before she could speak, she heard a noise come from down the hall. Fast, pacing, rough. It could only mean Queen Susanna had heard Bernie was not in her room.

She threw herself back into the chair with a gruff. "Great...Mother's coming."

"Forgive me if I have gotten you in trouble," Emmerich said.

"Don't be sorry. I'm glad I've been so sinful. It's not every day I get to beat a fellow smarty at chess!"

Emmerich lifted his brow and smirked. "Let's not be boastful now. That was only one game."

"Oh please. I could beat you again with my eyes closed."

"You could try."

"Yes, I could."

Mother was at the door. Before she could say anything, Emmerich quickly whispered to Bernette. "Will you speak to your sister for me? Arrange a meeting so I can speak with her?"

Of course-the plan. Bernie had almost forgotten about it. She gave him a quick nod. "Of course. I'll let you know what I find out."

"Thank you," he mouthed quietly as Susanna stepped into the room.

Chapter 22: Before the Storm

It rained when they arrived in Verloris and it would rain when they left.

Edward stood in the rain as he oversaw the carriage being loaded with Malina's things to be moved into Reigal. She packed heavy-cases and cases of frivolous things-and more than a few carriages would be needed for the journey. Edward sighed, wondering what his parents would think of the cargo load they would see coming up the road to greet them. What shock their eyes would show when they saw the carriages were not full of people, but of boxes.

Malina was nowhere to be found. In fact, Edward saw little of her all week. It had been twelve days since their wedding and he found that Malina was more willing to waste her time with others instead of him. He didn't mind it. What moments he had to himself became a treasure; a time to enjoy the peace and quiet before life would be plunged into chaos when he returned home.

Home. He dreaded the very word of it.

The last few nights had been restless for him. Tossing and turning alone in his bed, his wife uninterested in her new husband now that she had him, and all he could do was think-think of the faces he would see lashing out at him for what he had done in Verloris, think of the voices who would call him "failure" and "a disappointment" because he was nothing like his beloved brother. He would think of the quiet figure in the corner, his fiancée...the woman who could have been, *should have been,* his wife, weeping with no one to comfort her.

The wetness of the rain began to soak into his clothes, making him cold, but he paid it no heed. His thoughts had gotten hold of him once more as he stood there amidst the servants and their loading of the carriage. Antoinette, the most wonderful woman he had ever known, was about to have her heart broken.

He closed his eyes, dreading what was to come.

She would cry for days...weeks even. Antoinette was a woman who loved deep or not at all, and when she loved...it was with everything. She had never known heartbreak. She had never known the pain of loss. She had never known the suffering of rejection.

But now she would, and he would be her teacher.

Edward knew he hated himself the moment Stephen had died. He never told anyone and never let it show in his being. Now, with what he was about to do to Antoinette, his hatred grew, but he vowed to hold it in. She could not feel sorry for him, not feel any compassion for him after what he had done to her. He wanted her to hate him as much as he hated himself because that's what he deserved.

In the end, he wondered if fate was being kind to her. The woman who never knew sorrow was certainly going to feel it, but in the long run, perhaps sorrow would be prevented. Who was Edward kidding when he thought he could be her husband? He failed as a brother. He failed as a son. Could he honestly have succeeded as a husband and father when everything else had fallen through?

She would find someone worthy of her goodness, someone who knew how to be a good man to a good woman, someone who honored the priceless gem that she was and treasured her more than anything else. She deserved someone who would mend her heart and not break it.

She deserved someone like Emmerich.

The thought of his cousin made Edward's heart sink, but he accepted it. Emmerich was the better man-he always had been. Never had Emmerich lied or stolen or prostituted himself with a woman. There was no blood on Emmerich's hands, no shadows in his past to haunt him at night. The man was a saint, someone worthy of an angel. Edward knew that more than anyone, Emmerich would be good for Antoinette.

Still, he found it difficult to accept defeat.

The last of the luggage was loaded and Edward nodded to the servant in thanks. The young boy replied that he would fetch Malina from her chambers and tell her the caravan was ready to go to Reigal.

Before Edward entered the carriage, he noticed Marcus Peterson on a horse, trotting to where the prince was at and stopping as Edward opened the door. Edward greeted him and Marcus unhorsed, his hood and cloak also sopping wet from the rain.

"Is everything packed?" Edward asked.

"Yes," Marcus replied. "Everything is ready to go. We only wait on Malina."

"It's going to be a long journey," Edward said, looking at the carriage behind him. "With this many coaches, it will take us longer to get to Reigal. It may take over a week when we're in the mountain passes."

"We are going straight to Reigal?" Marcus asked, confused. "What of your family in Hugellia and the rest of the royal guard? They must be sick with worry thinking something has happened out in the wild."

Marcus Peterson was always thinking ahead, Edward couldn't help but note. It was a trait he hoped would never leave the knight as it had left him.

"I sent a letter to my grandfather stating we were returning to Reigal," Edward said. "I told him to send the rest of the guard home by the end of next week. Let them have their days of rest before returning home."

"So the king does not know of our stay in Verloris?"

"No," Edward replied. "I kept it vague. Let them question what it means later. They will find out the truth soon enough. Gossip travels faster than any letter, anyways."

A moment of silence passed between them as the rain continued to pour. Edward looked to the ground, his eyes burning from lack of sleep, and he rubbed them to ease the pain.

"You look tired," Marcus said.

"That's because I am."

"You should rest on the journey back."

"I doubt I will get any, but thank you for the advice."

"Edward," Marcus began. The prince looked up from the ground, his eyes red from rubbing too hard. Marcus sighed at the sight of him. "I won't pretend our arrival will be welcoming, because I know it won't, but try not to think of the future right now. Try to rest while you can."

"There will be no rest for me," Edward said quietly as he watched the castle door open, Malina stepping out in a fur cloak and shielded by a servant carrying an umbrella. She waved good-bye to a few onlookers, her father and sister included, who remained at the door. Edward had not seen Malina's family since the wedding party they held a few days ago. Malina's sister barely said a word to him. Their father said even less, ignoring him and Malina as much as he could.

Edward turned to Sir Peterson one last time before Malina approached. It would probably be the last time he and Marcus would have any privacy before arriving in Reigal. The journey would be spent with Malina and she would not wish to share her husband's attentions to any other when arriving in her new home. Edward wanted to say one final word of appreciation before everything in his world would fall apart.

"Marcus," Edward began, making the knight listen intently. "I wanted to thank you for remaining by my side while we were here in Verloris. I have deceived you, I have mistreated you, and I have been anything but a leader to you and the other guards. Yet you have been nothing but loyal and honorable, and though I question your judgment on it, you have even offered your friendship. For that, and for so many other things, I am grateful."

"It's nothing," Marcus said. "I have made my vows, Edward, and I will uphold them."

"A vow can easily be broken, Marcus. I know this too well. But a noble heart can never go astray." Edward held out his hand, a token of his appreciation to his most faithful knight. Marcus took it, clasping it and shaking it warmly, and it brought the first smile Edward had given since staying in Hugellia. "My crown is lost to me. My family and friends will soon be lost as well. But do not think I will ever forget your kindness to me, my honorable friend. Though I can no longer give it, I will work hard to see you honored for your services."

Marcus gave a humbled bow. "You need not do anything for me."

"I know," Edward said, letting go of his hand as Malina approached. "But I am grateful, nonetheless."

"Why do you tarry?" Malina interrupted as she arrived, her eyes like stone as she glared at her husband. "I do not wish to stand in this rain any longer! Open the carriage door at once! And you!" She turned to Marcus sharply. "Mount your horse. The prince and I shall have this carriage to ourselves. Do not keep us waiting!"

Marcus nodded as he mounted, giving one last look of pity to Edward as he rode off to the front.

"Well?" Malina asked as Edward watched Marcus leave. "Are you ready to go or not?"

Edward nodded as he held the door open for her to enter the carriage. He followed her in silence, taking the seat opposite her and shutting the door back. He watched as she looked out the window impatiently, and he leaned back in his seat. It was going to be a long journey.

"I'm exhausted."

Antoinette fell onto the sofa and exhaled softly. It was late into the evening and she was too tired to sleep. Mother had kept her busy planning the wedding the entire week, and Antoinette didn't know whether to be thankful her mother was so precise or annoyed that she couldn't go a day without controlling everything.

There was one thing to be grateful for in Mother's madness. At least that "talk" Emmerich had wanted to have with Antoinette had been delayed.

Twelve days had it been since Emmerich's arrival and Antoinette had barely seen him. In fact, the last she saw of him was the day he arrived. She could say many things about

Emmerich, she thought, but she could never say he was impatient.

Antoinette glanced up from her spot on the couch as Bernie walked in carrying a few books in her hand. She plopped onto the seat beside her and gave a sigh.

"Fancy seeing you here." Antoinette chuckled. "Ever since your fake flu, I haven't seen you at all! Where have you been?"

"Running errands for Mother," Bernie scoffed. "Write a letter here, tell the servants this, go outside and run a few laps so I can lose weight…"

"I'm so sorry, Bernie."

"Don't be. I'm just glad my punishment was staying away from her."

"At least one of us is free."

Bernie rested her head on the sofa's back. "Is she ever going to give you a break?"

"She's tiring out now," Antoinette replied. "At least she's not keeping me through the evenings anymore."

Bernie stifled a yawn as she placed the books on the floor and gathered her knees to her chest. "Why is Mother keeping us so busy?"

Antoinette paused. She had wondered the same thing. It seemed ever since Emmerich arrived, Mother kept everyone busier than usual. Mother was never fond of the van Ketten family-that much, she remembered-though why Mother held such animosity towards them was anyone's guess. Surely she wouldn't be so crude as to look down on them because they weren't royalty like the others.

"You heard her yourself. She has it in for Emery's parents," Antoinette said as she closed her eyes, wanting to sleep.

"But why?" Bernie asked. "I get that she's a snob, but still…"

"She's always been a snob, Bernie. That'll never change."

"Well, let her be snobby." Bernie shook her head. "Although, I guess I should come clean."

Antoinette opened her eyes. "About what?"

"Faking the flu wasn't the only thing I got in trouble for."

"Oh?" Antoinette asked, sitting up straight. "What else did you do?"

"I talked to Emmerich."

Antoinette smirked. She figured Bernie was all talk about finding him so repulsive. "I'm curious now. What did you two talk about?"

"Nothing much," Bernie said, giving her a look that said "It's not what you think." "I ran into him in the library getting some books. He was playing chess so I thought I'd join him."

"Sounds like you two had fun."

"Trust me-I was only doing it because Mother told me not to. And I doubt it was fun for him. He's a terrible chess player."

"Strange. He's always been a brilliant chess player." Antoinette giggled to herself but stopped after Bernie gave her a glare. "You had no mercy on the poor man, did you?"

"None whatsoever."

"So that's all that happened? You played chess?"

"On the contrary." Bernie wiggled her eyebrows up and down as she looked at her sister. "He talked quite a bit about you."

Antoinette's smile faded into a shrug. No matter how hard she tried to pass the buck with Emmerich van Ketten, somehow it always came back to bite her.

"What did he say?" she asked.

"He wants to talk to you."

"I gathered that much."

"And he wants me to set up a meeting with you for him since he's basically being treated like the plague."

Antoinette frowned. "He said that?"

"Well, I embellished it a little bit. He didn't mention the plague." Bernie smirked.

Antoinette crossed her arms. What was so urgent that Emmerich wanted to speak to her about it? She could only guess it had to do with the wedding. Why else would he want to talk? Though Bernie jested about Emmerich being in love with Antoinette, she began to wonder if Bernie's musings were true.

She would be hounded until Edward's arrival unless she talked to him. If Emmerich was about to have his heart broken, he might as well have it done to him gently.

"When does he want to talk?"

The look on Bernie's face looked surprised for a moment. Antoinette looked at her, motioning for an answer. "Did he say a time that was good for him?"

Bernie shook her head. "He's letting you decide."

"Give me two days. Mother has me running errands at the reception hall tomorrow and the day after. We should be in the clear after that. He can meet me in the gardens after dinner. If you can distract Mother for me, I should have enough time to get this over with."

"I'll send him a note then," Bernie said.

"Don't worry. I'll do it," Antoinette said, getting up and heading towards the desk. She pulled out some paper and took the quill in her hand, writing.

Bernie stood and went to her. "If you don't want to talk to him, you don't have to."

"It isn't fair for me to prolong this," Antoinette said, pausing from her letter. "He may not want to break up the wedding, because that's not like him, but maybe he just needs to say something."

"Like what?"

"I don't know." Antoinette rubbed her brow. "'Congratulations on your wedding', 'You've been a great friend', 'Good-bye'…"

"Or, 'Please don't marry Edward because I secretly love you and my cousin isn't good enough for you.'"

Antoinette looked at Bernie, her brows lowered. "What makes you say that?"

Bernie smirked. "Please, Antoinette. Everyone's noticed it."

Bernie turned to walk back to the couch, but Antoinette called out to her. "Notice what? Did he say something to you? Is that really what all of this is about?"

"He didn't say anything," Bernie said as she sat on the couch and picked up a book, opening it. "I'm sure it's nothing, just like you said."

Antoinette remained silent for a second before returning to her letter. She sat there, unsure of what to write, but she forced her hand upon the paper and finished the letter. Whatever Emmerich had to say to her, she at least owed him the time to listen.

But if he had anything to say about Edward and the wedding, she would ignore every word.

Antoinette hurried her pace as she left the palace and headed to the gardens. Mother hadn't noticed she was gone, thinking she was still in the parlor discussing room plans with Queen Maria. It wouldn't be long before Mother discovered the ruse, but as long as Bernie stuck to the plan, Antoinette would at least have a half hour without interruption. Hopefully that would be enough for Emmerich to say what he had to say and be done with it.

It was a beautiful evening for a talk, though Antoinette hoped such a romantic setting would not take place. The sun was just starting to set and the sky was a beautiful hue of red, pink, orange, and blue. It almost reminded her of the evening Edward had proposed to her on, minus the cooler air.

As she glanced ahead, she noticed Emmerich standing beside a bench near a grove of trees. Antoinette met his gaze as he watched her approach, his hands folded in front of him and standing so straight he looked like he was a soldier preparing for inspection. Antoinette recognized the setting immediately, and it made her cringe. It was the same bench Edward had proposed to her on, near the same tree they had their first kiss.

Fate had to be laughing somewhere, surely.

As she arrived, Emmerich gave a quick bow. "Lady Antoinette," he said, his voice shaking. Was he nervous? He certainly sounded like it, and that made Antoinette's heart beat faster. "Forgive me that it took so long for us to meet."

"There is no need for apology." Antoinette forced a smile, trying to be polite. The smile apparently calmed him as he unfolded his hands and relaxed. "Mother has kept me busy. I'm sure you know how she is."

"I hope I'm not the cause of it," he said.

Of course he was, Antoinette thought, but she would never tell him that. "It's fine. Mother has her ways, and with the wedding so close she is starting to feel overwhelmed with planning. She wants to make sure everything is perfect."

"Of course."

An awkward silence followed, and Antoinette wrung her hands together. "So...you wished to speak with me, Emery," she began, her stomach tying itself in knots. "What is it you wished to say?"

Emmerich's face went from nervous to confused. "I was hoping you would enlighten me. You said you wanted to talk about us."

Antoinette's eyes widened. "Us?"

"Yes."

"What about us?"

Emmerich gulped as he started to pace. "I was hoping you'd tell me," he said. "Your letter was a little vague."

Now things were getting complicated. Antoinette put her hand to her forehead, thinking back to all the letters she had written. Had she sent one to Emmerich? She didn't remember that she did.

"What letter, Emery?" Antoinette asked. "I'm afraid I don't know what you're talking about."

Emmerich stopped in his pacing and pulled out a piece of parchment from his pocket, handing it to her. "You sent this to me some weeks ago. It's even signed by you in your handwriting. See?"

Antoinette took the letter in her hands and read it. It was her handwriting, certainly. Perfected and not an error in sight. But she didn't write the letter, and after reading the contents, she felt confused. Had Emery been duped into thinking Antoinette was wanting to leave Edward for him?

And then came the other revelation. Emmerich had arrived quickly. Had Bernie been right? Had Emery been in love with her all along?

"I didn't write this, Emery," Antoinette stuttered. "I don't know how or why this was sent to you, but I didn't write this."

"But it's in your handwriting."

"Then someone forged it."

Emmerich's face looked morbid, embarrassed, his face blushing to the point of wanting to hide. He turned away from her, covering his mouth for a moment to hide his own disappointment. Antoinette felt sick from his reaction. Pity entered her heart at seeing her friend so wounded and hurt. Soon pity turned to anger towards whoever wrote the letter.

"Who could have done this?" she asked.

For a moment, Emery remained quiet, but his face was beginning to harden. "I have an idea."

Antoinette began to wonder, too. Could it have possibly been Bernie? She had forged a letter from Mother before. Could she have forged a letter from her sister? No…no,

Bernie wouldn't have done such a thing. Why would she want to break up the wedding?

It would explain why she's been talking about Emmerich so much…

Antoinette frowned. She hoped she was wrong. She desperately, truly hoped her sister wasn't behind this deception.

"I wonder…" Antoinette began, but stopped when she saw Emery turn to face her.

"Forgive me, Lady Antoinette, for wasting your time," he said, his face so downcast that it made Antoinette want to cry. He held out his hand and she handed him the letter, and he stuffed it back into his pocket. "I was a fool for thinking…no. It's nothing. I…I should leave."

He began to walk away, but Antoinette took him by the arm, gently pulling him back. "Wait, Emery. Don't go just yet."

He looked up at her, his eyes confused. "What is it?"

Antoinette paused, unsure of what to say. She didn't want to lay the blame on Bernie just yet. She wanted to talk to her first, at least try to get the truth and the reason behind it, but that didn't mean she couldn't lessen the damage that was already done on Emery. Though her heart was with Edward and always would be, she still had a special place for Emmerich van Ketten. She'd never forget her childhood best friend.

"I'm sorry, Emery," she said. "Sorry that this deception has happened and sorry that you have travelled so long a way for nothing."

"It's not your fault," Emery replied warmly. "Regardless of the circumstances, I am happy to see you. I only wish…"

He paused, looking away. Antoinette waited for him to continue, eyeing him and holding her breath.

Emmerich sighed. "I only wish…" he continued again, "that this deception was not played on you. I am very cross with the person who has done it."

Had Emery wondered if it was Bernie, too? Antoinette felt her stomach sour at the thought. She was sure Bernie meant well, if it was her. There had to be an explanation. Her sister was never one for cruel jokes.

"Who do you think has deceived us?"

Emmerich crossed his arms. "It is better you not know my opinion."

There. It had to be Bernie. Antoinette put her hand on his arm and began to plead. "Emery, please don't be cross with my sister. I'm sure she didn't mean to…"

"Your sister?" Emery asked, his brow going up. "Why would you think your sister would do such a thing?"

"I don't know," Antoinette replied with a sigh. "She's upset about the marriage and she doesn't want me to leave her. She's afraid of being left alone with Mother, and I thought…I don't know. Perhaps she wrote the letter to stop the wedding?"

"Lady Bernette is clever, Antoinette," Emmerich said softly. "But I do not think your sister capable of such a cruelty. I know her well enough to know that she loves you dearly and would never wish to hurt you or take away your happiness."

"Then if it wasn't her, who was it?" Antoinette asked.

"Please don't ask me that question." Emmerich looked away towards the sunset.

"And why not?"

"Because it will hurt you to know the truth."

"Tell me anyway," Antoinette said. "I don't like to be deceived and I especially do not like to see someone dear to me be used."

Emmerich exhaled slowly as he turned to her with sorrow in his eyes. "I believe it to be Edward."

Edward? Of all people they knew to be cruel, Edward was not one of them. Antoinette scoffed at the idea. "Why on earth would you think that?"

"Because I know him and what he is capable of."

Antoinette furrowed her brows in anger. "There's not a cruel bone in Edward's body! How could you even suspect such a thing?"

"You suspected your sister," Emmerich countered back.

"Because I couldn't think of anyone else."

"Well I could," Emmerich said. "Forgive me, my lady, if this upsets you, but I know it in my heart that this is the truth."

Antoinette glared. "I don't believe you."

"Don't take offense to it," Emmerich said, trying to be gentle after seeing her reaction.

Antoinette didn't care about the look of remorse on his face for upsetting her. He *should* be sorry. How could he say such a cruelty about his own cousin?

"Antoinette," Emmerich said softly, sitting beside her on the bench. "Do not let this revelation upset you, for you are not the target of this jest. This was meant for me and only me."

"How could you say that?" Antoinette seethed. "Edward has been nothing but kind to you, Emery. You are kin. You are like brothers!"

"We have not been close since childhood," Emmerich said. Antoinette swallowed the truth hard, like a bitter pill, one that she didn't want to take. "You may find it hard to believe, but we are far from friends. We only tolerate each other for our family's sake."

"I don't understand," Antoinette asked, her voice weakening. "What drew you apart? You were always friends when I saw you together."

"We did not wish to upset you with our quarrels." Emmerich stood to his feet and faced the sunset.

"Then at least answer me as to why Edward would play such a trick on you, and why I would be included in it!"

Emmerich looked as if something pained him, like a hurt too deep and stubborn was being held down to keep from coming out. He looked at her, his eyes heavy and seeming so tired all of a sudden. "Is it not obvious in the note?"

Antoinette bowed her head, her hands still knotted from the wringing. She wondered about the letter, how it made her sound like she wished to leave Edward for Emmerich. If Edward had written the letter, which she *knew* he didn't, then why would he make Emmerich think Antoinette wanted to see him? Would Edward really think Emmerich would be gullible enough to think Antoinette would leave Edward for him? Unless...

"Emery?" She didn't want to ask the question, but had to know the truth. "Do you...do you have feelings for me?"

The look on his face told her the truth even though his lips tried to hide it. "Feelings?" he asked.

"You came here so quickly thinking I was going to leave Edward for you," she replied. "You wouldn't have done so unless you felt something for me."

Emmerich crossed his arms, turning away. He didn't want to answer, it seemed.

"Emery, please tell me the truth," Antoinette said. "I won't be angry. I just want to know."

"It doesn't matter what I think," he muttered.

"It does to me," Antoinette said. "We've always trusted each other. Trust me now and be honest."

He sighed, bowing his head in silence before facing her again. "Yes," he said quietly, his sight falling to the ground.

She felt her heart flutter at the thought, but at the same time it sunk. Bernie and Mother were right, and she had been so, so blind. Why did she not see it? Or perhaps she did, and didn't want to admit it. "How long have you felt this way?"

"A long time," he whispered. "Since we were children, really."

"Why didn't you tell me?"

"I tried to," he said, the hurt in his face transparent, "but Edward...he got in the way."

"What do you mean?"

"I mean he didn't exactly act like family should." Emmerich rubbed his brow and began pacing again-a sheer sign he was nervous and was debating with himself on whether to be honest or not. Antoinette felt sick. Whatever was about to come out, she had a feeling it wasn't going to be good.

"Do you remember the day he told you he was in love with you?" Emmerich asked, his voice hoarse.

Antoinette nodded. She remembered it well. They were in Reigal, the three of them, and she had only known Edward for a few weeks.

"Do you remember the letter he gave you to confess his feelings?"

Antoinette nodded again. She still had the letter. It was the most beautiful confession of love she had ever read. "You have captured my heart and mind," she began, reciting it, "like summer captures the beauty of nature, or the night captures the beauty of the stars."

Emmerich lowered his head to the ground as he spoke the words along with her. "Not a day goes by that I don't think of you, and not an evening goes by that you don't fill my dreams."

Antoinette felt a lump in her throat. The letter. Had Emmerich read it? How did he know what Edward had said to her?

He looked up as he continued to recite it without her. "I have little to offer you. No looks. No charm. No future. I can only give you what I have, and that is my heart. A heart that will work every day for your welfare, a heart that will do anything for your happiness."

No...no, how did he know it all...*every word*?

"I take no shame in telling you, Antoinette Maria van Echt, that I am in love with you, and forever shall be."

"Emery..." Antoinette whispered, her lip quivering. "How...?"

Emmerich stood before her, facing her with sympathy. "I will never be a king, but you shall always be my queen."

It all made sense now. Everything. For so long she thought Edward had written it-he wasn't the heir to the throne when they began courting. It was Stephen. He didn't have as much to offer as he did now.

No, no... Antoinette scolded herself for doubting Edward. Of course he wrote it. It was in his handwriting. He gave it to her and recited it himself! But how did Emmerich know? Unless he somehow saw it first.

"How did you know what the letter said?" Antoinette asked, looking at Emmerich, her expression hardening.

"I know what the letter said because I'm the one who wrote it."

"Then why didn't you give it to me?" Antoinette asked. "It was Edward who gave me the letter. Edward who told me everything. You did nothing on that day! I didn't even see you!"

"You don't believe me?" Emmerich's face went from sorrowful to defensive. His eyes narrowed.

"Those were Edward's words, not yours!" she said, her voice rising.

"He has you fooled, Antoinette!" Emmerich replied as Antoinette stood to her feet and glared him down. "Did he tell you he wrote it himself? Did he tell you it came from his heart? Then he lied! It was I who wrote it, I who had planned to give it to you and ask for your hand in courtship. But I was the foolish one. I told Edward of my feelings for you and I thought he was going to help me in telling you. Instead, he took the letter and copied it in his own hand. Before I knew anything, he went to you himself!"

Antoinette stood there, her mouth agape. Edward was never deceptive. He never could be. Those words were from *him*, not Emmerich.

"I don't believe you," Antoinette said as she started to walk away. She was done with the conversation. She didn't want any more of it. But Emmerich was far from finished, and he jogged to keep up with her.

"Your husband-to-be is no saint, Antoinette. I don't tell you this to spite him or hurt you. I tell you this because you should know the truth!"

"If what you're saying *is* the truth, Emery, then why did you not come to me sooner? Why did you not tell me the letter was from you after Edward gave it to me?"

"Because I saw the look on your face," he said quietly, and suddenly Antoinette stopped. Emmerich sighed as he ran his fingers through his hair. "You were so happy with him. Happier than you ever were with me. Why would I destroy that?"

"Because it's honest," Antoinette seethed, her eyes watering.

"Antoinette, when you truly love someone, you'll give up your own happiness just to see them be happy."

She had no words to berate him on that.

But before she could counter the argument with him, she heard a horn sound in the distance. They both turned towards the road, noticing a caravan of about six carriages heading towards the palace. They flew purple banners, an obvious sign of royalty, but otherwise there was no sign of where they came from.

"What is that?" Antoinette asked as she narrowed her eyes, trying to get a better look.

Emmerich shielded his eyes from the sunlight and gazed into the distance. "Were the king and queen expecting any visitors?"

"No."

"Then I don't know who they are."

There was only one way to find out. Off Antoinette hurried towards the front of the palace, Emmerich following beside her. As they approached the front steps, the caravan became clearer in their view.

"I can see the front carriage!" Antoinette exclaimed. "It looks like Edward! And look-there's Sir Peterson riding at the front! Though I don't know who the other riders are. Would they be from Hugellia?"

She didn't notice Emmerich's face harden at the sight. "If they are from Hugellia, I don't recognize them."

"Maybe they're newer guards."

"Or they aren't from Hugellia at all."

Antoinette glanced at Emmerich, confused. "Where else would they be from?"

"Those carriages look like they're from Verloris, my lady." Emmerich said quietly. "I saw them once as a boy when my father met with their messenger for peace talks."

"It's probably a coincidence."

Emmerich shook his head. "I don't think so."

Antoinette ignored him. Despite the revelation of the letter, whatever the truth was, Edward was *here*. Edward was *home*. He loved her enough to come back to her early and surely he had an explanation about the letter. Surely...

Antoinette hurried to the front and Emmerich followed. "Antoinette, please-something isn't right about this," he said, but she shrugged his words off like the wind that bounced off her shoulders.

The carriage stopped just as she and Emmerich arrived on the steps. One of the new guards dismounted, heading to the first carriage door. Antoinette grinned as she headed down to greet her beloved. Doubtless he would be happy to see her, and she was happier than ever to see him. She would find out the truth from him-hear his side of Emmerich's fanciful stories.

"My lady, please..." Emmerich said as he reached out to her, and she shooed his hand away. Sir Peterson had dismounted and suddenly approached her, calling her name, but she ignored him as well.

The carriage door opened and out stepped Edward, looking handsome and regal as ever, although his eyes were baggy with exhaustion. She wasn't surprised. He was never a good traveler, always having trouble sleeping while on the road.

But when she smiled, calling his name, he didn't answer. He only looked at her-hard, almost like a glare-and kept his mouth shut. She thought it odd he wouldn't say anything, but she ignored it once again. *He's tired,* she thought to herself. *He just needs his rest, that's all.*

She went to embrace him, to take him in her arms and prove to him she was loyal and faithful and trusting, no matter what Emmerich had said. But before she could reach him, two of the guards came in front of her, brandishing spears and crossing them, creating a metal wall that separated her and her fiancé.

The sight was strange to her. Surprising. She didn't expect to be treated as a threat.

She heard Emmerich's angry voice like a muffle at the end of a tunnel, and she thought he said something about why the guards dared to brandish a weapon in front of a lady. She felt a tug on her arm, Emmerich's hand trying to pull her away, but she pulled back as she looked at Edward's face.

The man who left her was not the same man who came back.

No…it's Edward. He still loves me. He doesn't see me as a threat…

But all doubt was cast aside when a woman stepped out of the carriage with him.

To be continued in

Book 2 of The Ripple Affair series,

"Reign of Change"...

Turn the page for a preview of chapter 1...

Chapter 1: The First Wave

When Edward saw Antoinette run towards the carriage, his heart stopped. Not out of awe in her beauty or in love from seeing her after so many weeks apart, but out of despair...and disappointment.

Because Antoinette wasn't alone when she walked down the steps to meet him. Emmerich van Ketten was with her.

Why is he here? he wondered to himself through gritted teeth. For a moment he thought that somehow Emmerich knew of his secret marriage and had come to Reigal to warn Antoinette, but seeing her reaction to his arrival, the joy on her face and the hope in her eyes, he thought otherwise. She didn't know what was coming. Emmerich was there for other reasons-or coincidence.

Or maybe it's fate mocking me.

Edward supposed he should be thankful. He was about to break his love's heart. At least Emmerich would be there to pick up the pieces.

He just wished Emmerich wasn't there to see him fall.

The carriage came to a stop and Malina gripped Edward's wrist. "Are you ready, Edward?" she asked, pointing out the window. "And look! Is that Antoinette? It must be, from the green she is wearing. Typical forest land garb. But oh, the

Edelandian girl is happy to see you! Perhaps you should say hello."

It was the part Edward was dreading the most. He didn't want to hurt Antoinette. He'd rather cover his mouth to keep his hurtful words inside, to keep her from hearing his voice confirming betrayal. But it had to come out. She couldn't feel any remorse for him. She couldn't love him like he loved her. He was worthy of Malina. He was never worthy of Antoinette.

And it was time she saw the truth.

He hardened his face to stone when he stepped out of the carriage. There were barely any greeters; the family must've been busy and weren't expecting company. They would arrive within the minute, though. It didn't take long for word to reach the household, and Antoinette and Emmerich had to have seen him coming. Perhaps they were in the garden or taking a walk and saw him from the road.

A pang of jealousy crept through Edward's heart at the thought. Why were they together in the gardens, the place where Edward and Antoinette shared so many memories alone?

When Antoinette approached, calling his name, the Verloris guards that traveled with him stepped forth and blocked her touch with spears. She looked confused, almost frightened, yet he kept his face hard. Emmerich came to her defense like the noble lion he was and his face contorted into a snarl as he tried to pull Antoinette back to him.

"You *dare* brandish weapons to a lady of the court?" Emmerich spat. He clung to Antoinette's arm, looking as if ready to strike. His words were meant for the guards and went unnoticed, and as Antoinette stood there, still silent and processing the events around her, Emmerich turned to Edward, his eyes piercing.

"What is the meaning to this, Edward?" he demanded. "Tell these men to lower their weapons *now*!"

"No." Edward's voice was low, but Emmerich heard it as if it were a scream.

Emmerich's face soon matched Antoinette's and they both stood there, befuddled. Emmerich tried to pull Antoinette back again, but she remained firm. She didn't change at all until Malina peaked out of the carriage, taking Edward's hand as he helped her off.

Malina squinted at first, looking around and gazing at her surroundings. "My, what a quaint palace you have! So majestic with the mountains. I think I shall love it here, Edward." She turned to Antoinette as she took off her cloak. "Here," she said, holding the cloak out for Antoinette to take. "Feel free to have this cleaned. It's so dusty from the journey and I can't afford to get a cold in my condition."

Edward held his tongue. He wanted to take the cloak himself and burn it, scattering the ashes over Malina's head, but his anger was quenched as he saw Antoinette's lip start to quiver and her eyes fill with water. She held it together, the dear woman, as she was starting to put the pieces in place. Edward could only turn away. He didn't have enough strength to meet her estranged gaze.

"Darling, we'll have to talk about hiring new help. I think this girl is dumb," Malina said as she took the cloak and tossed it to one of her guards.

Emmerich's anger flared at Malina's words. "You *dare* speak to Lady Antoinette in such a disrespectful manner?"

"Who?" Malina asked as she turned to Edward. "My, he's defensive of his lady friend, isn't he?"

Defensive, indeed. It made Edward's stomach churn.

His eyes managed to look up and finally meet Antoinette's. She looked as if she was trying to hold her breath but having a terrible time with it. At first Edward thought she wouldn't be able to speak, that somehow the shock was so great she would become mute, until he heard her voice, soft and quiet like a summer breeze.

"Edward…who is this?" she asked.

About the Author

Erin Cruey once laughed when her mother told her she could be a writer one day. Nearly twenty years later, her mother's prediction came true, and Erin has learned to never question her mother again. When she isn't busy, you can find Erin trying to teach her betta fish new tricks. She currently resides in the United States of America with her family.

For the latest blog posts, news, and book releases, visit http://erincruey.com.